Rising Heat

PRAISE FOR *ONE PART WOMAN*

'Murugan works his themes with a light hand; they always emanate from his characters, who are endowed with enough contradiction and mystery to keep from devolving into mouthpieces . . . It's not just the physical world Murugan describes so vividly—the way a cow clears its throat, for example—but the rural community, a village of 20 huts and a thousand ancient resentments, where there is no privacy and your neighbor's suffering can serve as your evening's entertainment . . . I'm hoping for a whole shelf of books from this writer.'—**Parul Sehgal,** *New York Times*

'Intimate and affecting . . . Throughout the novel, Murugan pits the individual against the group. How far are you willing to go, he asks, in order to belong? . . . Murugan's descriptions of village life are evocative, but the true pleasure of this book lies in his adept explorations of male and female relationships, and in his unmistakable affection for people who find themselves pitted against the world.'—**Laila Lalami,** *New York Times Book Review*

'This subtly subversive novel examines the pang of childlessness experienced by Kali and Ponna, a couple living in rural southern India. In simple yet lyrical prose, Murugan shows how their standing in the world depends on offspring . . . The novel considers the constraints of tradition and beautifully articulates the couple's intense connection, even without a child.'—*New Yorker*

'Beautiful . . . Plunges readers into Tamil culture through a story of love within a caste system undergoing British colonization in the early 19th century . . . Murugan's touching, harrowing love story captures the toll that infertility has on a marriage in a world where having a child is the greatest measure of one's worth.'—***Publishers Weekly*** (starred review)

'With a backstory as fascinating as the narrative, this intriguing work, longlisted for the National Book Award, will undoubtedly be appreciated by internationally savvy Anglophone audiences.'—*Library Journal*

'Perumal Murugan brings a playful, fable-like quality to his tale of traditional values and their subversion.'—*Vanity Fair*, **'Fall's Best Books from Around the World'**

'Perumal Murugan's *One Part Woman* contains the sweetest, most substantial portrait of an Indian marriage in recent fiction. A touching and original novel.'—**Karan Mahajan, author of** *The Association of Small Bombs*

'Perumal Murugan's Tamil is vivid and terse, an instrument he uses with great care and precision to cut through the dense meshes of rural Tamil social life. The result, in this novel, is a brutally elegant examination of caste, family, and sex in South India.'—**Anuk Arudpragasam, author of** *The Story of a Brief Marriage*

'The life of an innocent couple who are led to believe that the expectations of the system defines their own personal pursuit of happiness forms Perumal Murugan's captivating story of love and desire. With his brilliant artistry, he captures the ups and downs of their lives. Works such as these have the power to subject contemporary value systems to intense introspection, it is for the same reason they are met with resistance. This work of art by Perumal Murugan can be acclaimed as modern mythology for its unusual access to cultural memories of the land and language, and the extraordinary courage with which it is dealt.'—**Vivek Shanbhag, author of** *Ghachar Ghochar*

'Murugan's writing is locally-grown literature, not a canned object sold on a supermarket bookshelf. It is rare to come across a writer who enjoys such intimacy with a land and those who live in close contact with it. *One Part Woman* is so rooted in the soil of tradition that its rebellion against it is all the more unexpected and moving.'—**Amitava Kumar, author of** *Immigrant, Montana*

'A major Indian writer . . . Dark currents run through *One Part Woman* . . . Kali and Ponna, a couple who are erotically wrapped up in each other, withstand waves of derision because they have not conceived a child after a decade of marriage . . . When describing the farming communities of South India, Mr. Murugan is neither sentimental nor harsh.'—*New York Times* **(profile)**

rising
heat

PERUMAL MURUGAN

Bestselling author of *One Part Woman*

Translated by JANANI KANNAN

PENGUIN

An imprint of Penguin Random House

HAMISH HAMILTON

USA | Canada | UK | Ireland | Australia
New Zealand | India | South Africa | China | Singapore

Hamish Hamilton is part of the Penguin Random House group of companies
whose addresses can be found at global.penguinrandomhouse.com

Published by Penguin Random House India Pvt. Ltd
4th Floor, Capital Tower 1, MG Road,
Gurugram 122 002, Haryana, India

First published in Tamil as *Yeru Veyil* by Kalachuvadu Publications 1991
First published in English in Hamish Hamilton by Penguin Random House India 2020

Copyright © Perumal Murugan 1991
English translation copyright © Janani Kannan 2020

ISBN 9780670093663

Typeset in Adobe Caslon Pro by Manipal Technologies Limited, Manipal
Printed at Replika Press Pvt. Ltd, India

www.penguin.co.in

This is a legitimate digitally printed version of the book and therefore might not
have certain extra finishing on the cover.

To Kannaps and Giri, the centre of my universe

—Janani Kannan

Contents

Translator's Note

Eru Veyyil, Perumal Murugan's first novel, is a timeless work of art that remains as relevant today as it was when it was first published in 1991. A poignant story of a young boy who witnesses his ancestral lands being taken away for housing development and bears the socio-economic consequences as he grows into adulthood, this novel made the world take notice of the then twenty-five-year-old writer.

My own paternal grandfather was a farmer all his life. During the frequent visits to our ancestral village, I remember him being surrounded by labourers all the time. Pongal festival meant shopping for scores of saris and veshtis to give away to the people who worked on the land. That was not only their livelihood but also their way of life. However, starting in the late eighties, the children of the labourers began to leave the village for the closest city or for Chennai, seeking other opportunities. By the turn of the twentieth century, the dearth for help in the farms was tangible. Many farmers in the neighbouring villages were forced to sell their land to housing developers. This personal experience connected me with the characters and the events in the novel intimately. Indeed, after I embarked on this translation, I learnt that Perumal Murugan's ancestral lands were also taken away for development.

The realism of the events in the novel is intricately woven with the way he develops the seemingly simple characters. These are characters with layers of emotions, desires and insecurities, defined by their experiences and circumstances, that make them act the way they do. He seamlessly but never overtly narrates the various characters' extreme actions and the dire situations they find themselves in, without evoking the sense of right or wrong. As one character in the novel puts it, everyone only needs an opportunity to present itself to not be scrupulous. I have strived hard to capture these subtleties as closely as possible to the Tamil work.

I have stayed true to Perumal Murugan's style of narration with simple and direct sentences. However, the dialect used in the original work, Kongu Tamil as it is known, is a sub-regional dialect, known for its unique words and expressions that are not part of Tamil spoken elsewhere. In the Tamil work, the author has included a glossary for the benefit of the larger Tamil audience. I was also fortunate to have the help of Indumathi Mariappan to help me navigate many of the nuances in the Konga Tamil language and cultural contexts. This English translation is homogenized but I have strived to preserve the intent of the narrative. Ambar Sahil Chatterjee helped tremendously in preserving this intent and avoiding the pitfall of literal translation. In some places, I have left some expressions as such, in cases where I found them to paint the picture better. Such contextual expressions are so integral to the speech and adds colour to the context.

As normal with translations, there are cultural references that often need more explaining than the space allows. An example is when the village head is described to be in such a rage that if he were given a bunch of neem leaves in his hands, it would complete the image of him being possessed. Readers familiar with the cultural context would know of the practice in south India where women and some men vow to fast in penance for a period of time before a festival or holy day to a certain deity, most commonly the goddess, in exchange for forgiveness or favour. Almost always, there is an episode of the divine Mother descending on one of them to soothsay or simply show presence. The person who becomes the medium for the spirit would evoke an aura of fear, shaking vigorously, their hair getting undone, their eyes rolling back and forth and their voice sounding guttural. They usually have a bunch of neem leaves in their hands, neem leaves being a symbol of the goddess herself. Such elaborations are not included to keep the preserve the fluidity of the narrative.

The Tamil language particularly lends itself naturally to the interweaving of tenses in storytelling. I found this aspect that seemed effortless and very appropriate in the original text quite a challenge to maintain in the translation. I thank Shreya Chakravertty with the editorial team for helping me keep the translated tenses consistent.

I first met Murugan at the launch of his books *Ardhanari* and *Aalavayan* in 2015, right before he declared himself dead as a writer. I was deeply struck by the simplicity of the man who by then was already world-renowned. I devoured his books and remember putting it out to the universe then that I wish to be associated with his writing sometime in future. When I received the email that asked me if I would be interested in translating his book, I had to pinch myself several times to make sure I was not dreaming. It is a deep honour that has given me immense joy to undertake this translation wok. For entrusting me this work, I am extremely grateful to Kannan Sundaram of Kalachuvadu.

Los Angeles   Janani Kannan
22 February 2020

Rising Heat

Chapter 1

'Mani, Mani . . . Mani, Mani, Mani-i-i, Mani-i-i-i!'

The boy's cries subsided, his voice losing steam as his throat shut in pain from having shouted for so long. His heart got drier, his eyes welled up. He gritted his teeth and fought to hold back his tears, in vain. Tears gushed like a mighty spring. He paused briefly, swallowing to release saliva in his dry mouth, and called out again.

The dog came bouncing when it heard its name, stopping a few feet away from him with its tongue dripping and its tail wagging so hard that it seemed ready to fall off. It then sat down, lashing its tail against the ground as it stared at the boy with a bewildered look in its eyes. When it heard 'Mani, Mani-i-i-i . . .' again, it twisted its body to look away and produced a groan to signify refusal. And yet, it rolled around in the dirt, evidently expressing its affection for the boy.

But he was so enraged that he wanted to beat that devil of a dog to a pulp. Thinking he could stealthily advance on the dog and then suddenly grab it, he softened his voice, letting it drip with sweetness, and inched closer. He stretched out one hand—with a few fingers folded as if they held something to eat—and gestured to it with the other. But the dog, alert to the boy's ploy, straightened its twisted body and ran over to the top of the elevation around the well in the Veera forest. The dog didn't want to get caught. Nor did it want to leave the boy and run away. It stood there, torn.

The tracks gouged by passing trucks glittered bright white in the rays of the evening sun. The razed forests were replaced with sprouts of grass. At a distance, more trees lay fallen with their arms spread wide. It was the time of felling. The boy was so angry that he wanted to get hold of the dog and annihilate it. For the past couple of days, it had been the same sequence of events with this dog—the chase and the slipping away had now become a habit. But how could he explain to the dog that they had been completely uprooted from this soil? That they had no claims left on the property. That not even a clump of soil belonged to them any more. He did not know the dog's language, but even if he did, he would still have found himself unable to reason with Mani. Or even to whisper in its ears, 'Those people whose laps you laid on and played with like a child are no longer here. Those houses in front of which you lazed around and ran barking towards at the slightest sound stand ruined, empty and motionless. There is no one here to provide food.' This dog would still choose to run away instead of coming into his arms.

The more he thought about it the angrier he got. But exhaustion softened him. Nearby was the temple bolster. He sat down, leaning against it. Let the dog go to hell. Let it die of starvation.

The breeze blew hot on his face. The little bells hanging from the tips of the lances planted at the temple's gateway swayed with the breeze. The delicate chiming of the bells sounded like a lullaby to him at that moment. *I should go to the gateway and watch the gentle movements of the bells to my heart's content,* he thought to himself. He went past the exterior structure of two timber columns, painted red, towards the inner plinth. Atop the plinth, sanitized with cow-dung paste and enclosed within bars, stood a small stone god. It had age-old deposits of oil that resembled the layers that form on top of dried cow dung. The deity was housed in a small, niche-like room. Memories of going round and round the room in circles touching the walls, of overcoming his shyness to run around and play catch with other children, of falling down—all came rushing back to him. This was where his friend Selvan's front tooth had snapped in half. He had fallen face down from the giddiness of running around when his tooth hit the ground and broke upon impact. His mouth was choked with blood. His cries had sounded shrill, like the bleating of a baby goat with a bloated stomach.

Days were spent in vain playing *thaayam*, which was not unlike a game of checkers, on the lime-plastered front yard covered with a pandal shelter. Important men, big adults, used to kneel down and grind their teeth as they rolled the dice. 'Single . . .!' 'An eight, an eight', 'Look at this perfect six!' The clamour and commotion. Contemptuous laughter. Whenever Appa lost, he spat on his pawns, circled them around his head and threw them away. Even today, those pawns could be found, if looked for, under that tamarind tree. And his father's sweaty face was sure to flash on the bright surface of the eighth pawn, ashen with anger.

The temple stood to the south of the road that connected Karattur to Odaiyur. To the north of the road was the Aattur *valavu*, a cluster of houses, about a forest's distance away. And then there were the forests that slipped around the temple. This proximity between the village and the temple was the reason the children had made the temple their playground. During harvest season, not a soul came to this side. The deity sweltered alone in the heat. That changed only once in a while, when the village priest came by to sprinkle some water on it. Even the sweeping and dousing of the front yard reduced to once every couple of days during that time.

It was his grandmother, his Paati, who cleaned and dampened the front yard of the temple. They paid her an annual budgeted amount from the village's account. She gathered all the dried leaves from the tamarind tree into little piles with her own hands. She specifically brought only a cow's dung to sanitize the front yard. A couple of the little ones usually followed Paati to the temple. If they did, they played there until someone called out to them that it was getting late for school. During holidays, it usually took someone from their homes to come over, land a couple of blows on their backs and drag them home. Caught up in the throes of their play, the children seldom noticed when Paati left or when the sun moved over their heads.

Since the temple sat right off the main road, the back wall was often destroyed by a wayward bus or lorry that ran into it. The village had grown weary from clearing the debris and rebuilding it over and over again. Aren't God's collisions always with man's creations! The worst was when Kannaiyah's bus rammed into the wall. The bus came to a halt after its snout had gone through the wall. Oh, the wailing of the driver who had got caught in the mangled steel! He hadn't lost consciousness throughout. Even though they cut through this and that to get to him, they were still only able to remove him in parts. He died when they were about halfway through. About four or five people had died in that accident. His Chithappa, Appa's younger brother, had gone in and out through the debris without a trace of fear. His body was like the trunk of the black babool tree, he could lift and hurl anything effortlessly.

The boy had stood there watching, holding the loose end of his mother's sari, withdrawn like a fledgling. The gruesomeness from that day had led to a carnage of his sleep for several days. From then on, he was quite afraid to come by this side alone. The temple's rear wall seemed to bear an impression of the heart-piercing cries of the driver, as if that agonized voice was somehow trapped in it. Coming here by himself was really scary. Belief in ghosts usually trumped belief in God.

The yard lay wide open like a threshing ground, where piles of grain fibres get twisted into ropes. A couple of fallen tamarind fruits lay on the ground. During the Karthigai festival, it was under this tamarind tree that the

lamps were placed. The lamps were kept on conical pearl
millet plates in which the flames crackled bright. They
stroked and licked with their tongues the docile branches
of the tamarind tree. A part of the tree trunk still stood
blackened from the heat of the lamps. To the south was a
platform studded with some holy stones. And surrounding
them densely were offerings of prayers in the form of
figurines of those requesting to be protected. The more he
stared at them, the more he wanted to laugh.

He spotted his mother among the figurines, standing
with him tucked on her hip, holding Annan and Akka
by their hands. The nose had chipped off, flattening the
face. The arms had fallen down. It had hardly been—
what, three years—since they set that figurine? For
reasons unknown, she used to carry him on her hip all
the time, as if he was a small child, although he was
already in fifth standard at that time. They even prayed
for Mani. The dog's figurine stood there still so new, its
sheen untainted. With its tongue sticking out and its
tail pluming up in the act of wagging, it looked like a
real bell, a *mani*. Once, when its body was covered with
blisters and it was fighting death, prayers and offerings
were made to God on its behalf. The *pandakaran* who
made the mud figurines always added a collar for all the
'escort' dogs but Mani alone didn't have one. Maybe
Appa described Mani to him. He had made a beautiful
and perfect image of Mani. The boy's hands twitched to
caress the dog's back as soon as he saw its figurine. The
pandakaran's workmanship deserved an award.

Nearby was the well adjoining the Veera forest, its massive mouth gaping wide open. The well did not belong to the temple; rather, it was his grandfather's younger brother's and they had allowed it to be used for temple purposes also. Every time he saw the well, his mind conjured up the image of Valliakka wearing her sari drawn up like a man as well as the screeching sound of the irrigation structure as she drew water with it. That Akka had since been given away in marriage. The forest had disappeared too, and the irrigation structure had been completely dismantled without a trace.

Mani was still sitting on the mound of the well. Neither was the dog coming to him nor was the boy able to grab it. 'If it continues to run away like this, it is going to wither away right here.' He should have made a habit of keeping it on a leash. This was all his father's doing. 'Why keep it leashed? It will behave without one,' Appa had said. Not that keeping it unleashed was a bad thing. The dog would lick its food clean and find itself a spot next to the goat shed. There was no need to tie it up at night and let it loose in the morning. Even so, it never cooperated at times of urgency, like right then. When it sensed that it was being summoned to be taken back home, this was how it stalled for time. He didn't even have the leash in his hand, yet, the dog perceived from the way he called its name that he had come to take it home, and it fooled around.

'Mani, Mani-i-i-i . . .' He put his hands together and went closer. The dog wagged and twisted its tail affectionately. As he drew closer, it dashed away, its twisted tail still showing its affection. 'Let it die without food.' *The mind that wants to take this dog home deserves this*, he thought, and smacked himself on his head repeatedly. He bit his lower lip and flung a stone at the dog. The animal closed its eyes, facing the boy directly, and avoided the stone by shrinking itself and turning to its side. The boy ran around and gathered more stones. His bare upper body got stickier with sweat. His khaki shorts pinched around his hips. He was as mad as an angry piglet. With the pockets filled with stones, he began to throw them in a volley, one after another. But even when a stone hit its target, the dog made no sound. 'You filthy scoundrel of a dog! Is there not an iota of fear in you?' Mani ran further away, seeing him so angry.

'Where will you go? Even if you run all around this entire forest, I am not going to let you go today. You think you can escape eating your food today, you rascal!'

The dog ran through the thorn-laden forest. The erstwhile foot tracks were covered with undergrowth. The bunds on the boundaries of the fields were strewn with branches. The forests that used to be richly verdant like a large green blanket now stood bare, as though persistently gnawed at. He couldn't run in any direction with his bare feet. The dog deftly slipped through the brambles and disappeared. The boy panted for breath loudly as he found himself deep in the forest. Which place was this? If people had traversed through these places like before, there would be recognizable landmarks. Everything was in ruins. Was there anything around to help identify precisely where he was? He spotted the fences that divided the Veera forest from the mango forest. They were made from kiluva trees and were all but destroyed. Walking along them would lead to the path to Itteri. Even though the tar road that ran past the temple went all the way to the lake, it was this path that the pedestrians frequented.

He walked along the fence. His skin was wet with sweat and glistened in the sunlight like a gleaming piece of wood soaked and darkened with rain. His feet were completely covered with dust. His eyes roamed everywhere. Hugging the temple on the east side was the Veera forest. On the west was the Minna forest. Where the two forests ended the mango forest began, right in the middle. Farther and higher away were the Veli forest and the Manuva forest. The mango forest ended at the lake pit that was shaped in the form of an unearthed brick. It spanned over a hundred acres or so. The rest were open lands bearing pearl millet, corn and groundnuts.

There were a few wells across the forests with meagre amounts of water in them, not unlike water inside a coconut.

Within this region had lived twenty families. His was four families. Then there was his grandfather's younger brother and his sons, his grandfather's older brother and his sons. Other than them was an *evaari*, a merchant, from Karattur who owned two acres. His looms and sizing business fetched him abundant money. He looked just like a piece of sun-dried coconut. He had filed a lawsuit against the government for taking his land. Well, he had the muscle and money to spend on lawsuits, but what could the rest do? They and their families were displaced from their lands.

The innumerable generations of his family that land had borne! That land which had been cooled over and over again by their sweat and transformed into fecund earth. That land which had embraced securely the life of every dispersed pearl millet grain and corn seed. The laughter of the cotton flowers. The strength of the groundnuts. Everything had turned lifeless. Edifices sprung everywhere from a land where crops once flourished. Boulder-like buildings, everywhere. Across the entire hundred acres.

He hadn't come by here since the displacement a month ago. What was the point anyway? Just old memories all over again, reducing him to tears whenever he caught sight of the denuded land. That was why he always fixed his gaze on the road every time he passed by this side. He had no desire to even steal a glance. What was left to see in a land that was turning barren? But his feet still longed to walk around the entire land one more time. The dog was nowhere to be found. It must be sitting on top of some mound waiting eagerly to see if he came looking for it. If only he had brought a little rice he could have left some for the dog. Mani would have gobbled it up after he left. *Let it be. For how many days more will it continue running away like this? Let it come home when it does. It must return home sometime.* With such thoughts, he abandoned chasing the dog and instead walked towards a cluster of roofless houses whose walls seemed headless from a distance.

The entire stretch of land from the mango forest all the way to the Veli forest had belonged to them—his Thatha, Periappa and Chithappa. Standing in front of the rest, his Chithappa's house could be seen even from afar. It was a big house—eight *ankanam*, measured by strides. On the front was a large plastered area to dry grains and ears of corn. The veranda extended along the east side of the house. Now, with the roof demolished, it was just a lifeless, headless house with exposed walls. Behind that was Periappa's house. That was also a big house. He had to get help from a grown-up even to push open its doors. The ferrules were knob-like that one could grab and hang from, swing from, like the doors of the temple. All around that house were walls the height of an adult. Just a little away from it was an open shed thatched with dried coconut fronds for Thatha and Paati. At the front was a work area. His house was to the west of Periappa's house. It wasn't as big as the other houses. There were two sheds right across each other—one to cook and keep things in, the other to sleep in and store things that were used only occasionally. In one corner was a cowshed.

So many cows and buffaloes had been kept tethered in this cowshed, one next to the other. Young calves had bounced and played around. There had once been piles of cow dung everywhere. Mounds of grains, covered with cow-dung to protect them from the elements, had covered the ground like large vats buried upside down. But everything had vanished within the flick of a finger. Now termite nests and anthills proliferated over the shattered plates that lay at his feet.

Very close to the north side of the cowshed was where the old buffalo used to be kept tied. The buffalo had been with them ever since he was a little child. His father's sister, Atthai, had given it to them when it was a little calf. It was very meek and easily scared. If someone new approached it, its eyes filled up with an unfounded fear. It would circle the cowshed over and over again, not stopping even to be milked. The same thing happened when it was taken out to the farmland or to be impregnated—it would gallop around, neigh, horripilate out of fear. But it never tried to pull itself free and escape. It identified everyone from his household but particularly loved his sister. She was the one who grazed it, fed it, did everything for it. She even understood the buffalo's language. It made a particular sound when someone from the family returned home after being away. It had different sounds for different things— for food, for water, to beckon its calf, if it was time for milking, if its fellow buffaloes were taken away for any reason, if it needed a male buffalo. It was so attached to the family. No one other than his mother could milk it. It would smell the person and run away, kicking. It would allow itself to be milked until the next calf in its uterus was seven or eight months old. Only when they decided to stop milking it would it stop lactating.

They had sold it only a month before they were displaced. What could they do with it thereafter? They couldn't keep it in the valavu, in the house that they were going to move into that was one among a cluster of houses with a common street running through. Some people from

Karattur bought it and took it away. The very next night, his mother thought that she heard the old buffalo and got up to check. And sure enough, there it was standing outside! It had come running back in the middle of the night. Amma couldn't hold back. She hugged its face and started crying. The whole household woke up and rushed outside wondering what had happened. Such a dear old buffalo and he didn't even know where it was any longer.

Memories alone stagnated like the rainwater that collects in the crevices of rocks.

He walked away from the cowshed towards the old house. The last bit of cow dung that Amma had smothered on the floor was still discernible in dried patches. Amma always applied more cow dung on the western corner. It was in the same corner that he and Annan stacked their books. That was the corner where Saraswathi, the Goddess of Learning, ostensibly resided. They had brought a table and a stool from his Atthai's house. There was fighting galore the first week after these items arrived because each of them wanted to use them. Those pieces of furniture might have been old, but they were so smooth and shiny, like a snake's body. Until the night before the table and stool arrived, neither ever sat down to study. Once the furniture arrived though, it was study time all day round. Annan was older and had a lot more to study. So, Annan got the table and stool. But the boy was little at that time—and everyone's pet too. He demanded that they belonged to him with obstinate tears. Appa finally brought another old stool from Chithappa's house and arranged for them to

sit across the table to study. From then on, both of them
stopped studying altogether.

~

They had removed all the roofing and the substructures.
Next, they would raze these lonely walls floating in solitude.
Amma used to stuff everything on the shelves in the
western wall. The eastern wall was quite deep and hosted
all the things the boys had. Here sat the little money boxes
got from a stall at the temple chariot festival. The box that
looked like an orange was always his. Annan had the one
that looked like a mango. It was quite ugly-looking, with
a tip that stuck out like the beak of a parrot. He never felt
like putting money in that one. These collection boxes were
filled bit by agonizing bit—for collecting neem seeds or
for digging out groundnuts and such. The Karattur chariot
festival was celebrated every year in the Tamil month of
Maasi, between February and March, and celebrations
went on the whole month. They would hire a cart to go to
the festival. Their relatives would give the children some
money to buy something for themselves from the stalls
there. Thatha, Aaya, Appuchi, Atthai . . . all of them. That
was when these boxes were full of money. Amma also gave
them money once a week on Thursdays to spend in the
market. Annan would buy himself something or the other
to eat and spend it all. The boy's money would go directly
into the box. And the money he collected was used up at
the time school reopened, to buy books and notebooks.

Memories of incidents were spread across the walls. Every spot evoked images that filled his heart. At the earthen hearth that lay wrecked, dishonest actions were uncovered. Amma had terrified Annan as she held both his hands, threatening to pile burning charcoal on them. Annan had apparently taken money without anyone's knowledge. If he had taken the money, the charcoal would burn him; if he hadn't, the sizzling coal would have no effect. With sweat pouring over his entire face, Annan had admitted to taking the money. Amma had tanned his hide that day.

The noise of the crows interrupted his reverie. They had begun to settle on the tamarind trees. These birds that used to brush their wings against the vadhanaram trees in the goat farm as they flew by appeared like little dots. Apparently, there was a goat farm there a long time ago. But now, only a plaque that commemorated Kamarajar's inauguration of that goat farm still remained.

It would soon get dark here. Amma would look for him. He should leave now. When he returned from school, he had come here straight without informing her, furiously determined to somehow get hold of that dog at least today. His mother would have assumed that he was playing somewhere. But where could he play now? There had been so many games to play in the forest. When he joined with the children of the farm workers, they kicked up so much dust in the air—enough to wonder if the late afternoon sky got its colour from the red soil. They played with no heed to the dimming skies.

He could barely play anything ever since they had moved into the valavu. Other houses choked theirs from both sides. Under the pretext of renovation, the houses had eaten into the streets too. Whatever was left after all this was the only space to play. Boys who were learning to ride bicycles constantly kept cutting across into that space. There were always people on the streets too—those who went to fetch water, those returning from the forest. On top of all that were the girls who sat on the thresholds of their homes under the pretext of combing their hair or delousing it, only to watch all the boys who were out playing. And the frequent chides. 'Don't touch this', 'Don't touch that', 'Don't go there', 'Don't come here'. How could anyone even feel like playing in this environment? The only thought that occurred to him there was to scoop up some dust, sprinkle it on everyone's faces and run away somewhere.

A gentle darkness enveloped him. Only his light-coloured pants were visible as he walked. He could see the loggers arrive far away. It was indeed quite beautiful to see them in the dim light as they walked with their axes and saws balanced on their shoulders. But these were the people who gruesomely chopped to pieces the tall standing palm trees that were until then full of life and health.

The flourishing crowns of the palmyra trees that produced ice apples and palm toddy in abundance were being ripped off and discarded. Little boys who liked palm hearts came running for the last bit of goodness before the trees withered away. The trees that spread across the forests and stood with stately elegance were all succumbing to the deathly blows of the bulldozer. These people came to do this job from somewhere far away. With unrecognizable faces. They kept axing down the trees and sending them to the brick kilns. The sight of the workers boarding the bus with their food containers and hands hanging loose or else riding away in their bicycles became a daily event.

How many trees! Like the palmyra tree near the water irrigation channel that had led to a fight between him and his Chithi. The fruit from that tree was so sweet, it was like eating jaggery. The top of the hard shells had husks smooth like butter and bunched together. The bottom was covered with coarse husks that hung torn and fibrous. It was these shells that had the sweetest fruit. Thatha would annoy everyone by repeating this every time they ate palm fruits. His description of the husks was repulsive to hear. Still, he would say it with such relish.

There were always fights involved when it came to the fruits from that tree. The tree was right outside Chithappa's house. The boy used to wake up to the call of the rooster and gather all the fruits from that tree that dropped with the breeze. In the morning, Chithi would look around the tree for the fruits and, finding none, scold him. She would say anything that came to her. But he wouldn't hold back either and would yell back at her. Chithi went on disregarding the fact that she was fighting with a little boy. Then it became a fight between his mother and Chithi, and soon Appa and Chithappa were butting heads too. For a long time, no one talked with each other. Even if they chanced upon each other, they growled.

The tree at the northern end was the best for palm toddy. Kandhan could climb that tree. If he climbed up once, he came down with a *puradai*, a dried-gourd container, brimming with theluvu, a non-alcoholic, sweet palm toddy. If he climbed a second time, another container full of toddy came down with him. Just that tree alone could fill a whole pot with toddy. The sap seeped out non-stop until the frond dried up. It was on top of that tree that Appa furtively drank kallu, fermented toddy. He snapped a frond stalk and made a straw out of it. He climbed the tree and drank nearly a quarter measure from the containers held between each of the frond knuckles. He then climbed down the tree swiftly, just as he had climbed up. He climbed without any rope or harness, and drank seating himself amidst the spathe. Since the tree oozed enough sap to make the containers overflow, no one knew that some went missing. Kandhan never found out about this secret operation till the end. The palm jaggery that his wife made—that she boiled in a large open vat with her hair pulled up in a large bun—tasted just like honey. God knows which forest they had gone to now, scouring for hooch.

In the grip of darkness, the whole forest evoked the scene of a massacre. The bulldozer had razed all the plinths and was filling the pits with the debris. The borders were all erased without a trace. There were no landmarks to identify one's land from another's. The bulldozer was approaching from the direction of the lake, levelling everything in its path it went along. Its bloody hands and demonic fangs had not yet touched the stretch of land right at the front.

Just seeing it approach with its iron jaws that levelled even the strongest walls was terrifying. It was an image of a juggernaut that swallowed anything and everything in its way and rolled on. One that pulled out the richness of the earth from deep inside and spat it out.

The roots of the felled trees came out like gigantic tubular root crops. Creepers, boundary trees and thorn shrubs were all severely uprooted. A crowd had collected around them. They practically crawled on top of each other in a furious bid to grab as much as they could. As if this was going to help fuel their kitchens for the rest of their lives. Perhaps they were gathering good pieces of wood and herbs for their own pyres? Whatever the reason, this was the last bit of fortune from this land for these people. The land that had once begot in abundance field after field of lush pearl millets and fertile green vegetables. It spilt out any residual trace of vegetation to the ruthless assault of this bulldozer.

Ensuring that every last bit of life was sucked out of the land were the supervising government officials in their spick and span outfits. They hovered around with notebooks in their hands. As if they wouldn't move on until the entire earth was excavated and exposed. As soon as the land was taken by the housing board to build a colony, the officers began swarming around. The way they drove everyone out was as cold-hearted as the God of Death. As if they were reclaiming their ancestral properties. An officer with no moustache arrived one day. His face was perpetually sullen. Whether it was Thatha or anyone else in his household, they all folded their hands out of respect when they spoke to this man. He only spoke in commands. 'He has power in the government. It is we who have to obey him,' Thatha would say. Once everyone left the forests, the bulldozer crept in. The officers were stoic like Death in handing out orders and measures to the workers. This was what had been going on for a month now. What other actions would they take to completely destroy these lands?

The boy sat on the mound around the well. The boundary marker was still standing. And so were two coconut trees. The hired hands had slit the throats of everything here and, like children on a rampage, left it all to writhe helplessly to death. Under a coconut tree was a dog pit. Looked like that was where Mani slept. The shade of the coconut tree was cool. The dog had dug out some soil and made a round pit. The soil was still cool. What would it do when they chopped down these trees too? Would the dog come to the valavu or would it give up its life here? He couldn't decide.

Poor cat, he suddenly recalled. It grew up like a child with the family. As soon as they began to pack all their things, it turned mad. It meowed incessantly. No one could catch it. Appa had suggested that it be put in a gunny bag and carried along. They tried cajoling it, tempting it, chasing it, chiding it. It ran away somewhere. The next day, it was found right there in the forest, dead, with its throat bitten off. It seemed like it had been caught by the dog. Akka used to feed it from her plate. The cat ate from one corner of Akka's plate. If it smelt curd and rice, it came running from wherever it was. It gave up its life the very next day after they moved out. All the creatures that played around were gone. Only the dog still remained, but in a calcified state, and kept coming back into the forest. The whole lot of goats from the pen had been taken to the market. Only the people and their limbs still remained.

Would they keep collecting firewood until they cleared the whole forest? Women, boys and children were all running with baskets in their hands. They didn't spare even the aloe leaves. He could check there to see if someone was going back to the valavu. He could go back with them, he decided, and got up.

The mound around the well was quite tall. For irrigation purposes, it was built to be a foot taller than the Pamberi well. One could see all the way to the lake from here. His Atthai used to make a visit from Maniyur once a month. They'd all stand on the mound to look for her. Each wanted the brag, 'I spotted her first!' Whenever Atthai visited, everyone was happy. 'You must eat with me', 'You must drink coffee with me,' they said as they pulled Atthai in all directions and troubled her.

Whenever the temple festival was announced, Atthai arrived driving her white goats. Along with her came her son too. Atthai's husband had passed away at a young age. She had only one son. If she came for the festival, she stayed with them for a week or ten days. They invited all their relatives to come over. Amma's relatives arrived in bigger groups—a crowd from Amma's younger sister Chinnamma's family from Karattur and Maama's family from Kollur. The flour made specially for the festival was quite distinctive. Whenever kadalaimaavu was made, it got over quickly. Occasionally, they cooked a goat too. Would that sort of happiness ever come back again? If Atthai were to visit thereafter, how would they all be with each other, together in one place, now that they had all moved away, each in their own direction?

To see their own, they would have to plan a visit going forward. Not that there was no bickering or fights when they were all together. There were always fights between Amma and Periamma or Periamma and Chithi or Chithi and Amma on little matters—if the goats strayed into the cultivated fields or if the chickens shat somewhere. Often, there were fights for no reason. But after a few days of them ignoring each other, things returned to normalcy. There were fights with Paati too. Paati didn't get along that well with her daughters-in-law. Still, it could never be like living with everyone together! On the west side was Thatha's older brother's family. On the east side was Thatha's younger brother's family. If anyone needed anything they just had to call out once. There would be a response no matter what time of day or night. Going forward, it would come down to a polite smile when they ran into each other in the streets.

He walked around the well. He couldn't quite see inside it. Darkness had deposited itself like char. The folks who had come to pick firewood were beginning to use the tar road to get back to the settlement. There were footpaths in all directions. No distinctions remained on cultivable lands. Anyone could go in any direction. He changed his pace to catch up with them. The well slowly receded farther and farther away—the well in which he used to swim; into which he fell twice and was rescued. It was quite a deep well. Eight *muttu*. It was someone's goodwill that he was saved that day. His mother and he had tied a pot to the irrigation apparatus to draw water from the well. It was always faster when two people worked on it together. So his mother drew from over the sluice. He drew it, weaving his legs around the water-lifting apparatus with his crotch against the pillar. It was a mud pot. A pot that had a bulging middle. It held twice as much as a regular pot. He had drawn it all the way up. Amma leant over to grab the pot. The pot kept sliding down. 'I am not able to reach,' she said. At that instant, he fell in along with the pillar and everything. The iron in the apparatus had rusted. If he had fallen on his head, that would have been the end of him. Luckily, only his hip was injured.

The other time was when everyone had gone to Karattur for a funeral. They had just installed a brand-new motor at Chithappa's. A centipede came out limping from the water channel the motor pumped into. Engrossed in making a path for it to go on, the boy kept moving backwards and got himself dangerously close to the edge. He slipped and fell into the well, but managed to grab on to a rock sticking out of the wall. Selvan called for help and Chithappa pulled him out. He has been rescued twice but if he fell in once more, that would be the end of him, an astrologer had predicted. Though, anyway, now they had moved away once and for all from this place.

Memories and events would remain buried, and concrete structures would be raised over them. The fragrance of the soil would be sealed with concrete. It would deny the land even drops of rain. Where were so many people going to come from? To whom were they going to sell these homes that they were building? The more he thought about it, the more perplexing it was. Steeped in his thoughts, he hurried towards the baskets of firewood, half walking, half running.

Chapter 2

It had been more than ten days since he last visited his Thatha and Paati. If he delayed any more, he'd have to endure Paati's incessant bickering and her tears that rolled down suddenly as she kept talking. He couldn't blame her, though. After having her sons so close to her and seeing them all the time, she found it unbearable that, like a thatched roof wrecked and strewn around by a cyclone, they were all brusquely scattered and thrown into different corners. He had resolved to pay them a visit at least once a week.

As soon as he returned from school, he flung his school bag into the house, stretched and cracked his hands and left. If Amma was around, she would tilt her head a certain way in disapproval. It meant, 'If you don't see the old woman, won't you be able to swallow your food?' Her anger and irritation at her now frail and drained mother-in-law were yet to subside. He had never understood this unending fight. It was good in a way that Amma was not home then. Akka was getting the stove started in the veranda. He called out to her, informed her about where he was heading and left immediately.

Beyond the fenced forest area, by the banks of the lake, was some unassigned land that the boy's grandparents had paid some money for. When the builders took their cultivable land for the colonies, Thatha and Paati built a small shack for themselves on that land. The boy's house in the valavu had remained unused when they lived in the forest. Periappa and Chithappa also used to own individual houses in the valavu. They had since sold them to build themselves larger houses in the forest. Now, the whole family was forced into a state akin to that of the Indian roller bird when Kandhan destroyed and threw out its nest along with its eggs and fledglings. Should they fly around the same tree lamenting their broken nest or should they look for another place to build a new nest? Nothing was clear. The boy's family decided to move into their house in the valavu. When Periappa's father-in-law promised him a tiny parcel of land if he moved closer, Periappa took the offer and built a small house on it. A house only as big as his old workshop. Chithappa too went to his father-in-law's house. But he didn't build himself a house there, he moved in with them.

During those days, Thatha looked like a meek dog. He would be lying on the cot but vanish suddenly. He would sit on the stone mortar outside the house and stare at the sky. He would roam around somewhere all day. He wouldn't engage in a conversation with anyone and only yell irritably at Paati. 'The food is terrible! the stew is tasteless!', and a thousand more such complaints. It was quite sad to see him like that. The sons were all relieved that they somehow found a way to settle themselves down but none of them showed a breath of concern for their father. They were all afraid that the parents may insist on staying with one of

them. It was Paati who broke the uncomfortable silence
and came up with an idea.

'Why are you being so stubborn? As if there is not a
little space for us under this vast open sky? Won't it suffice
if we built four pillars and a roof over that on the unassigned
land by the lake? At this age when the family is waiting to
get rid of us and the cemetery is waiting for us, do we need
a mansion to live in?'

Thatha took her word literally and built a hut in that
location. The only concern there was the potential flooding
of the lake. But that could be addressed if it happened.
That land was elevated enough. Only if it poured non-stop
for several days would the water reach the brim. They'd
manage as long as they could. When they announced that
they were leaving, none of the sons said anything. There
were long, deep sighs of relief all around.

Only when he reached their place did Paati return home
too. She had gone to pull out weeds in the kiluva forest. It
was the season of weeding in the cotton plantations. Paati
never stopped working. If she did, it would mean starvation
for those two beings.

'Kuppan promised to come by in the evening. Why has
he not come by yet? Till they lived in the forest, they had
something to fill their stomachs with but, apparently, he
has no food at home now. He's really struggling to make
ends meet, he says.'

Paati kept talking as she lit the stove. The wrinkles that
surrounded her eyes were like dried jujube fruit. He sat on
the mortar and chatted with her.

'But how's that, Aaya? He supposedly goes to work someplace in the town. He must be roaming around there, wasting time or getting into trouble. Otherwise why would he be in such a dire state?'

'No, Payya. He's not that kind of person. He was the farm lead for us since your Thatha's Appa's time. He has never stolen anything, ever. He never asked for more than what he was given. He took on tasks and toiled hard. He always kept the monies in order. He must be going through a rough patch.'

'What is Ramayi up to these days?'

Paati blew gently into the fire at the stove to get it up and put a griddle on top of it. She went into the hut and came back with a pot of red millet flour. He pulled out a winnow and the *arivalmanai*, and scraped some palm jaggery.

'Ramayi's husband is good for naught. She's come back here for good. That's another burden on him.'

Just as she made a batter with the red millet flour and poured a dosai, they spotted Kuppan and Ramayi approaching from a distance. Kuppan's body was shrivelled. Was he already that old? The boy was astonished. That body used to be strong like the dark trunk of a palm tree. A body that picked up a gunny bag the height of a man with ease. As soon as she saw him, Ramayi's eyes welled up and her lips spread into a smile. She increased her pace, flashing her betel-stained teeth.

'Ada . . . little master . . .! When did you get here? Don't you look healthy and tall, like a big boy! Oh, I may cast an evil eye on you if I'm not careful! Well, my master, which class are you studying in now?'

She never knew how to stop with one question. She would keep talking without a pause. She had to be bridled and pulled to a halt at some point. It was on her hips that he grew up. If he'd say, 'You look so dark, like you were immersed in a truck full of black ink', she'd draw her hip out and point it out to him.

'It is because I bore you all the time on my hips that they have tarnished and blackened like this. And if one worked in such heat out in the open all the time, what will the body do but get tanned?'

She worked in the farm until she got married. With her tummy sticking out like a basket, she was brought to the farm to work when she was barely a foot tall. Maybe she was shrunken because of all the blows she received from his mother. Her frizzy and discoloured hair used to be matted like a net. His mother would knock hard with her knuckles on that mess of a head. Amma's words crackled throughout the day, from the time Ramayi gathered all the cow dung early in the morning to when she drove all the goats into the pen at the end of the day. Moreover, the 'status' of being Kuppan's daughter only led to her being taken for granted. Still, Ramayi was the one who brought him up, enduring all that.

He responded to her with a smile, looking at her eyes that were still reeling from the surprise. A response that addressed all her questions.

'I came here only a little while ago. I'm in ninth standard now. So, have you come back here for good?'

She pursed her lips and smacked them noisily. She held her sadness on her face as she sat herself in a corner. Her face shrunk to the size of a fist. Kuppan too seated himself next to her.

'Um-hm. That rotten dog, I was suffering from a stomach ache for four days. Did he even ask me, "What is wrong with you?" Not a word. Whenever I looked for him, he was at the landlord's house. As if they reward him lavishly. All they do is point out a thousand problems before handing out the trifle of a salary. Those landlords are nothing like the ones here. They are soulless. And even the little they give, he drinks and drinks and squanders all of it on alcohol and beats me up for more. That's why I gathered the children and moved back here.'

She wiped her nose with the loose end of her sari. Then, she blew her nose, wiped that on the ground, looked at her father and spoke, cracking her knuckles as if to curse. She had such a unique way of talking. She turned her head like a chameleon, twisted her face, made gestures like cracking her knuckles and intonated her words like a song. He simply wanted to ignore what she was saying and just watch her talk.

'It's not as if my father has bundles and bundles of money stacked away. On the contrary, he doesn't have a penny. My life stinks here too, dear.'

Kuppan's pride was wounded. He moved away to spit out all the tobacco he was holding in his cheek and came back.

'She doesn't have what it takes to take control of the situation and thrive. And she mocks me. Look how much she talks. She isn't my daughter, she is a devil who has come to eat me.'

'Kuppa, she is just ranting with frustration. Just let her be. Here, eat these two hot, red millet dosai. I made them with palm jaggery.'

Paati handed one to Kuppan and one to Ramayi. She received it in the loose end of her sari. Paati put one on a plate and gave that to her grandson. This was Paati's standard food. It didn't cost anything to make. And it was quick too—she could make a few in a jiffy.

Darkness filled in lazily. There was no sight of Thatha as far as they could see. The boy couldn't leave till he saw Thatha. *I should just stay the night*, he thought to himself, and began to help Paati. Someone jumped over the colony compound wall. The wall that was laid out and being constructed per measured plans. That completely isolated this shack on the banks of the lake. One had to find the foot track near the compound wall, follow it all the way to the end of the wall and make a 'u' turn in order to get to the shack. Strong men would simply jump over the wall to get there. The man who did just that was Murugan.

'Is the big master not here?'

He sat on the mortar outside. He was so tall that seeing him seated on the mortar was like seeing a full-size pestle perched on it. He had a bushy moustache that completely covered his mouth. Once they started digging the foundation for the colony homes, many men like Murugan settled around here with their families. They came from near and far. They were mostly bricklayers and earth workers.

Murugan's job was to dig foundations for each of the houses in the colony. The labour charge was a lump sum that the contractor had negotiated per foundation. Murugan couldn't ask for more than that. If he did, the consequence would most likely leave him and his family starving without a job. So he took on part-time jobs like digging wells and building mud walls in the surrounding villages. Murugan had a lot of children. About ten or twelve. Even now, his wife was pregnant. Once, a fight almost broke out between Appa and Murugan over how many children he had. It happened when he was building a wall in Munnur. The heat was on the rise. The toddy that Appa had drank that morning sent a hot kick to his brain, making him ask Murugan a question that was burning within him for a while.

'You've become old enough to lose all your teeth and you still yearn to make more babies?'

His wife burst out sobbing loudly. Murugan grabbed a crowbar and rushed towards his dad. 'If I have them, I will feed them. Am I looking to you to support us? If you want, you make a few too.' Thatha had to get involved to calm Murugan down.

Paati served Murugan a dosai too. The boy found it amusing to watch Murugan's gigantic cup-like hands move up to his mouth and down.

'So . . . will you please let me know when the master returns. If he brings mutton, I would like two portions.'

'You live right here, don't you, Muruga. Why don't you come back in a little while and tell him this yourself?'

'Okay, I will come by after the nine o'clock horn.'

Murugan left, leaving no trace of his visit. He was quite a remarkable man. If not, could he have moved here from far away and survived with all the little children he had? Like a wildcat, he arrived quietly. He finished any job that he was tasked to do. Anyway, that he lived close by to Thatha and Paati was such a big help for them. All they had to do was call out for him and he would come over. There were about ten or fifteen families around. After all, didn't the thousands of houses waiting to be built need foundations to be dug out?

Paati poured water for Kuppan and Ramayi. They held their hands together like a palm leaf as they drank the water. If it was brighter, he would have found a palm fruit shell to drink from. Kuppan caressed his moustache and belched.

'Where in the town are you working, Kuppa?'

'Pccch, what can I tell you about my woes! If the farmlands were still around, I would have stayed put right here protecting master's feet. That was an unfortunate calamity. Now, I go to chop lumber at the sizing unit. But you see, there are mounds and mounds of them. No way can I keep cutting them, I feel my chest getting congested. The young fellows chop them up with so much vitality. I am not able to do so. Moreover, only if I slog till the end of the day can I see a little bit of money. Our lads are all doing only this kind of job these days.'

The longing and sadness that his voice suggested seemed genuine. Paati and Ramayi went to a corner of the yard to shave thorns off stalks. Paati's eyesight was getting worse progressively. Still, she didn't shy away from working. She never sat still; she was always meddling with something or the other. After they moved here too, she began to rear chickens. There were a lot of snakes along the lake's shore. They slithered into the houses more often during the dry season than when there was water in the lake. Paati never heeded any warnings about them.

'Why don't you see if there are any other farms you can work at, Kuppa?'

His question must have triggered Kuppa's frustration.

'What are you saying, how many farms are around nowadays? All the farm owners have moved to the town. What sprouts in this mountainous land? Only if you can irrigate with the salty water and toil away are you going to see something. Isn't everyone moving towards other things, owning a lorry or weaving or this or that? People who used to have farms here are themselves without one these days. Why would the ones already taking care of those let someone in? As is it, they are all worried they will lose their jobs.'

'Oh well.'

Paati gathered the thorn twigs that she had chopped up and piled them in a corner of the backyard. They were of the black mesquite variety. They crackled as they burned. Ramayi came back and sat down again.

'Ask about the big Saami. Let's leave. It's dark, look.' She nudged Kuppan. He raised his voice and said, 'Saami, we will take leave. It's getting dark. Don't know how she is faring with the children. They won't stay a minute without Ramayi.'

'Are you leaving, Kuppa? But there's no sign of the big Saami.'

'Let him come back when he does. I can meet him tomorrow or the day after. Would there be a grain of rice to spare? If you have something, please give anything, Saami.'

'I only have some finger millet, Kuppa. Wait, I will bring some.'

Paati went in and brought out the finger millet basket. The millet glittered a deep red in the light of the kerosene lamp, like ripe jujube fruit. Paati scooped some into her hands; she could well be measuring gold.

'Kuppa, all these years, we took millet home only after we measured a share for you. But look at what things have come to now. We ourselves don't know what to do for the next meal in this house.'

'Saami, big Saami . . . how can you say such words? Are we all not here for you? We will work like dogs for you even if all that is left is our skin. You are god to us. Can such words come out of your mouth?'

Kuppan lamented like a man who had stepped on fire. Everyone's eyes were filled to the brim. Paati measured the finger millet. Ramayi held the loose end of the sari like a bag to receive it.

'Kuppa, leave aside all what you said. Will just talking about past glory bring fodder for the cattle? I'm no longer a landlord. I'm now only a labourer. Only if I work in a few fields will I be able to feed the two stomachs. You know the big Saami very well. Ever since the fields were taken away for the colonies, his spirits have completely diminished. They gave us five thousand for the fields. A thousand of that has gone into this little structure of a house. What can we get with the rest of the money, tell me? Buy the kids two buns each and that's the end of that money.'

'Saami . . .'

'Let this be the last time, Kuppa. Come any time you want to. Would you like a meal? I will happily pour you a ladle of whatever we eat. But don't come every day with some excuse or the other. What else can I say.'

Paati's voice subsided. Like the quiet after a downpour. They kept walking farther and farther away. In the darkness, Kuppan's soft sniffling muffled by the towel covering his mouth alone was heard.

~

It was getting as dark as char. The boy caught the chickens as they clucked their way back into the backyard and put them on top of a tree. Chickens that hatched out of the eggs that Paati had incubated. She reared them with great care, as if they were human babies. The hens were at the onset of their next egg-laying season. The chickens weren't yet used to climbing the tree. They still didn't know how to hold on to the branches with their beaks and stay put. They kept falling down as he put them on the tree. Leaving the ones that stayed on the tree, the boy and Paati put the rest under a basket.

Thatha had not returned yet. In such darkness, where did he go instead of coming home at a normal hour? Paati grumbled on and on.

'Total disregard for time and tide! Are we so full of vitality that we can take down four men with one kick? Doesn't the man know how to use his brains and senses? As if the road that leads to our house is laid in tar. What if he falls into a pit or something? If he dies, well that's a matter that could be taken care of. But what if he breaks a leg or an arm, who will take care of him? Not the wonderful sons that we have borne. They left us out here in this pit to fare for ourselves whether we are able to or not. Doesn't he need to be aware of all this? If a tree matures, it becomes firewood, if a man matures, he becomes useless like a monkey, said Selvandharan, and it is turning out to be right . . .'

'Ada Aaya . . . why are you sitting here going on and on blabbering out whatever comes to your mouth?'

'That's right, I blabber. At least you come by this side once in ten days or so. Which other dog visits us? We are left with no one to check on us, even to see if we are dead or alive.'

Only if she dragged every person in the family into her monologue and threw into the air a few questions intended for them would Paati feel content. Once Thatha returned, though, all this would subside. She prepared some kali alone for him. To make saaru, the broth, Thatha had to be back. Which saaru? What all to put in it? He needed to stand next to her and provide instructions. In spite of that, he would still have a thousand gripes about it. They pulled out the cots and lay outside. A lamp was hung from the top. A frog croaking somewhere in the distance sounded like a fly trapped in a tin container.

'Payya, what if it rains? Maybe he has fallen somewhere, inebriated? Will you go look for him close by? You know my eyes are hardly good. Otherwise I would go looking myself.'

He got up and climbed down the platform from the front yard. At the corner of the compound wall—the wall went past the low-lying area and continued beyond except where it paused at the path that led to Karambakadu—a lamp flickered. Where did Thatha get a lamp from? He raised an eyebrow and looked attentively. He heard a blend of voices. He couldn't tell whose voices they were, but as he got closer it became clearer. It was his Thatha, with Murugan accompanying him.

'Leave it alone . . . the goat kid . . . as if you are some big shit. You want to hold my kid. Have I become that useless that I can't hold it myself? Leave the kid alone . . .'

'Please wait, Saami. I will bring it over for you. Please hold my hand for support. Careful, careful . . .'

Thatha was heavily intoxicated. He wouldn't be struggling so much otherwise. He would have staggered his way home somehow and wouldn't have needed any help.

'This is like the proverbial story of putting an old man on the dais just to have a wedding. Here we are with nothing to eat. In all this, this man had to drink to the point of unconsciousness.' Paati's prattle drifted over to them.

The boy ran over and held his grandfather. Murugan walked ahead with the lantern in one hand and a little goat in the other.

'Who's that . . . mm . . . Ponnaiyya, is it you? When did you come, my dear? Let the rest be however they are. You should be well. But that brother of yours, I brought him up bearing him on my back. He doesn't even visit me these days.'

'Thatha, he goes to the cinema tent to work at the soda stall there. If he leaves in the afternoon, he doesn't return home until twelve or one at night. How will he be able to sit next to you and spend time with you?'

'If you say so, my dear. Look at the goat kid, I went to Vettur to buy it. Why? To make mutton tomorrow. All for you, my dear. If I manage to leave two annas behind, those will be for you. No one can budge me, even by a strand of hair.'

When he was drunk, he couldn't control this gabble easily. He would keep spitting as he walked to clear his throat and talk non-stop. Paati's entire family would be spoken about. And if he wanted to kick anyone from the village, he would line them up in his mind and dole out imaginary kicks. Ever since they moved by the lake, he got into the goat-trading business. There were two markets that he went to every week— the Karattur one on Tuesdays and the Kalaiyur one on Saturdays. Every once in a while, he went to the one in Sillur on Fridays.

He also sold meat. He cut a lamb every Wednesday and Sunday. Naachan would come over to skin the lamb. When he cut up the meat, it was barely enough for the workers who had come to work on the colony. The meat disappeared in no time. And he would make his rounds and collect all the money. In some convoluted way, he too did his share and didn't stay idle.

'Check the man properly, Payya. See if he is still complete or is missing parts,' Paati yelled from where she was. There were thorns all around. The black mesquite shrubs grew even on rocks. Even a small prick hurt as if poison were smeared into the wound. He brought him on to the pathway carefully. Murugan went on to tether the goat kid to a shoot in the front yard. The goat was well-shaped. It would bear at least ten parts that would each sell for fifteen rupees. And the skin would fetch nothing less than thirty. *Wonder how much he bought it for. In his drunken state, he may have paid a lot more*, the boy thought to himself but didn't say it aloud. If he did, Paati wouldn't stay quiet. As it is, she was already yelling at Thatha.

'A goat? On top of all this, a goat?'

'Who the hell do you think you are? Spare the tempering!'

'If I don't, would you eat without it? Come in.'

'Ey, crone, what saaru have you made?'

'Why will I make any and have your stomach reject it. I was waiting for you.'

He made Thatha sit on the cot. He took his towel and put it on one side of the cot. Thatha removed his *veshti* and used it as a pillow as he lay down in his *komanam*. His body was shrivelled like a dried plantain leaf. At one time, his body was the envy of the people around. Only his Chithappa took after Thatha. His Periappa and Appa were similar—just a shove and their fragile bodies would tumble a few times before toppling over.

'I have made kali already. What saaru should I make?'

'Give her a kick, da! Constantly bickering.'

Murugan walked over and stood by the cot. 'Saami,' he cried with agitation, as if Thatha had fainted and he was calling him back to consciousness. 'What, da?' asked Thatha, taking his time.

'Tomorrow, please save two pieces of mutton for me. I will pay you back in a week. I am telling you now so you don't tell me later on that only one or one and a half pieces are available.'

'Okay, okay, go now.'

'Don't forget, Saami. I will come by in the morning.' And he left.

Paati lit up the stove and placed a pot on it. 'What saaru should I make? Tell me.'

'Why do you make it sound as if you have a thousand options? Can you make kuzhambu like at that Sera fellow's shop at least once? It is so good. Like that, can you?'

'Now, are you going to tell me or shall I go lie down? As it is, my back is so sore from chopping branches until the sun came down . . .'

'If you have flat bean seeds, use that. Put five chillies in there. You should grind them into a fine paste, like sandalwood. Then cook it well.'

Paati began to work with the flat bean seeds. As soon as the boy lay down in Paati's cot, Thatha called out to him, 'Ey, Ponnaiyya, come here. Did you see what your Chithappa has done?'

'Why, Thatha, did he pick a fight with someone?'

'Who dares touch my son? Will I spare him?'

He got up like a spring, biting his lower lip, making a threatening 'ummm' sound. He then calmed himself down after he cursed out loud and lay back down on the cot.

'The sire has bought himself a bullock cart.'

'Is that so! Well, as long as he can ride it smartly and make a living . . .' Paati commented as she rinsed out the flat bean kernels. She used some furnace oil and blew into the fire; the happiness from hearing that news spread on her face.

'What sort of occupation is that? Instead of buying an acre or two of land and farming on that, he is apparently going to buy carts and make a living out of that. Useless lad . . .'

'When time becomes favourable, he will buy not just two but four acres. Is it a two-bullock cart?'

'No, just one.'

Thatha kept getting up for every line he spoke. He had no control over himself. He finally sat up and rested his head in his palms. Otherwise he would have vomited.

'This is all he does nowadays. He sits here with his head like this and his livelihood gets deeper into losses,' Paati murmured as she chopped up some chillies. The boy peeled some onions. Thatha's sunken head perked up suddenly. 'Ponnaiyya, come sit by me.'

The boy sat next to him. Thatha gently stroked his head. His large calloused hands tremored. He was mesmerized by his grandson's growth. He rubbed his back as if to assure him. His words were indistinctive.

'What does she know, da. She came here yesterday. I know this land that was ours since my grandfather's days. And who knows how many generations before that . . . And today, they are building some paltry colonies on it. Worthless ticks. They wouldn't match up to my little finger . . .'

'Thatha, stop talking and lie down.'

'I will talk! Today they shut my well too . . . They shut it! That one that never dried even during the hottest years, da. How many cultivations we've reaped from that! The way the ears of millet swayed, like a lass laughing coyly. How much chilli and cotton! Every bit of it is gone. That bulldozer dug out the soil and heaped it right in front of my eyes, da. My stomach was on fire. They have buried everything in loads and loads of sand!'

He cried shaking like an old dog vomiting from its guts. The boy held his grandfather's shoulders and shook him, saying, 'Thatha, Thatha!' The sobs rose from the bottom of his ribs. The boy put his hands on his back and hugged his neck. Paati put the kernels aside and came over.

'Don't you drink and moan like this. Just how did that well give you a good life? It was possessed. You father put a rope around the irrigation structure at the well and hung himself to death because someone said something. The image of that mountain-like body hanging in mid-air is still fresh in my mind. That well killed a great man such as him. And what good did it do for the sons and their children? Saving Saamiyappan's only fall into the well turned out to be such a huge task. Ponnaiyyan fell twice and survived, thanks to the good heart of some god. And did we end up with a mansion from all the water we irrigated from it? We were always living meal to meal. The well was possessed with destitution! If they shut it, let them. Why are you going there to see what they are doing instead of going to work and coming home directly? Like we have any control over there any more. Just let go, won't you? Sitting here and lamenting like this.'

Paati put the kernels in the pot. From the treetop the rooster crowed an untimely call. With a sore and itchy throat. It was the first crowing by a new rooster.

Chapter 3

Whenever Amma's brother and sister-in-law visited, Amma couldn't hold still for a minute. He was Amma's only brother, older and, more importantly, slightly better off than them. That was why Amma was in a frenzy that morning, as if possessed by a spirit. How many times would she walk back and forth between the house and the veranda! She held a flask in her hand and walked into the house. Then she turned back and went to the veranda as if she had forgotten something. Then she stopped to talk to them. And to Akka. Akka mumbled something quietly to herself. Appa and Maama were in conversation. His Annan was on the cot, curled and twisted like a tied-up sack. Even though the boy was awake, he continued to lie down and did not get up.

It was all the exhaustion from the day before. The boy's irritation and anger at Amma had still not been assuaged. How sharp-tongued was this same Amma just the day before. Look at how she was fluttering about gleefully on seeing her brother and sister-in-law! If not for Appa, he would have lost control of himself in his ire. And wouldn't have recovered from the fizzy light-headedness. Or the shame he was subject to—as if he was stripped naked, tied to a pole and whipped. All this over a paltry issue.

It all started two days ago in school. The boys were chasing each other around playfully in their classroom. The maths teacher had not yet arrived. The boy and Ravi were very close. They had plenty of petty fights and angry exchanges between them also. Sometimes they threw blows at each other and brawled quite fiercely. When the maths teacher did not show up, these two suddenly began to chase each other around the class. He jumped over desks and benches but Ravi chased him relentlessly. The whole class was chaotic and no one knew what was going on. Ravi chased him everywhere and finally caught him in the corner of the class. In the giddiness of his victory, he pinched him on his hand. Once on his cheek. Once on his hip. And as he pinched him on his thigh, he shouted out, 'Dei, he isn't wearing any underwear!'

Senthil, Murali and Balu all got together, surrounded him and pinched him hard all over his front and back. They mocked and laughed at him. He shrank into himself and held on tightly to his shorts. His eyes were brimming with tears and on the verge of spilling over any minute. The pain from all the pinches was also unbearable. Until then, he didn't think that not wearing underwear was something to be made fun of. Ravi pulled him aside later and explained himself. With guilt.

'Dei, I did all that in the madness of the moment. Thoughtlessly.'

'It is okay, da . . .'

'Are you not wearing one only today or do you not wear one at all?'

'Should I be wearing one? I didn't know, da.'

Ravi gave a very awkward smile. He said after a little while, with some reservation, squirming the entire time, 'You are a total country bumpkin, da. We are in tenth standard. We are going to be in plus one next year. We have to wear full pants like college students. We are now older, aren't we? Wear underwear, da.'

At home, the boy couldn't ask just anyone to buy underwear. He was too embarrassed to walk into a store and buy any by himself. The commotion they had created in class the other day was eroding his peace. With extreme reluctance, he bought a few from a vendor at a street corner. He kept the underwear in a bin. Amma was gathering clothes to wash when her eyes fell on them. 'Whose are these?' she asked.

'These are mine, Amma. I bought them.'

'Why now, we seem to have crossed international borders here. Is your penis not staying down if you wear only your shorts?'

Amma's words fell like a scythe on his chest. He burst into tears and cried loudly. Appa came running and held him against his chest.

'Get lost, you donkey of a woman! Don't you know what to say to your son?'

'What does she know? I will buy you better ones. What does she know about current trends? Will you cry for all this now?' But Appa's words did not mend the wounds. He didn't eat dinner that night. Appa tried pacifying him in several ways and gave up after a while. Amma got a lot of scolding. That gave him some satisfaction.

'Let it go now. What would Maama and Atthai think if I keep lying down like this just because I am angry with Amma?' He got up and came out. Appa and Maama were sitting on the cot, Atthai was sitting on the plinth. She saw him and made a comment without moving her heavy body, tilting her head slightly from where she was.

'So, the master had to sleep in until now? Kids who study well would have woken up early and started studying by now. But you?'

'When did you arrive?' he politely inquired with a wide grin and tried to slip away to wash his face. His eyes were puffed up and red.

He didn't know why the two of them had come over so early. Maama was a masonry foreman. They lived in Karattur. Atthai always spoke in a chiding tone. Her eyes grew large, her nostrils flared up and her lips alternated between being bunched up and spread out when she spoke. She had a dominating demeanour. Maama was docile. Since the boy was so used to them, he wasn't being particularly mindful around them.

'Why don't you come by . . . Maama has brought half a dozen jackfruits. Who's there to eat all that? If you come over, you can bring some back, can't you?'

'I will come, Atthai.'

Appa and Maama were engrossed in their conversation about politics and paid no heed to them. Both of them were ardent fans of 'Thalaivar', 'the revolutionary leader', one of the two most famous actors of that time who went on to become the chief minister of Tamil Nadu eventually. There was not a Thalaivar movie that Appa had not watched. He did not watch anyone else's movies either. He didn't care at all for the other popular actor— 'Thilagam', as he was known. The actor of all actors. 'Thoppaiyan' was what Appa called him. Pot-bellied. Earlier, there was a Rama Talkies where they screened Thalaivar's movies back to back once every week. He always went only for the second show. Occasionally, he took the boy along as well. They would clean sand off the floor and watch the movie sitting on it. It was a miracle that the talkies had not exploded into bits with all the whistling and cheering from the fans. They were building a bigger movie theatre in Karattur town.

'From now on, there won't be any more dawns for the party with the symbol of sunrise. Back then, he partnered with that lady and managed to win.'

'That was a higher-level election. Even though that fell apart, it was Thalaivar who won here. As long as he is alive no one can move him from the position.'

'One should take heart. And look at that Thoppaiyan. An absolute miser who wouldn't even shoo a crow away while he is eating for fear of losing crumbs to it. But this man, he doesn't have any children, any successor. He will give away all that he has to the people.'

Because the two of them were in complete agreement, they could talk for hours on end like this. And if they started talking about movies, they would go over them scene by scene and relish every detail. They didn't need food, water. He seated himself next to his aunt. Atthai called for Akka.

'So, Pille, what are you doing here? Why don't you come home? Stay over for about ten days. You will be good company for our Geetha too.'

'How can I, Atthai? I am leaving to go to work now. They have started building homes in the colony. The plastering work is going on in full swing. There are groups of masons, people who have come here from god knows where doing this and that. What they don't have are labourers. That's what I've been doing these past ten, fifteen days.'

Akka was astonished even by the smallest of things. She would gather books full of pictures and pore over each picture with the fascination of a little child. Her eyes would grow big. In the excitement of seeing something that she had never seen before, a giggle would escape her. She couldn't contain herself even when just watching black ants marching by. 'Look here!' she would say, pointing out to them with the euphoria of having found the eighth wonder of the world. She knew all about the matters of the colony too. 'We have all seen a brick. But a cement block?' she exclaimed when she saw one for the first time. And talked about it the whole day. But her fascinations weren't worthy of Atthai's attention.

'They let you bear the burden of sand and stone in this scorching heat? Are your father and your mother going to live and feed themselves with the money that you earn? Mm . . .'

Amma served coffee to everyone. Atthai and Maama still hadn't brought up the reason for their visit. 'If you come home, you can bring back a few coconuts, can't you?',

'There's a ton of guavas at home. If you visit us, you can bring them back with you, won't you come?' Atthai went on and on, as if they had never seen any of that in their lives before. He grabbed a book and sat with it, pretending to study.

Atthai had two small measures of land in which they had cultivated a garden. She acted as if everything in the world was available there. If his family visited them, they returned with maybe one small bag of a fruit or vegetable. But, before their land was taken away for the colonies, every time Maama and Atthai visited them, they took back with them bags and bags of chillies, cucumbers, lime toddy, palm fruits—you name it! Only, they talked as if everyone's lives depended on their garden.

After rambling on for a while and beating around the bush, they finally came to the point.

'So . . . what brought you here this early today? Are you going elsewhere after this?'

'Where else would we go? We have come only to see you all, since it's been such a long time.'

Maama put his hand into his beard and fiddled with it. Maama always sported a long, unkempt beard, like a sage. It was white and looked like bleached palm fruit fibres. He would make a 'vrrk, vrrk' sound when he scratched it.

Atthai continued on. 'Why say all that? As a matter of fact, we have come here for a reason. He has spent so many years now as a masonry foreman. Going forward, we are thinking of setting up weaving looms.'

'Oho, that is a good thing. Have you already identified a location?'

'That's where I am short of a little bit of money.'

'You can possibly take a loan on your house, maybe?'

'Yes, we could. But we wanted to ask our family and friends before we did something like that. We all always have a few people who would never say no when sought for a favour. Don't you agree?'

'That is true, indeed.'

Maama was still scratching his beard. His mother and sister were sitting inside, in the midst of the smoke from the stove. Yet, their attention was on every word being spoken outside. The conversation continued between Atthai and Appa.

'From my maternal house to the place I am married into, there has been no dearth of trouble. I have lived a life worse than that of a dog. In spite of that, we don't have any debt with our relatives. Even if that meant us not having anything to feed ourselves.'

'Who is denying all that now?'

'I had already informed Pille about this. We want to ask you now. You have some money in exchange for all your farmlands, isn't it? If you lend us that money, we will pay it back with whatever interest people around here are paying. Or, if you want partnership, that is an option too. Even if we are very close relatives, this is a matter of money.'

'Look here. I don't know anything about weaving. I can't invest money in a business I have no knowledge of. I am also not sure if we are in a state where we can lend you the money. There are four acres of land that have come up for purchase. Out here, in Chinnur. I am trying to see if I can buy that.'

'But you will have some money left?'

'I got twenty-five for the farmlands. Two or three thousand went into repairing this house. When we moved here from the farms, this house was hardly inhabitable. So, whatever is left after that is all I have. I may not have enough even to buy the land. I too may have to seek a loan from someone.'

'What would you get out of the land? Why would you want to sink your money into that? If you put it in weaving, you can see money then and there. Right now, this is the busiest business.'

'Whatever is spent on a land will never go to waste. Are termites going to eat away the land? I will rear a few goats and live out of that. Our god is but this land.'

'Well, that's not what . . .'

'Why talk about this any further? Please talk to someone else to raise your capital.'

'Are we going to eat your money? Or take the money and run away?'

'Who said anything like that?'

'We came here because you are our relative and we thought that you would help . . . Get up now. Let's go.'

They both got up to leave. Appa didn't say anything. He sat staring still like a yogi in deep meditation. Amma came running from inside, calling after her brother. Atthai didn't seem to be bothered even a bit. She held her face tight like an inflated lorry tire. The boy ran in front of them crying 'Maama . . . Atthai . . .' But nothing changed their minds. They kept walking away. As they walked away, Atthai said, 'What difference does it make to have relatives or not, if they are no help in times of need? If they visit, that's two sacks of rice expended. If they don't, that's two sackfuls of rice saved.'

After that, Appa did not wish to spend two sacks of their aunt and uncle's rice. Only his mother talked ceaselessly about her family's grand stories. How else could she express the love she had for her sibling?

~

Amma lay curled up in a ball and didn't get up. She made something to eat only because she had to. She didn't go out anywhere. All day, the women would get together and play thaayam on the neighbour's plinth. Sometimes it went on into the night too. When one left, another took the spot to continue the game. Amma hadn't gone over to be part of it for a couple of days now. In fact, they all went to the movies the day before—all the ladies from Rosakka's house and Kariamma's house. His sister alone joined them. Ever since they had moved here, Amma always went with them to the movies. She would add hair extensions to lengthen her hair and make a large bundle out of it, much like an appam pan, on the backside of her head. And border it with a ring of stringed jasmine and crossandra twirled together. This set off Appa into utmost annoyance. He would say quietly:

The carefully braided hair bun is reeking of illness
The lord who went away still hasn't come back
The carefully combed hair bun is hosting bats now
The lord who promised to come back still hasn't
come back.

If those words ever reached her ears, wonder what all she'd have to say about that. And what troubles that would lead to. But she didn't go to the movies that day either. She remained lying down with a perpetually puffed-up face and teary eyes.

Appa didn't pay attention to any of that and went about his business. He had been leaving home at about the time the rooster crowed in the morning the last couple of days. Sevathaan from Seethakattu came to pick him up. He was the agent who was facilitating the purchase of the land. Quite a busybody, he was trying to secure at least two acres of land for Appa. It was his involvement in this effort that none of them at home liked. They feared that he would leave them in the lurch somewhere, somehow if they trusted him completely.

In reality, the whole village was wary of him. As soon as he was spotted a distance away, voices were hushed instantly and the discussions continued in murmurs. He was a big man. He had a thick, dark moustache and his eyes were always red, like the scarlet ivy gourd fruit. 'What does he have to worry about, he has clout wherever he goes. One needs to suitably fit a role to be like that,' said a man from Pottukaadu loudly once which Sevathaan overheard in passing. In fact, the man was speaking quite proudly of him and with good intent.

'How dare you suggest that I be called a loafer, a rogue, to my face?' he snarled and began to wave a knife that he pulled out from his hip. The man from Pottukaadu froze, completely clueless about how to react. He slipped into the forests as soon as he could. Sevathaan pulled out the knife for everything. Even though there hadn't been a scratch made with that on anyone, the fear was that he was big and rough and somehow harmful.

The days that followed his winning the card game were marked with his mockery ringing through the village. And there were days when vessels went missing in his house. Those days he bore a scowl on his face. His wife looked like a stick figure and invoked an image of a withered ascetic who barely spoke and spent long periods of time in meditation. She was quite pitiable.

Sevathaan was also involved in politics. He was in Thalaivar's party first. When the party with the sunrise symbol coalesced with the lady in national politics and won the local elections, he joined that party. When Thalaivar won, he moved back again. 'From now on, this is the one until death.' He often brought home men in veshtis that were marked in party colours and would create a din. Whenever he saw the wooden-legged Veeran alone, his face turned sour. As if he had just swallowed a shot of neem oil. Veeran belonged to the communist party. They acted as if their enmity spanned over generations.

Sevathaan usually arrived at their house right at the time the rooster crowed in the morning. 'Maama, Maama!' He sounded like a rooster calling out to a hen to feed on. With his basket-like head full of hair and sideburns that came all the way down his jawline, a look inspired by Thalaivar, he maintained quite a presence even at that hour of the day.

'And, Maaple,' he'd say to the boy, 'at least you should study well. We will find you a job. I will talk to Thalaivar and I will get you one,' and plant a strong pat on his face. One that made the boy's facial bones feel like they were going to crumble!

It was only recently that he was in town for ten days in a row. And that was very unusual. Two days, maybe three, but you couldn't find him around here for longer than that at any time. He travelled out of town for a week or ten days all the time. Sometimes he came back looking like a beggar. Sometimes he was dressed sharply and would sparkle. His family had somehow managed to keep it going all this time without depending on him.

Amma's contention was that associating with him was a precursor to losing all their money. 'This awful wastrel of a dog will blow away even the little money we have and bring us to the streets. If you join with the good, that's smart and makes sense. But if you join with the devil? That money will only end up funding drinks and dancers. This dog won't spare even the pyre pot.'

The part about not giving money to her brother never came up even by mistake. But Appa knew that that was the main reason for all this.

'Aammam, if I had dumped this money on your brother, you would have had no issues with that. You think

I will go to that miser? I will drink to that entire amount. And spend it on prostitutes. But not a single paisa of mine will go into your brother's hands. Remember this. And his wife, what sort of a woman is she? Feeding us two bags of rice every year, indeed! Like we are all lined up outside her house with our tongues sticking out in hunger. It was hardly meagre, the loads of things they have taken from here when we had the lands. Don't you think she should at least have a little sense of gratitude for all that?'

They fought like mongoose and cat, gouging and tearing each other to bits with words. Amma had another concern too. If Appa bought land, then they would move from the valavu to live on that land. Right now, Amma was very happy and satisfied where they were. There was no work to do as such. She didn't have to work in the farm. She didn't have to tend to the cows and buffaloes. Cooking and eating on time, chatting, going to the movies once a week and playing thaayam in her spare time. Would she want to leave all this behind and live in loneliness on some godforsaken land somewhere? That came up in the arguments too.

'Take a look at this man, wanting to buy lands, indeed! Why don't you just buy a cemetery then? You can bury me in there once and for all.'

Amma looked very different with her dishevelled hair, the way she swung her arms around and cracked her fingers as she lamented. Living in the valavu had changed her so much. Akka didn't show any concern for Appa or Amma. She heated up the water for herself every morning and spent half an hour in front of the mirror trying on different patterns of *pottu* before she left for work. She had only one thing to add: 'Appa, find some land in this general region. Not someplace far. Where else will I find a job like this?'

She spoke about her experiences of being a labourer with such relish. By the time the brick she described passed from one hand to another and reached the top, she'd behave as if she was there receiving it. She couldn't think of leaving that job and moving elsewhere. Appa took that into consideration.

'Why, dear, would we go away from here? We'll be somewhere close by. We'll find a place adjacent to this village,' he said, letting his love flow through his words. He had a soft corner for Akka.

For him, the very thought of moving out of this place was liberating. The torture of being stuck in a mouse's hole would be over. There were always people around all the time in the valavu. Nothing could be done in privacy. Someone would wiggle their way into the business halfway through and lead the effort in a different direction. Then turn the course completely. Slowly, they would make it their own. Living in this valavu was like being shackled. Fewer people worked in the farms; the number of people seeking work in Karattur town was increasing. They were perpetually in a hurry, frenzied like they were walking on hot water.

If Appa bought the land, the boy could play outside again. Jump into the well. The idea of being out in the open again filled the boy with excitement. The only person who was a little aloof from the whole thing was Annan. By the time he got back after finishing his work at the movie theatre it was late into the night. He woke up leisurely at ten the next morning and left again. He didn't have a clue about what was going on in the house. No matter what happened, though, he wasn't going to kick or scream or create a scene.

The boy left with his Appa and Akka early one morning to see the land that they were going to buy. They didn't breathe a word about it to Amma. Still, she somehow managed to find out about it. The land wasn't that far away. It was to the south of the valavu and Odaiyur main road. There was only a narrow separation between the lands they used to own and this one. They had to cross the lake to get there. From here, it looked as though the tail of the colony was broken. To the east of the panchayat road was Aattur. The west belonged to Chinnur. The land was to the west. But it wasn't a problem even if they had to switch villages. They all liked the land a lot.

There were portia trees everywhere they looked. They were very yellow and their petals looked like long fingers bunched together, with the fingertips alone slightly parted. There were about ten or fifteen vadhanaram trees too. Amidst the trees, in a curved shape bending in and out, was a palmyra shed. The walls had crumbled and the palmyra thatches were all but rotten and on the verge of sliding off. The old lady who used to live there was dead. She left behind two sons and a total of eight acres. The older son's four acres alone had come up for sale. He too had passed away. It was his wife who was selling the land.

The boy and his sister loved the new place. Appa was keen on moving ahead with the deal. He too had an important reason for that.

'Mamoy . . . you must taste the palm extract from this tree. It is nothing but nectar! Chinnaan does the climbing. He has the same lucky touch as his father. If I'm in town, I seat myself over here by midnight itself.'

Sevathaan made a salivating sound that shook his sideburns. He must have used that reason to get Appa to settle on the deal. He then pointed to the well and said, 'Maaple, this well used to supply water to the entire village at one time. It has gotten a tad bit salty lately. But that's no issue; if we get the irrigation set-up installed, water will come gushing out. There are going to be such lush crops of millets and cotton, you just watch.'

That there was a well was in itself significant. Some wells were conical—they were wide at the top and became narrower as they went deeper. One couldn't jump into those types of wells in any season. This well was of the same width all the way down. The water within stood still, touching the steps within. The boy wanted to jump in right then so badly. And as for Akka, the colony wasn't that far from there. 'I can lean over and grab it.'

Even before Amma knew about their visit to the land, she had already found out everything about the land. When they returned from their visit, she all but knocked them on their heads with an oar. She shook them to pieces.

'Would anyone who has ever set his eyes on that old witch want to buy the land she lived on? She died rotting, all alone. And all the drama she created when she was alive and well! Will anyone with family and children ever agree to live on a land adjacent to where she lived? And just because your father said so, you—you two donkeys—went to see that place now? Do you not have any sense? Does it hurt you to live in the cluster?'

Neither of them opened their mouths. If they did, they knew they would only get more of that.

'Look at how quietly they stand, as if they were born to a mute father.'

Again, there was a battle between Amma and Appa. But Appa didn't budge even a little. 'We are going and there is no change to that.'

'How long can I continue doing menial jobs? My Annan is setting up a weaving business apparently. Thambi is running a cart business. I will have at least four acres of land to my name. I will toil on that.'

'You could do something different like your Annan. Do you have to put all your money in that soil?'

'If I put it in the soil, where is it going to go? It only becomes treasure, di. Look, you can give me a thousand reasons. I am still going to buy that land. You can either come with me. Or you can stay here. The children and I are going there. We will feed you a ladle of porridge until the end.'

Amma's face was hot as a burning cinder. The force of her breath was enough to fell a person standing across from her. With all her pride, she ran to the cot and fell into it.

'Ever since we moved to the valavu, she has grown used to sitting and eating without working. Why would she want to exert herself and do any work? Let her lie there, ugly wretch.'

Two days later, Appa went with Sevathaan and sealed the deal. He paid two thousand up front. In six months, the deal would be completed. The boy brooded over the hostility that was going to last for six more months in the house until his head began to weigh like a rock.

Chapter 4

It was an ungodly hour. Must have been twelve or one at night. There was a knocking on the door. Appa would wake up to the smallest sound. He got up and opened the door. It was Thatha and Paati. 'Amma . . .!' he burst out in disbelief and everyone woke up then. The two of them were standing drenched to their bones and shivering like fledglings. Thatha was shedding more tears than the water on his back.

'Payya . . . look at what I'm reduced to! We came running all the way with just the clothes on our back.'

Appa didn't say anything. He held his father by the hand, brought him indoors and gave him a towel to dry himself with and a veshti to change into. Paati changed into another sari. They still could not grasp what had happened.

Thatha could not speak at all. He was sobbing and stammering. And seemed very agitated. He then cupped his cheeks and sat quietly, resting his elbows on his legs. Paati was the one who told them what had happened, little by little. It had been pouring for the last four days. Even though it went down to a drizzle occasionally, the rain never let up completely. If one stepped out thinking it was just a light rain, it became a dense downpour in an instant. The roads were all covered in mire. No matter which direction one turned to, it was wet all around. Nothing much was getting done. People still rushed to work with umbrellas and upturned wicker baskets. The lake that lay dried up and barren woke up suddenly from its slumber. But this rain definitely couldn't fill the lake. And even if it did, the water wouldn't come as far as their backyard.

It was a very remote spot that used to be under cultivation earlier. If the lake got filled up, this region got just a little wet. That's why they had built a platform there and put the shed over the platform. There was a two-foot-high pile of sand that was above land level. No one expected the water to reach the shed. Thatha and Paati had put their cots indoors and gone to sleep. Even though it had rained for three days continuously, they knew that the lake was not even a quarter full. Paati woke up in the middle of the night to relieve herself. When she put her feet on the floor, they were met with ice-cold water everywhere! If the water had reached beyond the levee, this was surely a big storm! She woke up Thatha frantically and went out.

It was roaring outside. As though a large mob was fuming loudly and rushing towards another mob. It was a massive flood raging with the mission of filling every vacant spot in and around the lake with water.

'As soon as we placed our feet outside, the water crashed upon us in waves. There was no other sound around us. Only the crashing and piercing roars from an invisible corner. I was frightened to the core. Didn't think of any of our belongings. There were ten chickens but we didn't look for them either. We didn't think of saving anything else.

Only our lives. We held our lives in one hand and held each other with the other throughout. The water level was above our knees. We could barely get in and wade through it. You know how the black mesquite thorns are everywhere too. We placed each step carefully, and till we slowly climbed out of that place, we weren't sure if we were going to die or survive.

'It seems that they may have opened out the waters from Karattur. Otherwise how will so much water get here? It has been so many years since this lake was built. I have never seen water like this before.'

There was a large pond right in the middle of Karattur town for all the waste from the surroundings. That pond always stood stagnant, topped with a coarse froth. All of Karattur's waters drained straight into it. Only when that big pond was full did they open it up. When they did do this, it ran over the roadways and stank up the city as it moved away. It then flowed via Keeravur to reach the low-lying area and make its way straight to the lake. It was only during such times that the salts from the leather hides were washed too. The lake had overflowed because the pond water had been released.

Paati's body could not handle the cold from being drenched in the rains. She shook violently. Her teeth rattled. It was a strange sound. The boy and his father wrapped her in a blanket, laid her on a cot and set out in the rain. If the water was still not high, they could, maybe, save the chickens and some things from the shack. Thatha wanted to go with them too.

'You just got here and were soaked through. Why do you want to be in the rain again? We will go over and check on things.'

Even though Appa tried to dissuade him from joining them, Thatha did not listen to him. They took a kerosene lamp, covered themselves and their heads with sheets made from jute sacks and set out in the rain. They struggled to walk on the roads as they were copiously covered with puddles blended with softened soil and slush. How had those two poor souls waded through all the mire without any light? The boy held his grandfather's hand protectively. Appa walked ahead with the lamp. It was still drizzling, with tiny raindrops. The skies were black and made the eyes giddy. They crossed the dense thorny shrubs by the goat sheds and walked on tar roads into the colony.

The cart road had vanished and a wider, newer mud road had been built on top of it. On both sides were half-built structures. In the dark, some looked tall and some others were shorter; they looked like the ruins of cities of the past. In all directions were piles of sand and gravel like men crouched in the open, defecating. Just the thought that the two of them had crossed all this by themselves made the boy's eyes well up.

In their old age, they had been left isolated, punished by imprisonment on an island. From the comfort of having their sons close and grandchildren crawling over their backs and heads they were forced to endure the torment of complete separation; the whole family was shattered like a coconut that is smashed to smithereens as an offering to a temple deity. In all the dangers of wading through the treacherous rains, they didn't have even one hand to hold on to for support. 'You are my support and I am yours.' How much their hearts must have cried as they walked alone on that path full of potholes and slippery ground in the nearly pitch-dark night. When one slipped the other must have held on tightly. The boy was struggling to walk even with the light from the lamp right now. How hard it must have been for them to take a step away from their dwelling place with only what they were wearing to save themselves. Their minds must have been filled with concern for the things they had left behind. Even if it was a tiny toy, would anyone have the heart to abandon it? How proud Paati was of every item she owned. 'These were all given to me as gifts by my mother for my wedding!' Every object bore a little bit of Paati. In spite of having three sons there had been no one to turn to in the middle of the night. No hand to hold for support. Not a dog would have been out when they entered the valavu. They would have gone looking for a warm and dry spot away from the rains. Even a dog had a better life than his grandparents . . . 'Appa!'

He held on to his Thatha's hand tightly. He wanted badly to have him rest on his shoulder and give him a big hug. Fear taunted him even though he was walking in the company of his father and grandfather. How did the two of them conquer their fears when they were walking alone, wandering in the open, on streets devoid of people? And the kinds of fears they must have seen in their lifetime! Perhaps the experiences that life had handed out to them had chased any fears far away. There was a flood. And the waters had entered their house. They had had to hold their lives in their hands and run for safety. All that wouldn't have affected them much. Sufferings are not always difficult when there are faces nearby to utter words that can soothe the heart. Let the misery weigh like a mountain on the mind. A chisel in the form of a tiny hand of solace is all that is needed to destroy that mountain. When they were standing in the middle of the roaring floods that rushed to attack them there were no hands offered in support. There was no one to talk to. The incontinence of old age would have hurt them even more. When they waded through knee-high waste, avoiding thorns, their solitude would have pricked them harder.

What sort of people were these sons who pushed the elders to the pit and entertained themselves by watching them from atop hills? Just what were they going to lose if they had them live along with their families? They didn't need a palace. If they were given a space as small as the palm of a hand in a little corner, they would still live within that. Thatha's erstwhile tall figure had shrunk to the span of the thumb and the pointer finger. He moved like a buffalo calf that, shrivelled from deprivation of milk, dragged its body as it walked—even his own body seemed a burden to him.

If people like Murugan were around, at least they would have come forward to help them. Once the foundation work was done, most of them had packed their bags and left. The few that were left had found places for rent elsewhere and moved away. The masons and helpers who had come to erect the buildings had all found a hut or a hole to rest in after they left work in the evening. There was no one left in the vicinity even to notice their absence if Thatha and Paati were to be murdered. Just a few watchmen who'd be sleeping sprawled in one of the completed houses in the colony. Those lucky men.

The road was fully blocked by sand and gravel. They walked along its edges past houses that looked complete. The cement blocks appeared dark. The lamp burned anxiously in his hand. 'You call this a house,' murmured Appa as he gave a wall a kick. The wall crumbled down to nothing. The boy and his grandfather stepped aside. Appa acted as though he was possessed and kicked one more wall down. The lamp moved up and down, fell down, got back up and fought for its life. The sound of the falling blocks was dampened by the rain. The walls that stood proud were now turned into a pile of rubble. Once two walls fell, the house beyond opened up fully to them. Appa was at the crest of his anger. He moved towards the next wall. 'Payya, Payya . . .' called out Thatha worriedly. The boy, on the other hand, stood petrified.

'Go, bring your father back, go now!' The voice that was trying to shake the boy back to consciousness ended in tears. Thatha slid down right there and cried. Appa returned with burning breath that had touched mighty peaks of wrath before beginning to calm down. His singular ire was visible in his eyes. A force that could easily raze the entire colony. A fury that could destroy the concrete edifices with just one foot. Suppressing all those emotions, he joined his father and found his voice to sob aloud.

Unable to help either of them, the boy pitifully called out, 'Appa, Appa.' His voice drowned in his own tears. He lifted up his grandfather to his feet, saying, 'Get up, Thatha.' Thatha got up with a residual whimper. Appa walked ahead and they followed him. The rain grew stronger. The raindrops fell pitter-patter on the baskets protecting their heads. In the surrounding darkness the houses moved. As they approached the low-lying area, they heard the waves breaking on the banks. The water crashed loudly against the colony's compound walls. The sound of the floods gushing in at a distance still didn't cease.

As far as one could see, water stood gnawing on the darkness. Lightning flashed periodically to show the expanse of the flood. The boy wanted to jump into all the waters and swim to his heart's content. Swim without ever touching the shore. And at the dawn of day, sink into the waters. He walked alongside his grandfather, drowning in his thoughts. It had been ten or fifteen years since the lake was built. He had never seen so much water in it in his life. Usually, there were only little pools of water stagnated here and there. The locals fished in those puddles over and over again, mixing up all the mud and creating a quagmire. Some years, the water filled up to a quarter of the lake's capacity. Those times were a lot of fun. Once, Selvan, Mani and he had got together and chased a pygmy goose. It had put its face straight into the water and gone in quickly, as though performing a somersault. It had then come out from some other location at a distance. The boys had breathlessly persisted in their efforts to capture it; they had formed a circle around it and tried to grab it. Um-hm. Now, more pygmy geese would come along. They would build nests among the thorn shrubs that hung everywhere and lay eggs.

All in all, the nest that the two oldies lived in was torn asunder. The top of the front facade could be seen above the water. The lake was sure to subside once the water submerged the whole shack. The chickens would have climbed the roof and escaped somehow. But the things that were inside the shack? It was impossible to go anywhere close to that place in this darkness. The sky was still lamenting. They didn't know what to do. The rage from seeing Thatha and Paati arrive in such a state in the middle of the night had made them rush over, as if they were going to accomplish something by coming here. But nothing could be done now. If they got into the water in this darkness, they wouldn't be able to gauge the depth or the force of it. Nor would they be able to recognize it if something went floating by in the water. The water could wash away even snakes. They felt they should return to the valavu.

'It's almost time for the rooster to call. Let's go back to the valavu and come back again. It will be dawn by then.' Without removing the baskets from their heads, they kept the sacks wrapped around them and perched on the pile of gravel. The clamour of the rain beating down and of the flood was similar to the noise at a race that climaxes as the runner reaches the finish line. That, along with the excited croaking of the frogs, all spread into their ears as cacophony. The soft protests of the lake as it began to overflow slowly increased in intensity. The palm trees were now submerged in water. They once stood aloof as if they had nothing to do with anyone around. Thatha and Appa shrunk to squat like bats. The boy gently rested his head on his grandfather and closed his eyes.

Out of nowhere, Mani came running wagging its tail and licked the boy's feet with a whimper. Thatha rubbed its back but the boy was angry with it. The devil, he never came to the valavu. He kept roaming about in the colony. He would go to the low-lying area to eat what Paati fed him and then lie there for some time in a pit. And then he would dash away. Just what was so special about this colony? The dog kept stroking his leg. The boy kicked it fiercely, with irritation. He must have hit the dog quite hard. Without a peep, it stood in a corner, quietly.

'What did it do to you? Poor thing, you think it understands all that is going around here, like we do?'

As he said that, Thatha loosened his legs from his squatting posture and his lap became available. It was so comforting for the boy to lie there in the rain. But, in that state of neither sleep nor consciousness, satanic dreams took over. A pair of cruel hands was grabbing, tearing his body organs apart and throwing them around. His fingers fell into the water. Stubby and resembling temple floats, they were chomped on by schools of fish. But the flesh kept growing back as they ate them. Tickled, he shook his hands.

'Ponnaiyya, Ponnaiyya!'

That was Thatha's voice. The day had dawned and there was light all around. But it was still cloudy and there was no sun. The noises had subsided and the water ran normally. The only sound was of water draining. The running water stroked the thorn bushes, and embraced the palm trees. It ran over the mounds and flattened them. It flowed through one end of the shack and came out blaring through the other. All the blockades and fences that were installed hung torn, missing parts. Things that were submerged and moved with the water showed up waving their hands at various places. The chickens stood on top of the shed covering each other with their wings. They repeatedly put their beaks into the water to see if they could get in and pulled them out with a disappointed 'kekkeeekk'.

As the sky brightened, others joined them one by one. Paati, Amma, Periappa, Chithappa. From close, from afar. They trudged through the water to help save any life and any object that escaped the storm.

~

Periappa had arrived at dawn itself. It had been a month since he had set up the weaving business. He had rented some space from some weaver in Thenur, built a structure by himself and installed ten looms in there. Even when they lived together in the farmlands, he would go to run the looms when there was no cultivation work to be done. After the ancestral lands went to the colonies, he continued

working at the looms for two more years. But how long
could he stay a labourer? He had some money that he had
saved and he didn't want to miss the opportunity to start
out on his own, in case there was no other. Getting men to
work at the looms was posing to be the biggest problem.
Even the ones that came to work switched workshops
every week. No one was interested in running the loom
consistently at the same place.

Aalkudi Raman's son and Rangan's son-in-law worked
at his workshop. Raman's son Shaktivel hadn't come to
work for two days. Periappa wanted to see him at his home
and call him back to work. Because he didn't know where
he lived, he took the boy to show him the way. Before he
left, Paati called out to him and said, 'My eldest Payya,
before you leave, come back to see me.'

The water in the lake wasn't fully drained yet. It had
been more than ten days now. Paati and Thatha were still
staying with them. They went to work as usual and came
back to them. One day, Paati came back saying there was no
more farming work left and went with Akka to work at the
construction site. But she didn't like that at all. 'The hands
that worked with grains shake when holding the cement
bowl, Payya,' she said and didn't go back the next day.

Paati and Amma didn't get along at all. There was no
fighting out in the open yet. But some frowning here and
there. Some pouting. Ignoring food and accepting it later,
and so on.

Thatha didn't say anything. If he was offered food, he
ate. If not, he didn't ask for it. His policy was different.

'In a farmer's house, there may be plenty sometimes. And sometimes there may not be anything. I am just an old piece of log. But I'm not going to die if I don't eat a meal.' There were absolutely no complaints from him about the rice and saaru. The man who used to taunt his wife all the time about them didn't say a word here. If the food had less salt, he didn't ask for more. He made his extraneousness known with his silence. What could you do to a man who didn't react to anything?

'Do the old man and old woman behave themselves? Or do they sit there and harp on some trifling detail?' Periappa asked the boy.

'They don't do anything like that, Periappa. They behave themselves. Still, living together is tough.'

'I know that, da. Even though she is my mother, the old lady can be quite the nag. Why do you think she asked me to stop by on the way back? She is going to ask if they could live with me, just watch . . .'

He had that fear in him. He did not wish to take in the old man and woman, to give them some space and feed them. He had the excuse of living with his father-in-law. This time around, though, blaming him wouldn't be fair either. Even if he agreed to take them, Periamma wouldn't let him. It took Periamma an entire day just to cook rice. She moved around and worked very slowly. If there were two more people to feed, she wouldn't know how to handle that. Even with the three girls she had, she couldn't manage anything. If only Amma didn't fuss so much about being with them, both his father's plan and his plans were to ask them to continue to stay with them. But when she served coffee to everyone in the morning, Amma would make Paati's alone very watery. She would tell her there was no kuzhambu left and serve her only rasam. 'As if we alone are buried in wealth here,' she would mutter under her breath, just loud enough for Paati to hear. Even worse was when she grumbled to the neighbours who lived next door or across from them, while Paati was within earshot.

'They have three sons, why should we alone take care of them? We went to help them and now we are bearing the burden. It's like taking a lizard that was stuck on a fence and putting it on our laps to protect it. What will it do but bite? Why not amble over to the older son's house? But, she's no fool like me, that daughter-in-law. She would have stated it cut and dried to them not to dare come by her place right in the beginning!'

'And here we have a wretched dog for a husband. Does he ever listen to a word of what I say? No matter what it is, what he says is always right. If he wants, let him take his father and mother with him and celebrate them. Who is saying no to that? Why do I have to when I don't want to?'

'The old man and old woman have a thousand complaints—the food is not good, the saaru is not good. Like they are giving me cartloads of money that I should cook with any care to feed them.'

All these words reached Paati's ears time and again. But she kept her mouth shut. She must have figured a way out of all this when she summoned her oldest son to come by.

When Periappa and the boy reached Shaktivel's house, Shaktivel had not even woken up. A little beyond the back side of the Kudiyaan valavu was the Aalkudi valavu. The long huts sat like ducks in a row. Naked children ran around with their bellies sticking out. Women sat along the pathway with their hair spread out. 'It is but a rotten fate of mine that I have to come seeking him like this,' murmured Periappa as he followed him. He walked ahead and called out for Shaktivel. Shaktivel was one class ahead of him when he was studying in Thenur. Shaktivel came out rubbing his eyes. He couldn't open his eyes to the bright daylight. He kept rubbing his eyes and trying to open them. It took him a while to comprehend who had come looking for him.

'Why, the day dawned a long while ago and it is afternoon now and yet our sire here is still unable to open his eyes, is it?'

'No, Ayya . . .'

As soon as he realized that it was Periappa who was standing there, he untied the folded portion of the lungi to cover his legs and straightened it.

'Why haven't you come to the loom the past two days, da?'

'I had gone to Marakkur, to my Atthai's place, Ayya.'

'What festival is going on there that you decided to go? Loafing around without coming to work . . . who will run the loom that is under your responsibility? At least you could have informed me that you weren't going to come for two days?'

'I left in a hurry, Ayya.'

'Look here, you either come to work regularly, or you leave. I will find someone else to do the work. Don't try all these tricks with me. This is what happens when I invite lads who loaf around with goats in the farmlands and give them a salaried job at the loom.'

Shaktivel stood looking down. Raman came by just then from somewhere.

'Salutations, Saami.'

'Mmm . . . has your lad grown beyond your control? And you don't give him any advice?'

'Where, Ayya, he was roaming about here saying he wasn't feeling well. He doesn't pay any heed to what I tell him. He brushes me off if I try.'

'He says he was at his Atthai's place. You say he was roaming about here. What is going on? Who are the father and son trying to deceive? You are all getting more supercilious by the day.'

'No, Ayya! He is a young lad. Please instruct him to come to work.'

'You had asked for a thousand for your daughter's wedding . . . did you get it?'

'Only you can help with that, Saami. I will kick this useless lad over to work. You know how to give generously, Saami.'

'If he is going to be irresponsible like this, how can I give anything? I will give the money. The father and the son will blow it away and sleep in pleasure. And I will be the one to stand outside your house and beg like a dog for the money.'

'No, no, Saami. He will come to work properly from now on.'

'Mm. Let me see. If he comes properly I will give the money. And I can deduct the money every week from his wages. But he must come to work.'

'He will.'

'And you, why are you standing there with a sneaky look on your face? Will you come regularly?'

'I will come from today, Ayya.'

'Better get there in time for the night shift.'

Seeing him along with his Periappa must have made Shaktivel a little uncomfortable. He went into his house right after. He used to study really well. His handwriting was perfect, like print. If something had to be written on the school blackboard, Padma teacher would always ask Shaktivel to write it. He had stopped going to school after fifth standard to work in the farmlands for three or four years. Now, he had switched to working at the loom.

Seeing Periappa, the Aalkudi valavu folks removed their towels from their shoulders, held them under their arms and bowed to salute him humbly. 'Salutations . . . salutations, Saami.' 'Mm,' he acknowledged them as he pushed on his cycle pedal. The boy was seated on the carrier. The people from this valavu were increasingly less involved in farming. They had left jobs in farms to work in the town. People like Periappa had no choice but to seek help from them. Two mills were being built near Marakkur. Once those opened, the lands would lie empty with no one to work on them.

Amma was cooling her coffee when they returned.
Thatha was seated on his cot. Appa was sitting on the
interior plinth and Paati on the exterior plinth. Periappa
sat himself next to Appa. The boy went into the house.

'Was he there?'

'Yes, yes. I'm unable to deal with the trouble of putting
these sorts of lads to work. But what other choice do I
have? If I don't use these lads, there's no one else available.
All the weaver fellows have set up two or three looms in
their own homes. Or they have their own workshops that
they go to.'

'Somehow compromise and make it work. This is not
cultivation that if you miss one planting season you have
to wait until the next. With businesses involving iron, you
have to work with the others, or else won't it affect your
capital?'

Just then, Amma handed out coffee to everyone,
interrupting Thatha, or so it seemed. 'Why did you ask me
to come back here, Amma?' Periappa asked as he sipped
his coffee.

'Mm . . . to chop onions for dinner! What the hell are
you all thinking? At first you abandoned us in some pit.
That area has now gone to the heavens. Now give us, the
two lives, some options for a livelihood and then leave.'

'What can I say? You are both earning. You share that.
Why don't you continue to stay in this Thambi's house?'

As soon as she heard that, Amma rushed from the
veranda without even paying heed to her leg slipping on
the way and hissed.

'What are you saying? Are we the only ones enjoying the older man's property? What about the two of you? Is he the only son they have that he needs to keep them here the entire time and feed them? Or are they blind? Or maimed?'

Periappa answered without missing a beat.

'Okay then, should we feed them for a month each?'

Now Paati's pride was pricked.

'The two of us can feed ourselves as long as we can use our hands and legs. Do you think we want to eat the leftovers that your wives will feed us? Get lost! Isn't this like the story of how everyone is barely alive after the house burnt down and the village gossip decides to come seeking a bride just then?'

'Aiyyo . . . aiyyo . . . this old lady is making up all these tales. How many days did I feed her my leftovers? I do all this and I'm still the sinner. Will she ever prosper!'

Amma stuffed her mouth with her hands and pretended to cry as she yelled. Paati tightened her face.

'Who accused you of anything now? I said it in general. But look at how loud you get referring to me as "old woman" over and over again.'

Two or three people gathered on the neighbour's plinth and peeped in to see what was going on. And Veerakka, who lived across from them, pretended to keep working as if she was paying no attention to all this.

'Okay, okay, let it be. Now let's be practical. I don't have a problem with them staying here. But they won't be okay continuing like this. That's why we need to find another way to make this work,' Appa said, addressing everyone there. No one said anything to that for a while.

'Looks like no one agrees with me. Then you come up with a plan.'

Through all this, Thatha didn't say a word. Periappa tried to weasel his way out. 'What if they live with the youngest?'

Appa continued.

'All that won't work out. Say something realistic. He has used up all his money to buy bullock carts and is struggling to make ends meet. There is no point in asking him to keep them.'

Periappa refused to accept that explanation. Appa did not relent. 'Anna, let me say this, listen to me. I have already made an agreement at Kakkankaadu. That will come through in about two months. They can build a shack on that land and live there.'

Periappa was pleased that the burden was off him. His face lit up with relief. He heaped praises on the idea.

'That is the right solution! I myself am not comfortable living with my in-laws. I am trying to figure out if I can come away and live somewhere else. The youngest one also wants to do something like that. No matter what, how long can I live at the mercy of my brothers-in-law, tell me?'

'You say it will take at least two months for the deal to come through. It will take another month to build the shack. Until then . . .?'

Paati raised the question and went into deep thought. Thatha sat fidgeting with his feet.

'Until then, just stay here.'

'No need. Apparently, there is a house available in Kaliammodu. I heard about it yesterday. We will lie there for three months. The rent is ten rupees. We can afford that. What do you say?'

Thatha's face cheered up. There was no opposition to Paati's statement from anyone.

Chapter 5

Akka was going to work at the colony regularly. The houses were getting completed at a brisk pace. They were to be auctioned and occupied soon. Those who had come from afar specifically for the construction work were leaving one by one. Work was dwindling. Akka, who had gone to work as usual that day, did not return that evening.

No one thought of her till it was seven in the evening. There was a lot of work to be done. The buffaloes had to be tethered, leaves to be plucked, goats to be herded into the pen. Paati had gone to work somewhere earlier that day and was cooking dinner at that time. Thatha was lying on the cot in the front yard. It was six or seven months after the deal on the land had been completed. Thatha and Paati had built a little shack and moved in to live on the land by themselves at first. Two or three months later, the boy and his family moved into the house after repairing it. Amma had absolutely no interest in moving. But since she had no other choice, what could she do?

The coffee that was made for Akka sat on the stove untouched. Amma, who was gathering utensils to wash, noticed the coffee and asked, 'What is this? Has the princess not had her coffee yet?' Only then did they notice that she hadn't returned home. Appa, who had gone to drink toddy in the evening, hadn't returned either. Amma grabbed the boy and burst out an instruction to him, 'Go and fetch your father.' Appa rushed back, wondering what had gone wrong.

'She kept saying work was getting over, work was getting over. Maybe they have all gotten together and gone to watch a movie?' he asked.

'Has Komuri ever gone to a movie without informing us? Instead of sitting here and talking pointlessly, won't you go and look for her somewhere, check what is going on?'

The pain from the fire in her belly spread through Amma. She couldn't verbalize the doubt she had in her mind. Would she have eloped with someone? Appa went to Porasa's house to find out who all worked with her in the colony. Porasa also went to the colony to work.

'Two, three people have rented a place in Kolunjikkadu. It is with them that your daughter works. They call their mason Mani.'

He took his cycle and went to Kolunjikkadu. He had to find her without arousing doubts in others. Otherwise, the news would spread rapidly, with generously added embellishments. Luckily, the house that he went seeking was set inwards and away from the rest. There were three big grown lads there, all of the same height. The radio was blaring and they were lying like mounds.

'We came home in the evening right after work. We don't know anything.'

As he pushed his cycle and moved away, he heard their stifled giggles. If he turned around immediately, they might run away and hide, he thought to himself. Without turning around to look at them, he went straight to Sevathaan's house.

Ever since he had helped purchase the lands, Sevathaan had become very close to Appa. He got more than a thousand as the brokerage fee. Still, Appa had a lot of trust in him. 'He travels around a bit. He should know more about a lot of things than us.' Sevathaan boasted often that he could meet minister Kandhasamy at any time and ask him for anything he wanted done. Perhaps because he didn't think anyone was going to check the veracity of his claim. He made his rounds wearing a towel on his shoulder with the party-colour stripes, and soon gathered some supporters.

'If there was someone who could stand next to Thalaivar, it would only be me. Just so you know, he would put his arm on my shoulder casually while he talked. Even minister Kandhasamy has to stand a step lower.'

He would say the same thing a few times. He would then change it slightly and say the same thing in a different way a few more times. The women would gather around and listen to him so intently that they wouldn't have noticed if a fly wandered into their gaping mouths.

'Which Thalaivar did you stand next to?' asked one of them once.

He reacted as if they were mocking him. He turned around to give a dismissive look to the woman who posed the question and then responded, 'There is only one Thalaivar in my mind. Maybe you have others.'

The questioner got teary with emotion. She slapped herself on her cheeks in penitence.

Once, he paid money to screen a Thalaivar movie for the people of that street—either by selling his wife's jewellery or by pawning it.

Kattaiveeran, or Veeran, would say, 'That bottom-feeding dog. He can't get close enough to see even the dust on Thalaivar's feet. Look at how he boasts! Don't I know how he is jumping through hoops trying to meet Kandhasamy . . . mm?'

Appa seated himself on the plinth outside Sevathaan's house. Sevathaan hadn't returned home yet. He had gone out on some work and got back only a little while after Appa got there. He came back looking very tired. Appa hesitated, wondering if he should tell him.

'I am just coming back from an event by the minister. That's why the exhaustion. You tell me, Maama . . . Whatever it is, tell me.'

He told him about it hesitantly; Sevathaan's face grew red.

'What kind of lads are those?'

'Who knows all that. I left just as soon as I got there. They cackled away standing behind me.'

'Oho! Let's go break their knees. Let's report to the police, Maama. Only if the police show up will they know not to mock us.'

Late into that night, he cycled to the police station to file a report. He stuffed fifty rupees into the hands of two officers and brought them along to Kolunjikkadu. The policemen took the lads to the station. It took just a few blows at the station for them to confess everything.

Akka had gone away with a lad called Kannan. The two of them had been courting each other for over a year. He was from a village next to Therur. They gave them his address. Appa and Sevathaan went looking for the address in a car they arranged for, along with the two policemen.

Appa was absolutely stoic. He had brought her up with so much affection, she being the only daughter. No matter how many sons one has, when it comes to daughters, there is always a soft corner for them. A daughter will never stop taking care of her father and mother. Even when she is married and in her husband's house, the joy she feels from a visit by her parents is unparalleled. He wiped his perspiration with his towel. The more he thought about it, the more he found it unbearable. 'A son must be smacked when being brought up while a daughter must be protected, they say. I brought her up with so much care but now this donkey has run away with some stranger leaving everything behind. Did I bring her up so carefully for this? I should have never let her leave the house. I let her go to work since others were doing it too and now she wants a husband. The body isn't satisfied with just food apparently. It is not a daughter I begot but a prostitute. Let me get my hands on her. I will chop her up and bury her. The whore of a daughter.'

'Daughters should be married off at the right age, Maama. If sons roam about, that's different. What do girls know? If a lad is a little good-looking, that's enough for them. One tap on their hips and the girls will easily cave.'

'Maaple, she is not that sort of a girl. We never ever imagined that she would run away like this.'

'Maama, who thinks of their father and mother when transgressing? It is as if they are under a spell. You can't blame anyone for that.'

Sevathaan chatted on fervently. He was happy that he was able to show off his prowess. And everything happened to his benefit. When they woke up the residents of that address at such an odd hour and they saw the police, they were completely shaken. There were three or four little children. Must have been that Kannan's younger siblings. After a search that resulted in turning the house upside down, they gave them an address in Ellur saying that was where they went. The car left for Ellur. Sevathaan chatted with the policemen throughout. They joked about 'cases' of eloping like this. Listening to it all made Appa remorseful. 'What an awful fate this is! I should have just let her get away and be however she wants. I want to leave her alone and run back home.' Appa hung his head. By the time they reached Ellur and found the place, the day had broken. The occupants were shocked to see Appa and the rest. Akka looked up at them and turned her teary gaze downwards. No one asked anyone anything. They grabbed her and put her in the car. The policeman took that lad and two others who were with him in another car and followed them.

He had a medium complexion. He let his curly hair spread all over his head and cover his ears. Must have been about twenty-five years old. He had a pretty face. The kind suitable to dance around with an actress in a drama show arranged typically during the temple festival. To the song 'What's that glance that you are giving me?' That face shrunk to the size of a coconut kernel. Akka sat motionless. Her face never looked up. Appa kept looking at her as if he would burn her down with his looks. She did not look at him at all. Appa also did not open his mouth to say a word.

By the time they reached home, the entire village was waiting for them. Who on earth would have spread the word? In fact, they had returned the car in Karattur itself and taken a bus home. 'No one in the village will know about this; let's keep this whole affair under the rug for some time and then get her married off to some guy in a few days,' Sevathaan had said. 'The lad was severely beaten up,' he said, and chuckled over and over again.

'You should have seen how they made him stand naked and beat him up. Each of his balls was swollen like a pumpkin. Bloody boys from the low caste of percussionists. They think we wouldn't come after them if they run away with our girl. From now on, he will never look at another girl for life!'

A stinking laugh. He blinked his eyes, flared his nostrils and repeated it to everyone. He described it as if he had done it by himself. Getting a car, going to Thenur, and then to Ellur. He patiently opened up every little detail for everyone to relish, like a Thalaivar movie. It was as if he was saying, 'If anyone else has issues like this, come to me.' If Appa had heard any of this, he'd much rather have left

Akka to her fate with that lad instead of having to put up with Sevathaan's fetid words. Filthy words spilt out of his mouth, words writhing like worms.

Appa did not have the strength to face anyone in the village. Instead he moaned in front of his daughter constantly. 'It is but our fate that she should leave home and elope with someone. And that anyone and everyone should talk about it.' The boy felt bad for his father but he didn't know what to do either. On his part, Appa avoided any sort of gatherings at any cost and stayed cooped up in the goat shed. Amma, on the other hand, would talk out of turn about something or the other and somehow end up bearing Appa's wrath. They both argued a lot.

'Brainless corpse, all this is because of your doing. You are the one who took her to the cinema, to cut her hair, to do this and that. What age do you think we live in that you should wear bra and blouse and saunter around like a horse? Here, we barely have a piece of cloth to cover our buttocks but the mother and daughter find ten different things to adorn.'

'Yes, you penny-pincher! I'm the one who spoilt her. Why didn't you buy her bras and blouses and keep her with you at home all the time? You don't have it to earn enough for your family. Didn't you enjoy the money that your daughter brought in by doing cement work at the construction site? Don't you blame me for spoiling her!'

That was it. After that, he would just fling anything he could at her and beat her. He would grab her by her hair and drag her and kick her, calling her a whore until he grew tired. That was followed by him drinking himself out of his wits. Who could reason with him? Annan was never around at home. The boy sat in a corner like a mouse. Amma would not get up for two days after that. With her hair unbraided and unkempt, she'd live on her cot. No one even cleaned out the ashes from the stove at that time. Annan would eat at the movies and the boy at Paati's house. She would feed him, grousing about how well the family used to be and what it had come to, and lay out some food for Appa too. If he was inebriated, he wouldn't touch it.

Akka didn't talk to anyone. She didn't step out of the house either. No weddings, no festivals, no events, no nothing. The whole house bore the shadow of death. The boy too could not mingle with any of the other kids in the village. He was too worried that they might say something derogatory about his sister in the heat of their silly squabbles. Even while walking by himself, he imagined someone whispering behind his back or laughing mockingly at him. When having a normal conversation, if someone smiled at him, he could only assume they were jeering. He couldn't focus on anything. He couldn't be at ease anywhere.

At home, there were fights all the time. The ever-cheerful Akka was now shattered to unrecognizable pieces, spilt like water tossed towards the sky. She no longer grew her eyes big over little things and talked exaggeratedly about them. She didn't so much as look up at all. She lost weight and was down to her bones. She looked at food like it was medicine. If insisted upon, she ate just a few morsels.

When Appa and Amma fought, she hid her head between her knees and whimpered softly without anyone noticing. Like a large river that stopped flowing suddenly, the whole house was enveloped in a sudden silence.

He too didn't like being at home. He did not want to go back home at all, but no matter where he went, thoughts about home dominated his mind. Whenever he was away, he constantly wondered if something was happening at home. He couldn't stay still in school. Just how did Annan not pay any heed to anything happening at home and go to work every day? Would he too reach that state of mind of not getting affected by anything around him?

Paati only added fuel to the fire. If Akka didn't respond when she called for her, she would panic and bring the whole house down. If Akka went someplace outside for a few minutes, Paati would go looking for her. She would constantly check on her. At night, she slept right next to Akka. What if she resorted to some untoward action? Periappa and Chithappa and all visited quite often, with the gloom of attending a funeral wake. They too moped around with their doglike long faces as if there wasn't already enough seriousness in the house, and behaved as though there was nothing else in this world they knew to talk about except Akka. The boy felt so angry that he wanted to spit on their faces and drive them out.

In spite of the commotion all around, he was still going to write his tenth-standard board exams. Just thinking about it frazzled him. Whatever he studied, he forgot the next minute. Seeing the other boys study day and night made him want to bawl loudly.

~

They were busy finding a husband for Akka. It was a hushed, low-key affair, for, if word got out, there were people who would make it their business to spread rumours about Akka and stop any progress. Maybe it was payback time for Appa's past arrogance. Sevathaan helped look for a groom. These days, Appa and Sevathaan were very close. They went together to the liquor shop every day, drank a lot, came back and talked nonsense. All that drinking didn't even agree with Appa. Yet, he drank too much, shouted all night and vomited his guts out. He didn't eat properly. He was becoming skinny like a stick.

Meanwhile, Sevathaan was becoming insufferable. He would invite himself over as the rooster crowed in the morning. Even at that hour, he was heavily inebriated.

'This Kandhasamy fellow, is he even human? That rogue that licks leftovers! Is it enough to be born in a farming family? Doesn't one need to know how to make a living from farming? And he has the post of a minister on top of all that. Did he not go outside the caste and marry someone from a lower caste? No wonder his mentality is like that too. Let's see . . . He has to come to me someday. Adey . . . what do you take this Sevathaan for? If I give you one on your cheek, you will go flying all the way to your village. You better be careful!'

He would talk dramatically, as if Kandhasamy was standing in front of him. About three thousand rupees were spent in the fiasco of looking for Akka. Sevathaan would have surely pocketed at least five hundred from that. In addition to being a land broker he made himself a marriage broker too. Sevathaan bothered the boy very often, saying 'Maapille this' and 'Maapille that'. But because he was helping with finding a groom for Akka, he had to be tolerated. As soon as he arrived, Akka would look up, roll her eyes, give him a look and turn away. Appa's drinking, Amma's fights, Akka's silence, Annan's indifference, Sevathaan's annoyance all pushed the boy further away from home. He felt like being outside was a lot more peaceful. He remained functional by staying away from home as much as possible.

And he got a set of friends that worked perfectly for that. About fifty or so families had moved into the colony. And more kept coming. When he passed tenth standard and moved on to ten plus one, three boys from the colony joined his school: Gopal, Murali and Kathirvel. Gopal's father was an officer. Murali's father worked in a thread mill. Kathirvel was the son of an elementary school teacher. All four had bicycles. They went to school together, came back from school together, chatted and roamed around together.

In the evening, after school, they went to the bus stand to ogle at all the girls from the Girls' High School before having a cup of tea at Modern Café. After that, they took their time cycling back to the colony. There, they spent an hour or hour and a half sitting on the temple plinth chatting. The bus stop was right across from them. This bus stop to Aattur used to be beyond the goat farm. Once the colony was constructed, they moved the bus stop to across the temple. This became a prestige issue for the villagers. Kattaiveeran, who had already protested the spread of Hindi, took the move as a challenge to his status and decided to stand with his wooden leg in the middle of the road to protest the move.

'I will see which bus driver dares drive past me. I have already lost a leg. I don't mind losing my life too.'

Kuppan moved over to the stop near the colony and started mending shoes there. Chinnatha set up her palm shelter there as well. They were trying to make the best of the situation for their livelihood. Sometimes Ramayi came by and sat there. If she saw him, she smiled with her lips parted as if to ask, 'How are you, little master?' without actually saying the words. That was all.

These lads would chat, and chat and chat some more. But if they tried to remember what they talked about, nothing came to mind. Their conversations were mostly about the girls who came to the bus stop.

'Did you see the yellow half-sari today? What a beauty! Isn't she perfect?'

'Sure but when she stands showing her side to us, what a pose that is! That's what's bewitching.'

'She's just showing off that she is wearing a bra, da.'

'Stop that. Don't you guys talk like that about my girl. I'm going to go over and talk to her in person one of these days, just you watch.'

'What are you going to ask her—if it's a Mody's or Naidu Hall brand?'

Gopal would raise his hand to whack the boy but he would pull his head away from him. Gopal had started falling in love with that girl seriously. The other three had no particular person they were interested in; rather, they were interested in all the ladies. If there was a guru of nuances, that had to be Murali. He was two years older than the others. Words that the boy felt too embarrassed to say spilt from Murali's mouth unabashed. The boy would feel uncomfortable and laugh squiggling like a worm in response. Murali kept mocking him, calling him 'a coy girl', and eventually made him come out of his shell. At exactly seven in the evening, two girls would come to the bus stop after their tuition classes. It was only after they left that these boys returned home.

The boy needed all this badly. He believed he was truly happy only when he was with those boys. He could forget all his worries and feel light enough to fly. When it was time to go home, his heart raced with anxiety. A fright consumed him, as if he was going to hell. Sometimes, he would say he was going out to study but would go to see a movie instead. That there was no power connection in his home worked to his advantage. Gopal watched movies pretty often. Murali and Kathir couldn't just step out of their homes without permission. So, they skipped school once in a while to watch movies. When the movie *Alaigal Oyvadhillai* was being screened for the second time, they watched it in the morning show and the consecutive matinee show. Kadhir was very fond of the actress Nalini in the movie *Uyirullavarai Usha*. When it came to staying on top of all things related to movies, Murali was unbeatable. Like how the actresses Radha and Nalini often times fought with each other. Since his family subscribed to a lot of magazines, he read up about the movies and shared that with the rest.

Even though the problems at home weren't going to be resolved this way, the boy found calm in being able to forget about all that and just be carefree for a little while. Appa did not work like before. It seemed that his spirit would come back only after Akka was settled. Recently, he had done some odd jobs like mending fences and trimming lawns at the colony homes. Amma too supplied buffalo milk to two or three homes in the colony. But the household was still leaden.

One day, Appa, Amma and Sevathaan left for Kattur before dawn to see a groom. Even though the village had largely stopped talking about Akka, no relatives came forward seeking her hand in marriage. Who would agree to marry a girl who had tried to elope? 'Will someone walk into a pit knowing very well it is deep?' they would say. If they decked her up in gold, maybe some guy would come forward, but there were no means for that either.

The trip to Kattur was followed by a big fight at home. Even though he didn't know all the details, the boy gathered the essentials from the conversation.

'No matter what you say, I will not agree to push our child into a pit,' Amma yelled.

Appa and Sevathaan spoke calmly. 'Who wants to push anyone in a pit? Don't you think we would know the difference between a puddle and a lake?'

'Oh yes, do I not know how all this works! A lame or a maimed lad is still okay. If it was his first marriage, we could give her away. Even if he is the heir to a large inheritance, I won't agree to giving our daughter in second marriage to someone.'

'Don't talk foolishly. Your daughter is not the epitome of character. Who will come forward to marry her after what she has done? If you want, you go find someone nice whom you approve of.' Appa was livid with anger.

'What is wrong with him? It has been a year since his first wife died. He has no children. Must be only about thirty or thirty-two years old. The man looks young and seems to be a quiet and polite type. Maybe he is not like us in status. At least we aren't without a square meal a day, seems like that itself is a bit of a struggle for him. But so what? Does he not go out and work? If he was even a little more comfortable moneywise, don't you think people would have been lining up outside his house to get him married to their daughters?'

'There is no need to think any further. Let's settle on this one. If not, where else do we go looking for a better alliance?'

'You want to dump her into a pit so you can spare yourself the efforts of seeking a better groom. Instead of that, why don't you spend two rupees on poison and kill her?'

Amma yelled with bitterness as tears poured down her face. From inside came Akka's whimpers.

'Have the mother and daughter discussed everything beforehand and planned their moaning? If you argue against this, I will chop you both up and make a pickle out of that. If I need to go to jail, so be it!' shouted Appa as if he was possessed. Sevathaan slowly walked away from there. Once he left, the discussion stopped. That night, Appa sought advice from Thatha and Paati.

'If the boy is good, then give him the girl. Forget about wealth, bloody wealth. If the boy is good, he will make the money needed. This would be his second marriage, but the first wife isn't around, right? Then what is the issue?'

That was their response. The sky was lit up by the moon. Thatha sat on a cot, speaking emphatically. His back alone was drenched in the light of the moon. When she heard him, Amma grumbled under her breath.

'What do the old man and the old woman have to lose? It is I who is stuck in the stinking sludge of a murky mire. Should my daughter suffer like me too?'

In a flash, Appa rushed from the exterior plinth, grabbed Amma's bundled hair and punched her on her back till his fists hurt. 'Yes, beat me up, da, beat me good! Finish me off and carry the funeral pot for me,' cried Amma. Appa returned to the plinth with his tired hand.

'I brought this one who spent her time collecting cow dung at her father's house and gave her a living. Look at what she has to say. She has found her tongue, hasn't she . . .'

All of Amma's efforts to oppose the wedding were futile. Arrangements for it were made with grandeur. Five sovereigns of gold jewellery, five thousand rupees in cash. The entire expense was borne by them. The wedding took place in Kattur. What if they had it in their village and something unforeseen happened? This way, even if some gossip happened to reach the groom's party, they could still manage it. Sevathaan did mention that he had given them a vague cover story on that incident. The groom's people had also figured out that there must be something off about this bride that they should offer her as a second wife. The day was fixed. The invitations had arrived. The process of inviting kith and kin formally was going on in full throttle.

Even amidst all the din, Akka sat staring vacantly as though she had lost something precious. Was she accepting all this as her fate? Was she wondering if she should have continued on with the man with whom she had run away? Or was she glad she had escaped from him? She didn't speak a word about any of that. About being with him, going away with him—nothing. After she was brought back, Amma watched her closely to check if she got her period. The doubts never went away completely even though she asked her about it.

She may have felt a little sense of relief, in some sense, escaping the pain of being the centre of doubt and disbelief. Everyone was happy in some sense. After all, the devil had been defeated. Who was going to keep her home and feed her otherwise? For how many more days could they shut their ears, unable to bear the ridicule of the village? Happiness set in, as if all their problems were going to be resolved with Akka leaving home.

Lord Siva's Blessings

Do not miss this!   What you have been waiting for eagerly!
No entry fee!

Wedding Wishes

The date is January 18   Today onwards

Introducing through this movie

The Hero from Kattur   The Heroine from Aattur
Vengacchami   Rosayi

In an epic legend of two youngsters coming together
A new release by New Relations Productions

Trapped in Marriage
Colour (A)

Movie sets	: Wedding dais	Story/Dialogue :	Brothers-in-law
Cameo actors	: Guests	Screenplay :	Brothers
Support	: Groomsmen	Production,	
	: Bridesmaids	Direction :	Groom's Family
Fight sequence	: Parents/In-Laws	Editing :	Friends
Camera	: Eyes	Music :	Wedding Band

Also featuring scandalous fights between parents and in-laws and
a mouth-watering variety of food in this new genre. This movie
will be screened on 18-10-82 as a morning show

Our Next Production

A joint venture by Vengacchami and Rosayi will be an entertainment
movie that will launch tonight starting with melodious songs

'Coo, Coo! On Rosayi's Lap'

Studio: Bedroom   Director: Vengacchami   Producer: Rosayi

After the outdoor scenes are shot at cool places like theatre, park,
beach, Kodaikanal, Ooty, uninterrupted for ten full months, the
movie will begin production.

Wishing that the movie runs successfully for many, many years to
come are supporters

Gopal   Murali   Kathirvel
Aattur Colony (Housing Board)

Chapter 6

There was a lot of noise by the cemetery. Like crows returning to their nests in the evening. The boy was sitting on the platform by the lake studying at that time. He could not recognize any of the voices or comprehend what was being said. The noise reached him over the tall and dense vadhanaram trees. He shut his book, tucked it under his arm and began to walk towards the trees. He asked Papayi Paati, who passed by half-walking half-running after delivering firewood to the colony with an empty basket upside down on her head, about the noise.

'Not sure what is going on . . . Looks like something is happening at the cemetery. Even your father rushed over there from the Veera forest just now.'

When drunk, his father didn't know what he was doing. He spat out anything that came to his mind. 'No matter how big a tusker of a man, I will bring him to his heel!' he'd bellow. Did he say or do something that shouldn't have been said and get into trouble with someone? He walked faster. The lands had been recently tilled. His feet sank a foot and a half into the loose soil. From a distance each footprint looked like a bandicoot or a rabbit in a mound of turd. He ran, pulling his feet in and out. The red earth stained his feet. He reached the shore, regained his composure a little and ran through the next forest.

The book that was under his arm kept slipping and falling down. The voices at a distance seemed clear and unclear at the same time. Like the cacophony that followed the end of a movie show when people exited the movie theatre.

The Aattur cemetery was right along the cart track that branched off the tar road to Chinnur. Adjacent to it was a liquor shop in a tent-like structure. That is where arguments, fights with weapons and family issues often erupted from. There were also times when big fights ended anticlimactically, with the people involved in the fight simply dusting the mud off their clothes and walking away with their arms around each other's shoulders. Maybe today's was like that too? He stood on the mound at the well in the Veera forest and saw that the liquor shop was deserted. There was not a soul there. The road, though, was swarming with people.

'Let me see who dares set foot in here today!'

'As if this place was begging for you all to move here . . .'

'I will chop you all up into pieces . . .!'

A crowd stood blocking the road. They stood at the mouth of the path that led to the cemetery and spoke moving their arms up and down. Only four or five of them were from the village. The rest were from the colony.

'Where else can we bury it? Please tell us where.'

'Put it in the ditch in the colony, who cares?'

'I've been watching all this since morning. They come and they go as they please. They dug a hole here too. I was waiting to see how this pans out . . .'

The boy pushed through and went into the crowd. There was a corpse lying on a wooden hearse. It was of an older person. Seemingly in deep meditation, taking in all the noises around it. A coin was placed on a dollop of sandalwood paste right at the centre of the forehead. The coin sparkled in the sunlight. The whole fight was about the corpse. The cemetery belonged to the people of Aattur. Could corpses from the colony be interred here? Where did they come from anyway? And what kind of people were they? Were the villagers fools that they would compromise the sanctity of the cemetery?

'We have already brought it here now. Where can we take it now? Please let us this one time.'

'Today you will plead to get your way but tomorrow you will demand that this is your right. Don't we know how you colony people think?'

Appa, Thatha and the panchayat head were all there with hoes and staves in their hands. Standing across them was a crowd of about forty or fifty people. They were all talking softly amongst themselves and standing along the side. There was a certain wrathful glow about Appa's face. Every person standing across from him was from the colony. He seethed with the urge to chop up every one of them in front of him. The owners of the corpse kept pleading and requesting politely for permission. On their faces were the shadows of fatigue, more from the sadness of loss than from the scorching sun.

'Where can we take the corpse that we have brought with us?'

'Take it to your village. You have all moved here just now. This cemetery has belonged to us for generations.'

'Let it be so, sir. But do we need to have this discussion with the corpse lying in the middle of the road?'

'Why should we even talk to this fellow? What is he to us, a Maama or Maaple? When we say take it away, just take it away.'

'If you had said something when we were still digging the grave, we wouldn't have come back with the corpse?'

'Who did you consult before digging the grave? We were waiting to see how far you'd go before asking us.'

When he saw his father, the boy wanted to grab him and take him away. He couldn't bear to see the spectacle his father was orchestrating, complete with a staff in his hand. His grandfather stood leaning on a staff in his bare komanam. He couldn't follow all that was said but he had gathered enough to know what was going on. Suddenly, a couple of women surrounded the hearse. They tousled their hair and began the funereal wailing. Their matted hair lay in clumps, much like inverted palm sheaths, as they slapped their faces and cried.

'If we lived on our land, we would have at least a handful of people to support us. We have moved away from our land . . . We are left at the mercies of their rules . . .'

The village landlord, who was one of the important people in the village, and who leased his land to smaller farmers, was uncontrollably furious. He ground his teeth, stuck his tongue out like Muniswamy, the fearsome-looking god who frightened offenders, and pushed his way to the front.

'You think you can seduce us by putting these women in front of us? These headless whores . . . we will chop up every single one of them.'

Instantly, the wailing stopped and the faces of the women displayed fear instead. Somebody pulled them away and they disappeared from the scene. The crowd lingered on, waiting for the problem to be resolved. Some moved around to sit on the rocks or get some tea from the tea shop. More people from the village joined in. Over time, everyone, from the oldest to the little ones, had assembled there.

The son of the deceased was an officer at some urban bank apparently, and he had moved into the colony only two or three months earlier.

The villagers gathered around the hearse as if they were in a village meeting. The people from the colony stepped away to talk privately, and only two or three men came back to speak to the villagers. One of the men who resembled the deceased must have been the bank officer. He spoke in a feeble voice amidst all the clamour.

'Please listen . . . we haven't come here to cause any problems. We do not know all the ways of this village.'

A voice interrupted him. 'Learn now then.'

'Who is that now? That man is saying something, isn't he? Let's listen to what he has to say.' The village landlord thwarted the interruption. With all the people gathered there, the scene was a perfect opportunity for him. He removed the towel that he had wrapped around his head and put it like a garland around his shoulders. He waved his hand as he spoke and moved forward.

'You talk.'

'This is what it is—I belong to Asalur. I don't know the traditions of this village. They told me this was the cemetery for the village. That's why we brought the body here. Now, if you tell us to take the corpse away, where are we going to take it to? You have to advise us on what other options we have.'

'What else can I tell you? Taking it away is the only option.'

'If each of you says something, how's that going to work? Four of you come and meet with four of us. We will sit down and resolve this.'

'Sure! Go, get some puffed rice and peanuts. We will relax and talk about this,' snapped the landlord.

The crowd roared with laughter and claps. The officer was on the verge of bursting into tears. The village landlord was raging in fury, as if the officer had personally hit him below his waist. If only he held a bunch of neem leaves, he'd look fully possessed.

'You want to sit down and talk? What do you think is going on here? Who is going to talk to whom? Your devious manipulations won't work here. Remove the body now!'

'Ayya . . . if this was your father or son, would you allow the body to lie in the middle of the road like this?'

'Who's asking you to leave it here like this? We have only been asking you to remove it.'

'What we have said so far is what it is. We are not going to sit and chat with you. There is no need for it either. We will not allow it here. Just take it away.'

The women in the crowd began to yell too. But they made no move to remove the corpse. The colony people still harboured a baseless belief that they could somehow convince the villagers, and tried talking to individuals while thinking of other ways to convince them. If fifty of the colony residents forced their way through, the villagers would have relented. But the villagers resisted with so much rage that even if they managed to inter the body there, it seemed as though they would dig it out and chop it up into pieces. Lacking the courage to go against the villagers and bury the corpse, the people from the colony began to disperse little by little.

Veeran, who dashed to the spot pedalling with one leg, dropped his cycle right on the spot and stood leaning on a staff. His imperial moustache was throbbing. There were deep lines on his forehead. He callously brushed aside his long hair. He reached the front of the crowd with four long strides and asked loudly, 'Who the hell is that?' He then went up to the hearse with the help of his staff and crossed over the body.

'Dei . . . take away the damn body . . . take it away, da. The colony people have crossed the line. If you all try to show your prowess here, I will nip you all, leaving no trace behind. Didn't you rogues get together and beat up Sevathaan the other day? He is lying in the hospital right now. You think there is no one to question your actions? He may be from the opposite party but you think we will keep quiet if he gets beaten up? If anyone here has it in him, come forward and show me what you have got.'

His folksy moustache twitched. He pouted his lips and spoke sonorously, chewing on the words, almost to the extent of not letting them out and spraying his saliva generously with his words. There was absolute silence following his speech. Not even the sound of breathing from any direction challenged that. The village landlord muttered something to himself and spat on the ground.

Veeran narrated loudly and elaborately the story of how Sevathaan had gone into the colony the week before and got beaten up. Admittedly, Sevathaan, in his intoxicated state, went knocking on the door of a house in the colony where a lady happened to be alone that night. When the frightened lady didn't open the door for him, he put his hand through the window and knocked over a few things, all the while yelling and using words he shouldn't have used. The lady was so scared she couldn't even scream. The next day he was found after work with bloodied wounds in one of the unoccupied houses in the colony. Even he didn't know who beat him up. When he opened his eyes in the hospital, he simply cried, 'It's dark, it's dark!' One of his legs was fractured and bandaged. His hand was smashed. His head had a gash as deep as a finger. Putting aside what he did to deserve it, the fact that some person from the colony who belonged to some unknown place hit a fellow villager was not acceptable.

'That bastard of a bus driver . . . If a nubile girl from the colony dresses up a little and walks by the road, regardless of who she is, that fellow will stop for her. But if it were the girls from the village, he doesn't even slow down. These dogs have to be beaten into shape first.'

Then Veeran went on to talk about his valorous and unparalleled efforts to get the bus to stop for the village girls. The village landlord couldn't tolerate it any longer.

'Stop now. Let's talk about what needs to be done instead of simply wasting time talking about irrelevant stories.'

'Let him talk. The temerity of the colony people also needs to be subjugated. Otherwise these incidents will only keep increasing.'

Thatha, who came directly from the liquor shop, redid his komanam and straightened it before walking up to the hearse.

'Dei . . . are you going to remove this body now or not?'

The other team had now gotten a little cautious. They spoke in a polite manner.

'Where should we bury it?'

'Well, isn't the lake available in plenty? Burn it on the banks.'

'Water will get into the grave, sir.'

'Adada . . . will your father melt in the water? Who cares what happens to a corpse. Just go now.'

'How can we let go like that?'

'Why are we still talking about this? Now, are you going to lift this hearse or should we carry it and leave it on the other side of the road?'

A young lad who had been patiently waiting and listening to all that was said hurried to the front. The sun shone sharply on his face.

'Do you dare put it there? Let me see just how you would even touch it. The only talking then will be by the police, be careful.'

That pushed Thatha to the edge of his patience. He roared out loud. 'You fuckers! Why are we even talking to them any more? Come, grab this now!'

He kicked the hearse with his foot. The corpse rolled over and lay stomach down. Veeran shoved the barren corpse with his staff. There was a lot of commotion. 'Aiyo, aiyo!' A lot of cries of despair. They finally got hold of the body and rushed to the banks of the lake to bury it there.

After everything was over, the police showed up too. Fifteen prominent people from the village, including Appa, Thatha and Veeran, were taken to the police station. Their annoyance at the people of the colony was further exacerbated now that they had dragged them to the police station, along with their anger and enmity. These were faceless enemies. Every house and every stone was a fiend.

~

Murali tapped the ash from the cigarette with his little finger and blew smoke upwards into the sky. He asked, after a long period of silence, 'Shall we go to see *Billa*?'

'Will we get tickets now?'

Kathirvel never said no when it came to movies. He immediately delved into what needed to be done next to make it happen. Gopal was entirely oblivious to what was being discussed and stood leaning against the wall, engrossed in his own thoughts. The boy protested. 'Let's not go,' he said. 'We have a maths test on Monday. I haven't studied for it at all. Otherwise Paramasivam will burn us to ashes with his looks.'

Paramasivam was the maths teacher. He made no allowances for the fact that the boys were in twelfth standard and had no qualms insulting them in front of everyone else. He would even twist their ears. All through his class, the boys sat trembling with fear.

'He acts as though he is a greatly successful man. Just watch if I don't ask him some disparaging questions one of these days . . .'

'Okay, okay, stop. I know all about how your fearless words last only as long as we aren't anywhere close to him.'

'You get lost! You are so scared of him that you need to pee every time you see him. Funny that you should be mocking me . . .'

Gopal finally broke his silence. 'Let's go to see *Billa*, da.'

'The hallowed words have been uttered. What else do we need? Let's go!'

'That wasn't a prediction by Dhanappaswamy that it needs to be true, was it?'

Dhanappaswamy was a *samiyaar*, a godman, who had come to the colony. He was available only two days a week, travelled only in a car, and had a large following. And all his predictions had been famously coming true apparently.

'Should we go see him one of these days?'

'Let's go to see *Billa* now.'

'Tomorrow's Saturday. Let's go to the matinee show.'

A gentle darkness began to swallow them. Winged termites began to swarm around the temple plinth. Mosquitoes were biting sharply. A Swega moped went past them. It was Sevathaan.

'Look! A "*billa*" just went by us.'

Gopal laughed uncontrollably, his outstretched arm pointing at Sevathaan. He guffawed in spurts and sounded like the puffs of smoke when an oil engine was being started. The boy found it annoying. And he felt a tad bit of anger at the tip of his nose.

'Why are you calling that guy "billa", da?'

'Then what else would you call a lecherous loafer?'

Gopal laughed again. The boy's face was completely ashen. His speech was getting more passionate.

'Be careful with what you say. Don't think that you can get away with saying anything about my fellow villager and that I will keep quiet and put up with it.' He wagged a finger in his face as if to warn him. Gopal made a gesture of wiping his warning on his groin and laughed again. Murali joined him too.

'Isn't he quite the fellow villager? The one that entered the colony and got beat up? Just because he has a Swega moped now, he's now considered a model man?'

'He has now become the owner of a liquor shop too. He is definitely a model man!'

The two of them mocking Sevathaan spiked the boy's anger like a sprinkle of chilli powder. *Yes, he is a bad man. So what? Ever since he returned from the hospital after*

getting beaten up in the colony he has been behaving himself.
How dare these worthless fools talk about him? he thought
to himself.

Sevathaan had two acres of land up the road. He had
built a house on it and sold it for one lakh rupees. With
that he bought himself a vehicle. He renovated his house a
little and became a partner at the liquor shop.

'These are but alms from Thalaivar,' he would say.

If anyone went to him seeking help, he did as much
as he could. Of course, he would also make sure that he
gained something from it. 'Could a honey harvester be
expected to not lick his arm?' And then there were the laws
of politics, of course. On Thalaivar's birthday, he provided
liquor for free. The men and women from Aalkudi would
get drunk and roll all over the road that day. 'The great
Thalaivar has come to us in the form of Sevathaan,' they'd
say. Regardless, no matter how good or bad he was, what
right did the colony folks have to talk about him? the boy
thought to himself and a force took over him.

'Do not talk about him. I will get really angry. Mind
your business,' he warned them.

'Let's see how bad your anger is. Come, show us a
little of your anger,' Kathirvel teased him. He cracked the
knuckle of his pointer finger right in his face. 'Dei, we were
here on the plinth of his village's temple. He may even
break our bones.'

By now the boy was completely exasperated. 'Of course,
this is our village's temple. Why should we be okay with
you using it?'

'Temples are common to all, da.'

'How can they be common to all? How can the temple that has been with us for generations suddenly also belong to the plate-lickers who arrived yesterday?'

He spilt his words quickly. That year when they celebrated the annual festival day, they didn't collect any funds from the people who lived in the colony—because if they did, they could claim rights to the temple later. They would have to be consulted for any planning related to the temple. And one of them could even become the village landlord. And the whole village would have to listen to him with reverence. 'If you include strangers that's what you will get.'

Gopal spoke. 'You don't want to tax us. If we gave you the money as a donation you will accept it, won't you?'

'Look, they have installed a nice large donation box in bronze. Look at how big the lock is. If the colony folks put their donation money in there, you won't have any problems taking that money, would you?'

Murali contorted his body and did a little dance. The boy glowered at his face and said, stretching his voice, 'Of course! If we include you in this and a problem arises tomorrow, you all will shut yourselves in your homes. Not only that, you will shut the windows and draw the curtains over them. Just a little hissing sound and that's enough to scare the whole bunch of you. You all are like a flock of crows that fly around crowing. Will anyone trust you enough to include you in any activity?'

'Look now, don't keep saying things. Screw this temple. We will build a thousand temples, da. Wait and watch how we conduct the kumbabhishekam and open one in the month of Thai.'

'You all will? Sure . . .'

'We will launch "Arul Nayagan Thai pongal entertainment team" and even conduct competitions. If you have the guts, have your villagers send in a team to compete.'

With the rush from laying out such an elaborate plan, Kathirvel lit up a cigarette. Gopal grabbed it from him in a hurry and took a drag too. The smoke went around in a circle with an air of something being accomplished. The boy did not know how to retort. In the midst of the silence that ensued, he said, 'Let us see how you conduct it. You are a bunch of useless fellows who are all words and no action. Don't we know about you guys?'

'We need the words to set a purpose and achieve it. You watch, we will send an appeal to the government to take over this temple. Then your tails will all be cut off.'

'Let's see which government fellow will dare take over the temple. We will chop him up while his blood is still throbbing through his veins. You don't know about us.'

'Oh yes, we do! You are a bunch which doesn't have a penny to buy even a coconut but will have a pound to push your weight around. You are all a bunch of misers.'

'Dei, stop talking about my people.'

'You are the one who started it.'

'Okay, enough is enough, you fellows. Let's talk about something else.' A fed-up Murali intervened and spoke like a peacemaker. Gopal got up, stood on the road and tied his lungi high.

'So what if we talk about your people? I will stand in the middle of the road and shout out loud about them. Did you not call my folks plate-lickers?'

'Go ahead and shout! I will still call you imbeciles all the same.'

'Don't we know about you people. Aren't you all but a heartless bunch that kicked a corpse that was brought to the cemetery.'

'Yes, we will kick. We will hit. And if any one of you come by that side again, we will chop you up too. Why should we allow you in our cemetery? Why don't you go ask the government for one if you want one? Or better yet, bury them inside your homes. Or cut them up into pieces and eat them if you want to.'

Loafing rascals! You dare speak about my people! If you who have come running away from some other place to live here have so much arrogance, then think about how much we, who have lived on this land for generations, must feel? thought the boy, wanting to grab Gopal's neck and rip his jugular out.

'Okay, if you don't want to share the cemetery with the people in the colony, then that should apply to everyone in the colony. Why would you allow people who belong to your sect alone even if they live in the colony? They too have come from other places, have they not?'

'Yeah, they are from their sect, right? They are a fanatic herd.'

At that instant, the boy's ability to speak was blocked by his rage. He wanted to drag and kick them both. What could he do to stump them? What should he say? He couldn't think straight. But there was no way he was not going to stand up for his village.

'We will do that and whatever else we want. How is it your problem?'

'Since all his people sold their land recently and are suddenly rich with that money, they are acting like this, I say.'

'Dei . . . you are but a loafing mongrel who has come from some unknown land and you think you can talk about us? I will chop up your balls. And your father's too.'

He caught Murali's hair in a bunch and circled him around. He ripped apart his shirt and destroyed it. Gopal and Kathirvel pulled the two apart. For a while, no one said anything. They each felt a little guilt in their hearts. The boy heaved like a dog that was tired from chasing a cat. Murali fixed his ruffled hair and said, 'Let what happened be. Going forward, let's not talk about such things amongst us.'

They walked away without a dent in their kinship even though they had flung words at each other.

Chapter 7

Murali, who was walking along the edge of the road, slowed down with his cycle and fell back, and gestured to the boy to do so too. The boy let Gopal and Kathirvel walk ahead and fell back too. The potholes on the road that the cyclists were spread across threatened to make them stumble.

'Are you both going to talk about something secretly? Include us too, da! Otherwise we will meddle.'

'Better yet, are you guys going to "write with a pen"?' Gopal said and burst out laughing. For a few days now, Gopal had been going over the top. Thangarasu was their physics teacher who was recently married. He took tuition classes on the upper floor of his house, in a room that served as his bedroom as well. When Gopal went over for tuition in the evenings, he would look around intently. One day, he unravelled the wicker mat that was tucked away in a corner. A curly strand of hair fell from it. He picked it up with a little stick and showed it around to everyone else, chuckling the whole time. All the boys clamoured to see that strand of hair, as if they had never seen one. As if they could see their teacher's first night pan out in front of them. The boy grabbed Gopal's shirt, pulled him close and asked disconcertedly, 'Why this obscenity?'

Gopal pulled back his shirt calmly and said, 'Do you know anything about all this? Did you not read the series by Kamala Viswanathan in *Saani*?'

'No, I didn't, but what is the connection here?'

'In that series, they identify the murderer with a strand of hair from "that" part of a woman. All this is science, da.'

This made him want to read that series. But he simply said, 'The type of science that makes me want to vomit,' and walked away. This was how Gopal displayed his taste, through these sorts of little things. Lately, they were all he talked about. Sometimes, even if the boy wanted to listen to him, he got bored. He ignored Gopal's comment and fell back with Murali. They waited until the two in the front were but a dot, far away, and then Murali halted his cycle. While they both relieved themselves behind a tamarind tree, Murali asked him, 'Does your Annan drink?'

The way Murali asked the question seemed a little loaded. Why was he asking this question, the boy wondered. When they had gone to Vimala Theatre to watch movies, the boy had pointed to his brother and said, 'This is my older brother.' That was it. Murali might have seen him maybe three times in all. Now he was asking about him out of the blue. That too a question about drinking. Not comprehending the situation fully, he asked Murali, 'Why do you ask, da?'

'Just. Simply. Tell me now.'

'Earlier, he used to drink kallu in the forests. But now, where does he have the time for all that? He comes home after twelve at night. He has loads of work. He doesn't go there these days.'

Murali picked up his cycle and didn't say anything for some time. He seemed deep in thought. He opened his mouth a couple of times to say something but didn't. He looked up at the canopy of the tamarind tree, and then looked at the boy. He wiped his face with his hand, stopped his hand on top of his nose and stayed there, thinking.

'What is it, da? Whatever it is, tell me now.'

'Don't take this the wrong way. I have something to tell you.'

'Whatever it is, don't hesitate, just tell me.'

Murali rode his cycle with his eyes fixed on the front wheel and did not look once at the boy. His voice sounded feeble as he said, 'I too have gotten inebriated a couple of times, da. I'm not saying it is such a big sin. But . . .'

'Just say it, da. This is hardly the time to talk like a saint.' His beating around the bush was beginning to annoy the boy.

'I saw your brother completely drunk yesterday.'

Surely he must have confused his identity with someone else. How would he remember a face that he had seen two, maybe three, times? He has seen someone else and assumed it is my Annan. Cockeyed fellow! he thought, laughing.

'Do you know how my brother looks?'

His words sounded as if he was mocking Murali's capability to remember things. Even in school, Murali couldn't repeat what was said a short while before. He felt that the boy was pinpointing all that with his question, and that burned him. Anger and pride boiled over.

'He is a bit fairer than you. He combs his hair like Thalaivar. His cheeks are a little hollow. His moustache has only the end hair sticking out. His nose is withered and points downwards. His eyes . . .'

'Stop, stop. Tell me, where did you see him?'

The identification marks that Murali gave were all correct. But would he have been drunk? That too to the point of delirium? The golden boy. Reserved. Quiet. Was he really talking about him?

'Last night, I went to a second-show cinema with my Maama. It must have been around one, one-fifteen. There was not a soul around. And not a sound. It was only within the colony by the ration store corner that we heard two or three people talk and laugh loudly. We couldn't tell who they were so we went close by to find out. They completely ignored us. Then, suddenly, they began to fight amongst themselves. They hit each other even though not one of them could stand steady. Your brother was among them. The others were from Vettur, apparently. My Maama told me. I, too, was not very sure at first. But then I checked closely in the light from the lamp. It was surely your brother.'

Annan came in at night without anyone's knowledge. He left after everyone in the morning. Even if he was drunk, it was true that no one could have known . But hanging out in groups and creating trouble?

The boy's head began to spin. He wanted to stop the cycle and just sit down right there. What else did he have to bear the burden of? The house was just about returning to some state of normalcy after the thunder that had struck them. Now this? They had imprisoned Appa for a week after the cemetery episode. Because the whole village took responsibility, that incident died away without causing any further trouble. After Akka got married and left, they barely saw her. She came home on rare occasions, as if visiting some acquaintance. Unable to bear all this, Appa shut himself in the goat pen. Thatha and Paati spent their time bickering and fighting between themselves. They were both just bags of bones, though. They had as many wrinkles on their body as the bubbles in the rice water they threw away, and shrunk a little every passing day. But who was really flourishing anyway? Chithappa's story was similar too. He was in danger of getting pneumonia from all the loads he was lifting. He was always drunk because of his work. His eyes were perpetually bloodied.

When the boy wondered why it was all happening this way, he could only blame the loss of the land they had owned. How cheerful and energetic their lives were! They were flung away, out of their lands, and this was the state they were in now. How could Annan too do this?

He didn't sleep that night. It was a new-moon night and pitch-dark outside. He was lying down in the shed. His mother's cot was by the front of the house. Across from her and a little away was Thatha's shed, where the old couple slept, each in one corner. A small lamp flickered from the shed where food was cooked. Until then, there was no sign of Annan. The boy lay awake, determined to see when

Annan got in. He kept tossing and turning. The thornlike cot bothered him. The cock crowed. Was it crowing at an odd hour? His brother could blame losing track of time if at least the moon was up and bright. But why hadn't he returned yet on such a pitch-dark night? That rascal, he had been sneaking into the house in the middle of the night!

Mani stood by the well and howled. The howl he howled every three hours, or a *saamam*. The boy wanted to beat up the dog. It howled as if everything was lost. He should have just left it to run around in the colony. After Thatha and Paati lost everything and moved to the valavu, Mani used to come home too. But he had to circumvent the village to get home because theirs was the last house in the valavu and it would have to fight with the other dogs in the village if it went through there. They all ganged up to attack it as if it were a stranger. It was getting to be too much trouble for it to reach home, tucking its tail between its legs and escaping all the attacks. So, Mani found its own convoluted route to get to them. If they gave it something to eat, Mani finished that and then made its way to the colony again. And ever since they had bought land and moved, it was freed of having to deal with the village dogs.

Mani stopped howling and started barking. Other dogs began to join the chorus from afar. Mani went close to the cart track and barked harder—and then suddenly stopped as if nothing had happened. The boy lifted his head slightly to see what was going on.

There was the sound of a cycle. And he could see someone pushing it. Mani went close to that person and rubbed against their legs, whimpering softly. The person simply gave it a kick in the darkness and said, 'Get lost.' Mani withdrew into a corner, crying loudly in pain. Just when he was wondering if he should get up and help his brother, his mother was already up and walking towards him.

'Why are you creating so much trouble for me?' She gave him a tight rap on his head with her knuckles. His head couldn't stay straight. With his head hanging down to the front, he slowly managed to put down the stand of his cycle. Amma held the stumbling fellow by his hand and guided him inside. The boy, on the other hand, watched the whole thing happen in front of him and his ire grew beyond bounds.

Amma, you knew all about this and are keeping it a secret? What sort of mother are you!? You think you are protecting this spineless son by hiding his character? How long do you think you can protect him? As long as you do so, he will keep drinking. And cause nuisance. And eat without anyone noticing him and go to sleep. Amma, what you are doing is enabling him. It will get him out of the consequences of his actions. But that only temporarily. The more he drinks, the walls of protection you have built will crumble one by one. They will all come down and expose him to the world. At that time, he will stand naked, hurting; stop protecting him, Amma. Why are you feeding him? Is it because he drinks, and if he sleeps on an empty stomach, his intestines will get fried and his buttocks will explode? If there is someone to take such good care of him, how will he ever feel any remorse from drinking so much? He will happily drink more. He will drink until he doesn't remember anything. Are you afraid that he will drink openly if everyone came to know of it? Foolish mother . . . Let him drink openly. A person committing a mistake in secrecy will always feel protected. Take that away from him. Let some fear about life get into him.

Amma served Annan some food, scolding him in her mind. So, Annan did drink. It was also very clear that this was a daily affair. What should he do now? He had to expose Annan and include Amma too.

He walked stealthily to the goat pen. He heard Appa's loud snore. Appa sounded one with the goats. 'Appa, Appa,' he called out softly. Appa ground his teeth like stones rubbing against each other. If someone who didn't know about it heard this, it was sure to scare them. Why did he grind his teeth like this? 'Huh?' he said as he woke up with a start and climbed down. 'What, da?' His voice quivered.

'Come and see the state that your older son is in. Come.'

'Why, what happened?'

'He is completely drunk, Appa. It seems to me that he comes home like this every day.'

'Oh no! Has he also decided to drop a rock on this family's head?'

He followed Appa in the dark. The shaken body was quivering. His father couldn't walk faster. Even in the dark, the komanam shone like a bright white line. He was sagging like an old white goat that had had four or five kids. Amma came out to throw away the leaf that Annan ate from. She let out a soft cry as she saw them approach and withdrew to one side in fright.

'Why are you shouting? It's just us. Call your lovely son out.'

'He is already asleep.'

'Sure, of course. Dei! Get up and come out!'

Annan got up from the plinth of the house and came over. He tried hard to control his stagger. He stood up straight and pressed his feet down hard. 'What, Appa?' he asked loudly.

'How long has this been going on?' Appa asked without a trace of anger in his voice. Instead, it was laced with fatigue from the motley experiences he had gone through.

'What are you referring to, Appa?'

'This drunken state that you are in.'

'Who is drunk?'

Annan spoke loudly. Even his voice sounded as if he was going to beat someone up. Meanwhile, the stare that Amma gave to the boy as she stood with the still-to-be-discarded leaf in her hand was sparking with fire.

'You are a dupe who knows nothing. I know everything. You don't have to go to the cinema talkies starting tomorrow. Stay back and work in the farm.'

'That's not my fate! Why should I roam around with the goats wearing a komanam?'

His voice came out clearly and deliberately without a crack. Appa was a bit taken aback by his response. Until then, Annan had never argued against Appa. He was an innocent lad who listened to whatever was told to him. A simpleton. His father couldn't take it that he sounded so belligerent.

'Then what? You speak as if you are born into a landlord family. That you can do nothing and still eat.'

'Give me money. I will start a soda shop.'

'How will I trust someone who is so drunk that he is walking on his head with any money?'

Appa's voice shivered. Maybe it was the wind making it shake and crack a little?

'I will drink. And do whatever I want. Do I ask you for money? I earn. And do I give money for the family regularly or not?'

He sat himself on a rock and held his head in his hands.

'So, since you are earning, I shouldn't ask His Highness any questions?'

'Give me money to set up a shop. Then if you find me drinking after that you have every right to pull me up. But don't expect me to sit around and bear the burden of the land. I won't.'

'But you think you can run the shop yourself?'

'Won't I? Give me the money and watch for yourself.'

Amma couldn't bear it any longer and intervened. 'Is he not saying he will do it? Just give him the money. He will learn to manage it. He knows the trade already. It's not like he has to suffer in the forest like we do.'

'You shut up and stay out of this, di. This is between him and me. And aren't you quite the charitable goddess. Providing food to all the wastrels that come home drunk.'

'As if you smell fragrant, with no alcohol on your breath.'

He got up as if possessed, grinding his teeth loudly. With the first stick he could find, he beat Amma. Her cries broke through the darkness. 'Sinner, sinner, just kill me!'

He beat her with it until the stick broke into pieces.

'Why are you hitting Amma, leave her alone!' shouted Annan and pushed Appa back. Appa fell stomach down outside the house. The boy ran over to the father and helped him up. Thatha and Paati watched all this through the darkness. Appa's leg got cut by the rock and the boy's hands were sticky with his blood. 'Aiyyo, Appa!' he cried and found a piece of cloth to tie up his wound. Annan sat himself again on the rock and planted his head in his palms.

'Adei . . . are you so drunk that you dare hit Appa? You drunk dog!'

The boy grabbed Annan's hands in a bunch and punched him on his back. Annan grabbed his arm and bit him hard. The two of them rolled on the sand outside, fighting. 'Dei . . . dei,' yelled Amma and Appa as they tried to separate them.

'Why are you doing this? Everyone is bent on destroying this family even more. Learn to be responsible and make a living, you motherfuckers,' cried Thatha from the plinth. His voice was carried away by the winds, alone.

~

Inside the house, Amma lay with her hair spread everywhere. Around her, dirt and dust had built a boundary. Her undone hair lay clumped in unkempt locks with her having no time to pull them all into a bundle. She didn't bother making or serving any food. She refused to get up regardless of what anyone said. Evidently, the burden in her mind hurt her more than Appa's blows. Money earned through so much hard work! Everything got wiped away by greed. The boy found it disgusting to see Amma's swollen face. Annan was the only one who kept trying to make her get up. 'Get away!' she snapped, swatting him with her arm as she continued to lie down.

She didn't get up to even milk the cows. Appa would let the calf loose in the morning. In the evening, the boy milked the cow. He wasn't used to it, having not done it for a while. But the buffalo stood still no matter who milked it. And its udders were soft like a flower. Just touching them made them squirt milk. If it was blocked, even if he used both his hands to softly squirt, nothing came out. He gently knelt down, balanced himself on his feet and milked the cow. Appa stood in front, caressing its face. He would have milked the cow himself but he couldn't kneel down. If he did, it hurt like death.

Appa was raising his hand for everything. These days, his inadequacies seemed to manifest as blows and fights. And even the swear words he uttered grew worse. They wriggled like worms when he opened his mouth. Unable to bear Appa's anger, Thatha fought with him once.

To that, Appa yelled, 'Can the old man not shut up and stay out of it?'

Since then, Thatha hadn't opened his mouth to ask about anything. He remained 'like a beaten rock', saying nothing. His chidings at Paati alone could be heard well into the night.

Amma too began to want all sorts of things. The young women from the colony had no work to do. They had all the time to go to the movies and dramas. Amma too would tie up the buffalo and go away with them to gossip or watch movies. Should Appa take care of the lands? Or milking the cows? Or grazing the goats? All the work landed on his head. Unlike before, nobody came to work in the farms. Even if they did, the salaries they demanded could be met only by giving them the shirt off his back. But Amma did not care about any of that. She made herself up, combed her hair, made a bun out of it and wrapped it with crossandra flowers. To make up for her wispy hair, she added fake hair that went all the way to her waist. He found all of this to be very distasteful. Appa observed everything but didn't say anything. But some day—like how he had exploded in Annan's case—when he found the opportunity, he would beat the hell out of her to appease his anger. He had already begun to say something about it now and then.

'Looks like a man in the colony is waiting there with the gates wide open.' Or, 'Who invited you over there? You've walked back and forth from the colony seven times already.'

To all this, Amma would retort with, 'Why don't you come by? I will expose the man I cuddle on my lap. You are the one who goes to prostitutes from seven different villages. If you accuse me of anything, it will be your tongue that will rot, you watch.'

All that the boy could do was to cry within, hearing the exchanges his parents had. Who could he shut up? Both of them were pouring out the fires that were the agitations of their minds. And if they took joy in seeing the other charred from that fire, just what could he say? They were damaging each other so much with mere words. They seldom remembered that there were others around. And how many inappropriate embarrassing details they spoke out in the presence of their own son who now stood taller than the father. Is this what they meant when they said 'turn forty and the demeanour changes to that of a dog's'? They didn't have the guts to face the consequences and instead gorged on each other. He even harboured thoughts of leaving home and running away with nothing but what he was wearing.

Amma just couldn't do the work related to the land and stay quiet in that house. She would fetch two or three potfuls of rice-drained water for the buffalo. She would take cow dung for the houses that gave her the rice-drained water. She also had the job of delivering milk to the colony twice every day. And then she would deliver cow-dung cakes or castor plant twigs, and that was a couple of rounds of walking. She always managed to make some money every time she went to the colony. And if she gave Appa two paisa, two more went into her purse. The money she made went back to the colony as loans. Thirty-three per cent interest or forty-eight per cent interest. They even came home looking for her sometimes.

'Please give two hundred. Even if you charge forty eight per cent, that is okay with us. We will return the amount in two months.'

These were people who drew a fixed salary every month. Why were they finding themselves borrowing money so often? They all lived way beyond their means, then they borrowed money with interest. These were people who worked at the mill, who were office-goers, weavers. Amma loaned money only to families she knew from delivering milk.

In spite of her cautiousness, trouble found its way. Last evening, the women who delivered milk had all stood whispering amongst themselves near the lake's water channel. Appa, who was grazing the buffalo on the banks, couldn't contain himself and asked them, 'What's the buzz about?' For a few minutes, there was silence, like when the crows that were cawing away stopped suddenly. Breaking that silence, Velakka turned towards Appa, fidgeted with a corner of her sari and said, 'Nothing much. One of the housewives from the colony wrapped up her things and ran away in the middle of the night without telling anyone.'

'Then?'

'Yesterday, she was standing outside her house in her full figure, Thambi. She even asked if I had any milk left over. I said no and left. And before sunrise she vanished!'

'But why?'

'Looks like she couldn't bear the burden of all the debt. If you keep borrowing in all directions for sixty per cent and hundred per cent, you have to pay it back at some point, don't you? Otherwise your home will find its place in the street.'

Pavakka couldn't keep her mouth shut, and broke her silence too.

'Your wife is the one who provides milk for her. Wonder how much she lent her.'

'Some say it was five thousand. Some say it was two thousand. The village says all kinds of things, no one knows for sure. Do you know how much she had lent her, Thambi?'

'How awful! Wonder how much she lent, this fool. I know nothing about that . . .'

'But do you not ask her anything about all this? In that case, this is how things will be if a woman does things on her own!'

Velakka added oil to the fire and spread it even more. When Appa returned home with the buffalo, Amma was coming back from the colony with teary eyes and a reddened nose at the same time.

'I work so hard that my bones stick out but you give a hot fomentation to some unknown man instead?'

'How much did you lose, di?

'Do you know where that man is right now?

'Do you know which village he is from?

'Do you know if he has any relatives around here?'

For all of Appa's questions, tears were the only response. Her crying without explanation infuriated Appa and he beat her up to take out his frustration. If it hadn't been for Nachakka who happened to be passing by and came running to peel him off her, screaming, 'What is this, Maama!' he may have even killed her, who knew. He had destroyed Amma's fragile body. But who could be blamed? The couple who took the money had run away with it, leaving no name or address behind. No one knew where they had come from either. When they asked the neighbour, he seemed to be clueless.

'They never spoke much to us, so we also didn't bother with getting to know them. When they didn't want to know us, we too decided it was best to mind our business.'

The boy was the one who interviewed the neighbour. Hearing the neighbour's response made him very angry. What sort of logic was that? If the house next door were to get broken into, that's when the neighbours would suddenly be hard of hearing. If someone mentioned it in the morning, they'd probably say, 'I thought I heard something in my dream.' He cursed them in his mind, cleared his throat, spat out, and took his cycle to return home.

What was lost was lost. They still didn't know how much the loss was. 'What is the point in talking about it again and again? Let us move on and take care of what needs to be done going forward,' everyone said as if talking about someone's demise, and yet, kept talking about it reminding them about the loss over and over again. The milkmaids were secretly really happy. Those were the minds that couldn't wait for one among their own to fall. Their faces, though, dripped with innocence.

The boy was sitting on the plinth, writing something. Amma kept lying down. She wasn't ready to listen to anyone. He even took some food on a plate and tried to feed her. *Um hm.* No. Just then, Dheenambal came by with her daughter. It must have been about a year since her husband died. She was taking care of three little children on her own.

'Is Akka not around?'

Appa, who was gathering cow dung, looked up and said, 'She's lying in there. Call her.' She called out for her but Amma didn't budge even though she had heard her. She must have thought that Dheenambal had come to inquire about the missing money.

'Dheenambal Akka has come to talk to you about something. She's calling you. Get up and come,' the boy stopped writing and said loudly.

Amma straightened her crushed body, stretched it back and came out. She wiped her swollen eyes with her sari and sat at the threshold of the entrance door. She was blinded by the daylight.

'What is it, Dheenamba?'

'Only because you recommended, I let this child help with the daily chores in that household. Don't they know how much a ten-year-old girl can do? Didn't that lady also bear a daughter? That Satan. Wretched unlucky bitch.'

She didn't care about the state Amma was in. Her moans could be heard all the way to the road.

'What is the matter, tell me.'

'Look at this, how her back is swollen in lumps. Absolute lawlessness. She has hit the child with a branch.

May she bear worms instead of children! Such a small child, if she is asked to carry a whole pot of water, can she do it?'

' . . .'

'She fed my child spoilt food apparently. Not even a dog will eat that food! My child had to eat that food and then wash all their clothes. Doesn't that lady have any brains? That butt of a donkey. What is the point in talking about her? I have to curse that man out. The one who orphaned all three like this.' And she started scolding her husband. In between her sobs, Amma asked her, 'What do you want me to do now?'

'Mm . . . I left her there because of you. You should have to listen to my words at least a little bit.'

'Yes, you left her there because I said so. Who is denying that? That lady asked me if I knew any young child who could help her with her chores. I knew you were struggling to make ends meet. So I told you about that job. Now if she is treating her like this just stop sending her.'

'But shouldn't there be some sense of justice? The child from Singaram's house is also going to work at someone's house like this. Apparently, that lady takes care of her as her own. Doesn't she have any compassion? I may not have enough to feed her but I won't let her be beaten by that devil of a lady.'

'Stop it, Dheenambal. If I hear of any other good place looking for help, I will let you know. I too thought she would take good care of your daughter. But if she is like this, why send her there?'

Amma spoke while opening her eyes slowly. Her body had not seen food for two or three days and she was struggling a lot. Dheenambal walked away, scolding anyone she could think of along with her child. Poor little girl. Her face was shrunken and lacked any sparkle, like a copra being dehydrated to extract oil. Appa found yet another reason to vent his anger on Amma.

'Why do you need to be in others' business? If the colony people suffer, does that become your problem? Look at this face that is finding work for some other! Like we don't have enough on our plates already.'

And it began again. When would this stop? How many arguments were yet to happen? He shut his book and started walking. It was beginning to get dark. He went by the banks of the lake. And kept walking. What would happen if he kept walking like this? He did not ever want to go back home again. But where would he take a bath, eat, change his clothes? Were all those things important? Could he not roam around like a homeless person without having to worry about mundane chores? No matter how far he walked away, he knew he had to return home. But there was not a hand to assuage him. Not a shoulder to cry on. What should he do? Where should he go? Che . . . A rock looked inviting. He spread his hands on its surface and lay down. The warmth from the rock was soothing. He wanted to lie there and not move at all. The humming of the nocturnal insects began to get louder but he was oblivious to everything around him, including how much time passed.

Chapter 8

It was heart-wrenching to look at Kuppan. He was barely recognizable. He needed a stick to support himself and was barely able to pick up his feet from the ground as he walked. His skin was indistinguishable from his veshti, which looked like it had been soaked in cow dung. The body which was once tough as a rock was now dry and loose. He was breathing audibly through his toothless mouth. He had got himself a pair of spectacles from a free eye-care camp for his cataract. Yet, he couldn't see anything. He was managing simply with his familiarity of things and by using his fingers to feel. He had a vessel that hung from his shoulder with a rope. In it was a collection of foods from different houses of the colony that bubbled from fermentation. Gopal clapped and stopped the man who was struggling to make his way in the dark.

'Ey, Kuppa . . . any specials today?'

Kuppan paused, put his hand over his eyes as if he was protecting them from the midday sun and said, 'Who is this, Saami?'

'He is quite the conniving fellow, da!' murmured Murali. 'Is the "Vasantha Maligai" full today?'

Kuppan said, 'What was that, Saami?' towards the direction of the voices like a deaf person. The little tent-like structure that he erected to sew and mend people's slippers had come to be known as the 'Vasantha Maligai' after a movie in which a house with the same name was the breeding ground for nefarious activities. There were always four or five people in that shop. Farm labourers gathered there and chit-chatted in a localized version of the Telugu language.

'Mamoy, emi sangathi?'

'Ora ittanadu veli vecchiniki pillithiriya?'

'Peddhaiyya, aa itta kaadhi rugal icchana?'

Kuppan had the responsibility of passing information to everyone. If the colony folks needed labourers for any work, they would spread the word through him. The women would comb their dried and discoloured hair back and into braids and sit at his shop. Their mouths were always reddened from chewing betel leaves. The way they spoke, shaking their heads in merriment, and laughed, twirling their tongues, would draw people waiting at the bus stop to join them. Kuppan also did the job of pimping out women. Those who were collecting dust with no work after the forests were destroyed had become mere bodies. At least the men found themselves odd jobs like chopping firewood, building fences, sizing logs or weaving. What could the women do? If both husband and wife didn't work, there was never enough to fill a stomach. There were children too, one after the other, to feed. Of the salary earned, half went into Sevathaan's pocket via his liquor store. That was why Kuppan's shop became Vasantha Maligai.

Kuppan didn't identify the boy who was with his friends. He too kept quiet so he couldn't be recognized.

'So, shall we come by after ten at night?'

'Don't, Saami, don't do that.'

'Don't try to trick us. We came the other day too. You forgot about that, didn't you? You thought we were new customers?'

'You young children don't do it, Saami.'

Murali's ash-laden lip was twitching in the dark.

'Yow . . . you speak as if we are just old enough to drink milk. You do a job like this. And you want to advise us too. Come here now.'

He took him to a hidden spot behind the tamarind tree. At a distance was the sound of a blaring horn. Only the bus named 'Cho Vilas' drove by this fast. If the driver put his hand on the horn at Odaiyur where he started the bus, he took his hand off the horn only after reaching Karattur, the last stop. He always drove in such a rush. From out of the blue, he flew past them, flashing his blinding lights for a brief minute. Murali joined them after sending Kuppan away.

'This old man is a smart guy, da. He tried to pull a fast one on me.'

'So, yes or no?' asked Gopal eagerly.

'Yes, of course!'

'Should we take him too?' Kadhir, short for Kathirvel, asked, pointing to the boy. The boy's hands were shivering. He was nervous. He was sweating even with the cool breeze. The more he wiped his fingers on his lungi, the more they sweated. Should he join them and see what this was all about? They all had done this two or three times already. It was Murali's Maama who first initiated them. He had coined the phrase 'writing with a pen'.

'Where do you want to take him . . . So he soils himself?'

Their laughter in the darkness damaged his ear unmercifully. It echoed in his ears as if they were all mocking him. He got really angry. 'As if these guys know it all. Like only they have everything.'

'If we get caught in some awkward situation, he wouldn't know to run away, da.'

'Then it will be the story of the one who ran away and didn't get caught and the other who stopped to piss and got caught.'

Again, they all laughed, mocking him. Murali bent down and laughed so hard his stomach hurt.

Gopal had tears in his eyes from all the laughing. They all got such joy from teasing the boy. Kadhir quoted a tag line from an advertisement, 'Say that once again?', and laughed, hearing it all over again. The boy felt as if he was standing naked and being spat on. *Loafing rascals! You think I can't do it? You think I don't have the guts to do it. I will show you.* He stood in front of them and said sharply, 'Let's go right now, I'm ready.'

'He has pride for sure. Let's see what else he's got.'

Barely controlling his laughter, one of them said, 'Are you coming for sure? Think harder once more.'

He was close to crying at this point. He showed his fury on his face and said, 'Why, you don't believe me? Let's go right now, da.'

There was still time before 10 p.m. If they slowly circled the area once, that would take care of it. They got off their cycles and walked. In the boy's mind was an inexplicable guilt. He said all that he did in bravado. But was it right? What would happen if someone from home came to know? But he also wanted to do it. He was curious to find out what it was all about. It was an itch within him. But was it right? He assuaged himself, thinking, *This is hardly a habit like it is for them. It is only this one time. And then never after. And not only that. No more hanging out with these fellows.*

The streets were mottled with light. He had long stopped being able to identify any landmark to figure out where they were. Then he saw Muthu's handcart. Muthu ironed clothes for a living. He had stopped going to people's homes to take orders a long time ago. He ironed clothes only in the cart. Whenever the boy passed by, Muthu would ask, 'Why don't we get to see much of little Saami these days?' as he pressed his clothes. But his wife still went to every home to collect clothes without fail.

'Hey, they have announced the dates for the examinations. When are we going to study?' came Kadhir's saddened voice.

'Why are you thinking about that at this hour?' said Murali, wincing. 'My blood is heated and I am so turned on right now. Don't spoil it for me.'

When they entered a particular street, it occurred to the boy that his Periappa's house was on it. 'Dei, let's not go through this one,' he said. They went through the next street. Periappa had bought a house in the colony itself and

moved into it. He now owned two houses there—he lived
in one and rented out the other. If his Periappa saw him in
that area, he was sure to get reprimanded. 'What are you
doing with the boys from the colony?' he'd question him.

'Look at this fellow, still afraid of his Periappa, da.'

'Don't you act too smart. I know all about when you get
scared too. I will make sure to point it out then.'

The streets were barren. The vadhanaram trees
spread their canopies like umbrellas and cast shadows.
Watching them move gently in the light from the lamps
was fascinating. *Why not just stay here with this beautiful
moment*, he thought to himself. Did he have to go with
them? They went past those who were confined in their
homes. Gopal walked while talking about something with
his eyes open wide. What direction were they headed in?
Were they lost?

'Where are we going?'

'Right now, we are going to Kadhir's house. There is
no one home. There is some dosai batter there. We'll buy a
couple of eggs. By the time we finish eating, it will be ten.
We can go by the lake after,' Murali explained, batting his
eyelids. 'All this extra effort because of him. We shouldn't
have brought him along.'

*He has this pride that he is the oldest of us all. He is brash
and thinks he can take care of anything that comes his way.
He likes to stir the pot and trap us in his web by deceit. No
point blaming him, though. This is my weakness. Why this
weakness? Because I want to find out what it is all about.
My eagerness, my impatience to find out about it. But at this*

age, is it right to ignore studies and go after things like this?
Why are we after such things? But would I even be able to
study if I was at home instead? There are fights, arguments all
the time. This seems much better than being there and going
crazy with all the screaming. Appa is a drunkard. Annan is
an alcoholic. But I'm not going to drink and cause any trouble.
No one knows about this . . . but is it okay to do it just because
no one knows about it?

Incoherent thoughts dawned upon him. He was spiralling in and out of cognizance, barely aware of what the rest were talking about.

'Why are you walking so quietly? Are you afraid?'

Murali's mockery of him whenever he wanted to. That crooked smile that made his lips disappear. His constant belittling of him!

The boy denied it immediately.

'Not at all . . . I was simply listening to your conversation.'

'Well, if you are afraid, stop right now. Otherwise, you can't blame us for this and that.'

'Hmm.'

There was no one at Kadhir's house. The rooms were filled with picture frames, deer antlers and fake tigers. Even though he was a teacher, Kadhir's father had a lot of interest in hunting. Kadhir and Gopal went in to make dosai and omelettes. The boy lay down on the bed with his face buried in a pillow and asked Murali, 'Have you seen this movie *Unarchigal*, with Ilavarasan?' The movie was about a young lad who dies eventually of a sexually transmitted disease.

Murali gave him a look and said, as if he was advising him, 'That doesn't happen to everyone, da. That's just your fear. Why are you psyching yourself up thinking about such things? Am I not going to do it before you? We are doing this just for fun. At this age, how long are you going to be on my side, listening to my experiences? Tell me. If you go once, you will find out for yourself. "Chi . . . is this it?" you will say, and be able to concentrate on your work from then on. Otherwise you will find yourself wondering about it all the time. Sex is very important for your body, da. Most importantly, it will help with lowering your stress.'

'. . .'

'How long are we going to keep checking out the ladies on the streets and talking about wanting more of their midriffs? Only ones who don't have this sort of opportunity will talk like that. But why do we need to? All this is mere fun at this age.'

'. . .'

'Are we trying to grab the arm of another man's wife? Are we going to waylay a lady on the streets and carry her away? Those are unequivocally wrong. We are going to pay for this service. So, who is committing a mistake here? Take it easy, da. Don't overthink it. In matters like this, you shouldn't think so much. You want to do it now, you just do it. You should only think about this minute as real. You think this is immoral? Nothing is funnier than that . . .'

'. . .'

'Kadhir too was afraid like this at first. Now he invites me to join him when he goes! We aren't doing anything that hasn't been done already. And who really is that scrupulous, tell me? Everyone only needs an opportunity to present itself to not be so. Until such a time, they will talk as if they are the keepers of morality.'

The more elaborately Murali talked about this, the more confused the boy got. He thought Murali was alluding to too many things as he made his case and was contradicting himself. And that many things that he said were incorrect. But on the other hand, it seemed right too. So he unloaded his fears and began to walk with them.

The lake was behind the colony, and there were stagnant puddles all around. They walked carefully around the dugouts created for harvesting sand and soil. Murali led the group, Kadhir and Gopal were in the middle, and the boy trailed behind them. Piles and marshy puddles lay spread beyond the lake. There were little mounds in all directions. The dense unja trees looked melancholic in the dark.

'Why isn't anyone here, da?' asked Kadhir, pale-faced.

'Just wait, let's see.'

Hearing their voices, a figure emerged from hiding. It took a little while to distinguish them from the surrounding darkness.

'Oh, is it not the officer's son? Why dear, you are all so tender still. Yet, you want a lady every other week? All right, come on then. May your sins be added to mine.'

'Right . . . and you still haven't stopped your constant nagging.'

He felt an unbearable pain, as if his chest was being split open. Whose voice was that? A voice that felt like a sharp slap. A voice that had stroked him with comfort and protection. A voice that had embraced him, soaking in love. He took a step backward and began to walk away. Releasing himself from the grasp of that voice. Leaving them behind.

~

A centipede crawled all over his body, clawing him as it moved. On his face, his hands, his back, his hips . . . He wanted to grab it and hurl it away and kept reaching out with his hands. How big that centipede was! Where was it? It didn't get caught at all. He wanted to chop every body part off and throw it away. Not only this centipede, he wanted to lose everything around him. Not a single thought should still remain within. All he wanted to do was keep walking alone in the light of the moon on the long tar road.

The moon shone quietly. *Boy! What was I just about to do? Does nothing else matter in front of bodily desires? Does lust have a quality of making one act as if possessed? Can I not overcome that? In this moment of the night, they must be destroying Ramayi. How did I let myself be a part of that group? If it was not her, would I too have stayed? How she used to be! And now, she is driven to sell her body surreptitiously to make ends meet. Who is responsible for this? Is it the government who snatched our lands? Or us who shook them off our backs and left them behind? Is she doing this because she is unable to find another job? And Kuppan has accepted all this quietly and justified it? Was it because of her imbecile husband who left her? Was it the need of her children's stomachs? Why did she become this?*

Far away, a knoll glistened in the darkness. Behind it was the light from the rising moon. The lamps looked like a meandering snake. The bald rock glowed like a halo. He wanted to put his hands together in prayer right then. At the same time, he felt embarrassed to turn towards that direction too. He felt a sense of awareness dawn on him as the moon slowly rose up in the sky and the light around him grew brighter. The moon that rose to expel the darkness that had settled within him. Couldn't this have happened earlier?

He sat on the mound at the well. In the light of the moon, the well looked lazy. The water that rippled gently with the breeze seemed to stretch its arms and invite him to it. In a corner a little fish sprung up and down in a flash. Somewhere from a distance came the sound of a lone dog barking. The neem tree by the well nodded with its branches, beckoning him. He wondered if he should get in. Could this cool water help him unload the burden in his chest, the heat from his body and the centipede?

Little waves crashed and splattered along the edges incessantly. Yet the water seemed emotionless. *Why is the water in the well so agitated at this hour? Everyone is peacefully asleep somewhere, why is there so much excitement here? A cheer that can be heard only within the ear. Waves that crash only within the chest. I should get in.*

He took off his shirt and lungi and threw them on a rock nearby. The underwear irritated him too. Were his clothes the 'centipede' that had crawled all over him? He needed to embrace the water without anything on him. To hold his breath and sink slowly into it. Become one with the fish that were swimming around. He removed his underwear and tossed that aside too. An inexplicable peace seemed to envelop him. Everything vanished and his mind floated along, naked.

He jumped from the top of the mound. He heard the water part and surround him. The moonbeams splattered with the ripples. The coolness of the water freed him from all the dreadful hands of the night. He circled his arms gently in the water and swam around the well. This was how memories involving Ramayi swam around in his mind. Memories of him holding on to her skirt and running about in the forests, running after the goats, playing *anjaankal*, a game with five pebbles, and hopscotch . . . He used to think he couldn't do anything without her.

She, too, kept him safe in the palm of her hand as if she had borne him in her womb and given birth to him. As soon as she arrived with her two braids and an overtly oily face, she would pick him up and place him on her hip. He would go to sleep resting his head on her breasts. He used to curl himself to fit into her lap and be buried deep in there. Once, he got chicken pox and had sores all over his body. 'The goddess has seen him,' they said and didn't let him out at all. He lay inside on the cot the entire time. Amma collected neem leaves, made a paste of them and applied it with a chicken feather. That spread coolness on the otherwise itchy sores. Ramayi belonged to the labour class and wasn't allowed to see him in that state. She wasn't allowed to receive any food or drink from his house during that time. She was considered a defilement. That wouldn't be acceptable for curing chicken pox.

'Let the little Saami get better. May the goddess let him go. I will make an offering to the same goddess; I will circumambulate around her on foot. I am fine, I can live even on just water. I will bring some starch water from home and have that during the day. Let the little Saami get up.'

Until the sores waned and he was given his first shower after the sickness, Ramayi didn't come by the house even by mistake. She went directly to the pen in the farms to let the goats graze, put them back in the pen and went home. After he got better, she touched every scar from the sores on his body and kissed them. When he thought about that love and about how he was going to tear apart with lust the same lips that had been filled with affection towards him . . . he felt lesser than a worm.

Even the water in the well had turned tepid, or so it seemed. His body was burning with heat. In a corner, an avri fish slapped the water hard with its tail, spattered the water and disappeared. He lay on his back and looked up at the sky. He saw in the twinkling stars the tear-stained eyes of Ramayi.

Ramayi, what all you were for me. If you had noticed me in the darkness, what would you have thought? That your fate was driving you to sleep with your son? Or, that you were getting an opportunity to sleep with the little Saami, and would derive joy from that? Would you have bugged me for more money? Would you have invited me to visit you more often? Your poverty can make you think in whatever way it wants. And I am audacious.

He must have been ten years old then. His fever had not subsided at all. His body had become so hot it could have toasted sesame seeds. Amma had gone to visit Maama. Somebody in Thenur had been known to cure any illness with sacred ash. Ramayi had heard that if anyone was possessed or had spells cast on them, receiving the sacred ash would help expel all evil. She carried him to Thenur. He couldn't walk; his head was spinning and he had no strength in his legs or his body. If they took the bus, he was sure to throw up from his gut. He was adamant about not taking one. Ramayi gave him a piggyback ride, bearing his weight the whole way, four miles to go there and four to come back. The body that had borne the burden of a ten-year-old was now lying over sand and stones bearing the burden of unknown men.

Are you the leaf that the bottom-feeders lick the leftovers from? Are you in so much poverty? But I know. I can despise this water, but I can never despise you. When he felt tickled by the little fish nibbling on some wounds in his feet, he was reminded of her palmyra-sprout-like fingers tickling him. *Could you not have gone as a maid to assist someone? But then, who would hire you to assist them? Did you really not get any job? And here I am, helpless and unable to protect you. Even here, you are the one at the bottom. A labourer. The same slave that you were in the farm. You had to bear it all when my mother hit you over and over again. What do you like more?*

The life then that was filled with love and affection even though you were a slave? Or the life now where you part ways after you get your money for giving your body and do what you want? Or don't you like either? What are your wishes? Do you ever think about all that?

The water was getting too cold. His body began to shiver. Like he was going to get sick. Still, he continued to lie there even though he thought it was foolish of him to do so.

The moon slowly hid behind the swirls of clouds. The well was completely dark, and the darkness felt safe. There was no need to fear anything. No one knew, except the knoll that stood proudly at a distance and the hidden moon. He had escaped from humanity.

He smashed the water hard. His hand hurt. He sat on the mound and wept. And wept some more. There were no lips to console him. No hands to wipe his tears. He cried as much as he wanted. The moon came out again. At the same moment, the knoll shone brightly in a golden-haloed hue.

Chapter 9

That was the best time to study. The time when silence was broken into pieces and dispersed by the cawing crows across the sky like light. The sun had not yet risen. It would take some time for it just to cross Karattucchi. During that time, the mind was flat, unflustered and undisturbed. Like the still, clear water in a well. Anything he studied at that hour rushed into his memory and fought for a spot.

The boy was seated in the lap of a portia tree at the mound around the well. His book was open but his mind refused to stay still. Amma and Appa were in the farm across, distributing dirt. Appa was heaping the wicker basket with dirt. Amma tossed the basket into the air like a ball and spun it around almost a whole circle with just the tips of her fingers. The dirt from the basket spread uniformly, covering the land without a gap in a perfect circle. From afar, the tilled farmlands seemed bright red, as if they were all ablaze. Now, with the dirt, it was as if someone had covered the land with a dark blanket. It was clear by the way Appa was collecting the dirt, with his loincloth shaking, that he had forgotten himself. The boy put his book aside and kept gazing at Appa.

From the lumps of the manure out crawled tiny white worms, unable to make sense of the new environment.

The crows that came seeking the worms sat with them wriggling in their beaks as they bobbled up and down. The bright white flour-like worms squirmed in the beaks of the crows. There was so much noise! The dog charged at the crows, and after shooing away a few of them, made itself a little pit and nestled in it. 'You want to nap already?' Amma tossed a question at the dog as she tapped its head with the basket.

Poor thing. Mani still wasn't getting used to things. When they lived in the valavu, things were easier but it would still go to the colony. Even after they moved to the current place, it could not forget the ancestral place, and spent most of the day there, in the colony. There were two houses right next to the well adjacent to the mango forests that it liked. The people there fed it leftovers: soaked rice, something or the other. It slept under the hibiscus shrub all day and returned home right about the time when Amma left to deliver milk in the evening. All night, Mani protected them here. It wasn't shiny and healthy like before, and it was also getting old. Still, if it ever heard its name called, it would come running wagging its tail, kneel down and not let go until it was petted.

It got up because of Amma and moved away a fair distance from her. 'Mani!' he called out. It ran towards him. 'Instead of studying, you call the dog to play with it. Like the barber sat and shaved the head of a sheep instead of cutting hair . . .' said Amma loudly as she returned to scattering dirt. He patted away the dirt that was stuck on the dog's head. Seeing that, Amma shouted again.

'Why are you playing with the dog instead of studying? Why don't you come here instead? Come and scatter a few baskets. If I'm here distributing twenty to twenty-five bags of dirt, when will I cook food? We don't have any leftovers either.'

Without saying a word in response to Amma, he left the dog, picked up his book and lay down on his stomach.

'That's right. All this while you sat there, watching everything as if it was some entertainment show. Look at him, the minute I called him to help, he doesn't even look up. Apparently, children have work to do only when they are called to help.'

Amma flung the basket at Appa's feet, annoyed. He pulled the basket that fell towards his heel in front of him. He then cleared his throat and spat into the dirt.

'Why are you bothering him when he is studying? You don't feel like working, you want to call him. Bend your body and do the work. Otherwise it will explode like a cucumber fruit. Do you want to go pull the cot and lie down on it? And dress up nicely and spend time in the colony? All my fate! Like a big-headed crow that ate shit. And ended up with shit all over its wings.'

Amma's face turned dark with anger as she picked up the basket that came with Appa's words and put it on top of her head. After she had emptied it, she removed the cloth pad she had on her head, retied it and grumbled, 'If one has a spot to live in and a mistress's house to be in, what difference does it make if there is any income or not. Isn't that what I've become?'

'Who are you accusing of going to a mistress? You think I am like your family? I will pull your tongue out and stitch your mouth up, be careful.'

Everything crumbled like the dirt. When had they become like a mongoose and snake? They hadn't seemed like this before. If any of them opened their mouth, it ended in a fight. Listening to them squabble with each other was beginning to annoy him. He could not stomach this change at all. He felt like getting up from the spot and running away somewhere. Luckily, before he got up, Annan walked over. What a surprise, he was up so early!

'Appoy . . . come home. Thalaivar is calling.'

Appa planted the short-handled hoe firmly for support and looked up.

'M . . . what?'

'Thalaivar is calling you, Appa.'

'Who is Thalaivar?'

'Why, it is our Sevathaan Maama, Appa.'

'Oo! He has become Thalaivar these days, has he? For all the rogues on the street?'

'Don't say stuff like that. What do you know? The folks from the colony themselves stand with their arms folded in respect when they talk to him.'

Annan's face turned red, as if he was personally shamed. He stepped down from the border of the farmland that he was standing on. Appa took off his towel that he had worn like a turban and dusted it as he walked over. No one knew what was on his mind when he said, 'You go, ask him to come here.'

He then got busy again with the dispersal of the manure dirt. Amma sat down and didn't say a word. A fear dawned on the boy that something unpleasant was going to happen. He calmed himself down a little and rubbed the dog's back. He fixed his gaze on the spilt dirt lying on the ground.

Unable to bear the heat, the little worms displaced from the manure lay belly-up. They sparkled like pieces of bronze. But the crows went away, too tired to bend any more. The morning sun scorched him like fire. He couldn't bear the burn and wanted to jump into the well that instant.

Sevathaan walked in the front and Annan was behind him, on one side, alone. His clean white veshti and white shirt were blindingly bright in the sun. His hair was combed flat to his head. His haircut was like that of a policeman's. He looked better built than before. Holding the edge of his veshti up, he walked over with his belly protruding just a little. His face was full and glowing.

'What, Maamoy, dispersing manure dirt, is it?'

Appa dropped the hoe and came over. The half-filled basket sat there with its mouth open wide like a small rock cave. As soon as Appa stopped filling the basket, Amma put it upside down and sat on it right there in the field. A labourer was walking along the edge of the field. When Sevathaan saw him, he hailed him. 'What's going on, Payya?' The labourer left his cycle at the edge of the field and walked towards them.

'Whenever you tell me to, I will come, Ayya.'

'It won't be possible this week. Come on Monday next week. We will get it done. Why lock horns with your father in his old age? We will calculate a settlement somehow and finish it. You come then, okay?'

'I will. Okay, may I take your leave? I need to go to the colony on some work.'

He left. Sevathaan looked at Appa and said, 'What, Maama?' Appa looked him up and down and broke into a thin smile. Lately, they didn't see much of each other. Sevathaan had a lot of work to do. He had also become an important man. Appa didn't have any work with him. He looked at him with surprise and said, 'The great chief has come seeking me. Of what service can I be?'

He dropped his voice, like someone speaking subserviently. Sevathaan grimaced as if embarrassed.

'What, Maama, you too? A few of these ignorant fellows got together and keep referring to me as chief. But you too?'

'But if I don't, won't you get angry with me?'

'Let's leave those donkeys alone. I came here to talk about something very important with you. Have you already ploughed the fields?' Evidently, he wanted to divert Appa from going further down that direction.

'Hmm. After the manure is dispersed, the land will be tilled.'

Along the well were boulders just the right size to sit on, as if they were cut out to be that way. They all sat down on them. Sevathaan turned around to the boy sitting with a book and inquired when the exams were to begin before he delved into his main subject.

'You have four acres, don't you? Why don't you give away two acres, I will get you a great price for them.'

He asked without any hesitation and got straight to the point. Thatha came to join them, supporting himself on his walking stick, and sat down on the covered plinth. He stretched his feet as if a broad stone lay between them. Sevathaan, who stopped talking when he saw him, continued, 'Maama . . . you are an older person. Please don't oppose what I say.'

Thatha removed the towel that he had wrapped around his head and put it on his shoulders, slowly turning towards him. His face was puffed up. His body was dried up and shrivelled. His legs were swollen. He spoke while struggling to breathe normally.

'Maaple . . . you were the one who got us this field. We don't deny that. But that doesn't mean we have to give it up because you say so. Somehow, we gave away our fields that were like gold to the colony. Even though God took away my sight, he has given me this staff to be able to at least totter around. Please don't snatch that away from me . . . Maaple.'

His voice faltered. The tears were on the brink of bursting out. Very calmly, he composed himself. Annan stood next to him and spoke in a frenzy.

'What do you know that you've come here now? You miserable old man! Why can't you just lie on your cot and wait to be taken away? Why are you here sucking my life out?'

'What did I say now?'

'To hell with what you said. Just get lost.'

Thatha didn't say anything. Sevathaan scowled. Amma hugged the portia tree and glared at Thatha. Appa's head was hanging down. The boy, on the other hand, was so enraged he wanted to knock his older brother out cold. *That immature lad who picks leftovers in the cinema theatre! That drunkard! How dare he speak like that to Thatha!*

'Okay then. I won't say anything. You continue.'

He got up with the help of his stick and walked away, leaning on it. He looked like he could fall any minute. It would take only a small pebble. He walked putting so much pressure on the stick, as if he could bury all his burden in its strength. Until he crossed the well and went across the ground, no one said anything.

'You give small lads some rope and see how they behave. Don't they know how to talk to older people? Why does a foot-long dog need a foot-and-a-half-long tail?'

Sevathaan spoke as if he was chiding Annan. Amma reacted before Annan did.

'That is how people who are as good as dead should be spoken to. Otherwise they won't let you prosper, neither will they let you die. You continue, Payya.'

The sun was scorching. The goats in the pen were bleating. It was time to let them out to graze. If they were left to graze before the sun was fully up, they would fill their stomachs at least a little bit. Appa kept looking at the goats as he spoke.

'What is the urgency to sell the lands now, Payya?'

'We too have to understand the conditions of the village and be accommodative, Maama. Kids born yesterday are talking about rickshaws and lorries and finance companies. They drive around and see some money in that. This Payyan too is about twenty-five years old. Only if he has a shop or something to his name will the families with a potential bride feel he is worthy. And three or four of them will come forward to give him their daughters. We managed to give away the daughter in marriage in a good way. You took care of a necessity but there's another one too, isn't it? Can you forget him just because he is male? What do you think about what I am saying, Maama?'

He paused a little while, as if to check the impact of his words. Appa was crouched and meddling with a stick in his hand. The boy had put his book far away and was biting his nails, waiting anxiously to see what Appa was going to say. Amma and Annan stared at Appa without batting their eyelids. It seemed that Sevathaan had come over to have this conversation kindled by the two of them.

Sevathaan went on. 'This Payyan knows a thing or two about running a soda shop. He says let's set up a cool-drink shop in this hot season. I too think this is a good idea. What do you make from farming? In the end there won't be enough to farm, Selvandharan said, and you know that too, don't you? These days, the land value is pretty good. Right now, they will offer to pay forty thousand even for your land. I will get you fifty. If you give two acres, that will make it a lakh. What do you say, Maama?'

Appa nodded his head up and down. He was afraid to
look up in case the tears crashed out, breaking the dams.
He swallowed, wetting his throat with his saliva.

'Is selling the land the only way to set up a shop?'

'Then what? It's not like you have earned so much
and stacked away bags of money somewhere. If instead of
buying this land, you had entered into a partnership with
my brother in the weaving business, we would have been
doing okay today. Somehow, they saved a little here and
there and have made it good for themselves. But didn't this
man say there was no way he would partner with them?'

Amma's words kept falling like crumbling termite
colonies. Appa lifted his head and gave her a look. His eyes
were swollen and red as agave fruit.

'Go away. Go, let the goats out.'

Amma stood there mumbling as if she didn't hear what
he said. She bundled up the loose end of her sari into a
ball and covered her mouth with it. She looked like she
was in a house mourning a death. Sevathaan continued.
'Maama, we have to adapt ourselves to the changing times.
Don't keep saying "farming and fields" like your father did.
You know you are getting one lakh. Give twenty to your
son. Let him set up a shop. Put twenty in your younger
son's name. If he continues to study, he can use it for that.
Or else, he can do what he wants with it. It will be his
choice. We don't want to wish harm on anyone. Then use
ten to pay back any debt you may have. Give the daughter
one or two. She is pregnant right now. And he doesn't
come with anything. If it was some other man, he would

never have lived with her after what she had done. Put the rest of the fifty in financing and join that venture. Aren't finance companies doing so well these days? Every month you will get one or two even after paying interest. You will still have two acres of land, right? What are you going to unearth from farming, Maama?'

Appa pushed back. 'If the fields aren't worked on, they aren't going to go anywhere. Somehow we can see some money coming from it. Payya doesn't need to go to the shop to work. None of that. All he needs to do is take care of a few goats and deliver clean water to a few houses in the colony. They don't have good water sources and are desperate. If he goes the distance on his cycle, he will be done in an hour. He will make a hundred, hundred and fifty a month. If we set up a shop and it goes under, then we would have to sit and look at each other's faces with all the money gone.'

In spite of Sevathaan doing his sales pitch, Appa did not budge. He had no desire to part with the soil. Sevathaan sat cawing away, but Appa took his time to think and respond patiently. His thoughts began to try Annan's patience.

'Of course, and I will go to wash the feet of the colony folks. You keep coming up with ideas like this all your life. Just split up the property that is supposed to come to me. I will do what I want with it.'

Annan's words agitated Appa. He ground his teeth audibly. Tears gathered in his eyes. It was really sad to look at him. The boy wanted to run to him, give him a hug and console him.

'You were born to my dick and you think you can advise me? Get lost. If you are so smart, go to court and claim what you can. You won't get a single paisa while I am alive.'

'I am talking politely because you are my father but you put on a show! You think I will leave you alone? Just wait, I will break your leg, put you on a cot and feed you porridge.'

'Dei, dei,' cried Sevathaan as he grabbed Annan, but he still flung a rock at his father. A sharp stone, it struck Appa's leg. 'Aiyo . . .!' His leg was covered in a stream of blood. 'Dei!' Appa screamed as he got up, grabbed Annan by a flock of his hair and punched him on his back. Annan bent down and bit him hard, in an act of frenzy. The boy ran to them and dragged Annan away from Appa. Amma too came running and dragged Annan by the hand. Sevathaan held Appa. By the time they managed to separate the two of them, everyone was out of breath. The field was full of footprints, as if two street dogs had fought one another. Furious, they glared at each other and heaved.

'They are both waiting, determined to take me to the grave. Where can I go and cry my sorrows away?' cried Amma.

A month after that, they all went to sign the land deed.

~

The temple chariot stopped at the corner of the Kooli temple. A crowd held the large rope to pull it; the people surrounding the chariot moved with it. It was only when the gigantic chariot was pulled that the crowd was so big.

The faded fabrics used for decoration filled up with air like an umbrella and shrank back again. The chariot moved slowly, like an old man struggling to walk. The wheels of the chariot were akin to the back of a labourer who lifted sacks for a living. The priest who was seated on the dark legs of the chariot was drenched in sweat. The ones that sat alongside the sculpture of the deity lit camphor one after the other, allowing for a slight breeze between them. '*Aragaro!*' cheered the people as they pulled the chariot forward with their might; the people who propelled the wheel with thin planks ran along with them. The hands of the devotees existed only to be lifted above the heads in prayer and to pat their cheeks in repentance, or so it seemed. Children who were crushed in the crowds hid behind saris, scared stiff and too frightened to even cry.

Young men focused on weaving in with the young ladies in the crowd were reminded constantly by the big-bellied policemen, who were intolerant of their youth and eagerness, that they held the power with lathis in their hands. The fragrance of jasmine flowers was everywhere. Even really old women had some stringed flowers tucked in their hair. In the dry, discoloured hair of the village women, these flowers stood out sharply. Children who managed to gather balloons had no space to jump about and play with them, and wilted. It was more engaging to watch them than the slow-moving chariot.

This was the same chariot that otherwise stood parked, empty-topped. Once a year alone it gained a new brilliance; although, even otherwise, if you went by the chariot every day and observed it regularly, it would seem to have some life in it. When the festival season arrived, the pride was transcendent. People found joy in seeing it together. When a crowd gathers around something, even an ordinary feat becomes astonishing. The brass figurine of the deity used in the festival, the *utsavamurthi*, which usually sat in a corner of the temple with no one paying any attention to it, gained a new sparkle during the festival. The sparkle could be from the conceit that the utsavamurthi must feel knowing that minister Kandhasamy himself bowed to it in reverence and inaugurated the pulling of the chariot by touching the thick rope. While the power-wielding elite glittered in white, the commoners gathered all their strength and drew the chariot; it was their hands that had scabs.

People gathered like flies at the water and rest shelter that was located at the tip of Keezhur Road. Apparently, some youth association had had the good heart to set one up for the benefit of the crowd. In the olden days, water and rest shelters were located in each village. People who walked several miles to watch the chariot would stop along the way and drink water at the shelters. The bullock carts filled the streets with noise. Nowadays, those vehicles had reduced in number. People came hanging on the footboards of buses, spent a little time watching the crowds, and returned home hanging on footboards. Several of the water and rest shelters were removed since no one used them.

They stopped the chariot with the thin planks. There was so much fatigue on the face of the utsavamurthi that had sat on the chariot the entire way. He had to rest at least for a little while. The mid-afternoon sun was scorching like fire. It looked bearable in the morning but became intense as time passed. It was the season of rising heat. People walked towards the festival shops and carousels. The chariot would be drawn back out only in the evening, around the time that the sun went down.

The boy and Vasu walked towards Annan's cool-drink shop. It had been more than twenty days since Annan had opened his shop. The boy had gone there only a couple of times so far as his exams had been going on. After the exams were over, he detached himself completely from Murali, Kadhir and Gopal. He began to avoid them, fearing their teasing. In spite of that, they still managed to corner and torment him every now and then. But ever since he began to spend time with Vasu and Durai, who both worked at the buffalo agency, he didn't miss the others much. It was a good way for him to sever his ties with them.

On a piece of land completely covered with black thorn bushes, there had once stood a goat farm. But all that was left of it was a milestone that was installed by Kamarajar in the fifties in the corner of the road with the words 'goat farm'. This land came to the notice of the housing board. Immediately thereafter, the animal husbandry department woke up. They decided to use the land—that was otherwise not being used for anything—to house a buffalo shelter, and bought ten buffaloes to begin the operation. Vasu and Durai worked at that agency. Between going to the theatre or playing thaayam or simply chatting with the two of them, the boy's vacations passed steadily.

If only the results of his exams were announced, he could run away to some place. Until then, it was a big tug of war between him and the days that passed. The days were long. The nights were longer. His lazy mind was beginning to get covered with anthills everywhere. Loneliness made him think all sorts of thoughts. Empty dreams floated everywhere in his mind. At any time, the dreams dissolved into issues. Even a small incident got blown up into something monumental in his bizarre thoughts. Just a gentle movement of a leaf and he created a whole kingdom out of it. His imagination, though, showered on his lap victory after victory. Thoughts that were controlled and tucked away in some corner all sprung out with fervour and danced away unfettered. He lost himself. It seemed that loneliness was going to pull him apart into pieces and devour him like steaming hot food.

To everything, his answer was, 'Let the results come out, I can run away somewhere.' Into a crowd. Not a paltry crowd of four or five people, but of a thousand. He would be indistinguishable. He consoled himself with a variety of reasons.

'Is this your shop?'

'Mm, yes. Come, let's get something to drink.'

The entryway was fully covered with cycles parked by the people who had come to see the temple chariot. Amongst them was Appa's Swega. The shop was crowded. Appa was at the cashier's. Annan was inside somewhere, apparently.

A small lad was serving everyone. The boy and his friend sat on the front bench. Appa saw them and asked, 'Would you like some rose milk?'

The boy didn't say anything. Appa's eyes were the colour of red earth. Sweat covered his now loose and limp face and dripped down it. His mouth bore a crooked and split smile. His head rocked very gently. His hands struggled so much even to simply receive a payment, keep the money inside and provide change. He went inside a few times. The voice that had chided Annan was splattering words.

The boy felt disgusted to even look at him. He turned his gaze to the road and the bench. Some strangers were walking around. His heart was burning. *He comes and drinks here too.* Appa was getting worse by the day. Annan had asked him to come to the shop that day because it was going to be very crowded. Appa wore a shirt and veshti that he took out from a box and had come here on the Swega.

Riding the Swega made Appa think he was on top of the world. It made him feel that he had risen to the position of ruling a country. He drove it at an uncontrollable speed. The way he twisted the accelerator—it was only a matter of time before the vehicle was going to fall apart! He had already fallen from it twice. And Annan once—he hit his jaw and had to have two teeth extracted. His cheeks had swollen up like balloons. It was the boy who took Annan on his bicycle to the hospital. Annan sat with him on his cycle, covering his face. The shop had to remain closed for four or five days. Driving drunk—at times like that, what seemed to assuage him was the thought that both of them were incorrigible.

Appa behaved as if a large crown had found him and sat on his head. After he joined the finance company, the first month's interest and his share of profit for investing in the company all added up to more than three thousand. He would park the Swega at the liquor shop and drink. He couldn't tell the difference between the sky and the earth.

'No one can touch even the tip of my hair. No matter who it is, it will take only one punch. That won't change even if a lakh rupees are at stake.'

He said the same thing over and over again. Manna, who had come to the liquor shop too, was the one who asked him about it. He was a weaver, and drank only once in a while. But when he did, he literally went swimming in liquor.

'Why, Maama, are you talking non-stop? You don't have ten rupees in your pocket right now. But you wave your hands and show off when you have nothing?'

'Dei, what are you saying? I will stab you. Who are you challenging? Your father was a beggar. You are a beggar. You thought I am one amongst you all?'

'Don't say just anything. Even I can make tall claims.'

'Just what do you want, now? You drink, I will pay for it.'

As Appa kept paying, he kept drinking. He too was fully inebriated.

'Is this all you can do, Maama?'

'What else do you want, da?'

'You talk as if you have thousands in cash and you can buy anything that I ask for.'

'Dei, you loafing dog, look at this . . .'

Appa pulled out a wad of cash from his pocket and flung it at him. Fifty- and hundred-rupee notes flew up and fell everywhere in front of the liquor shop. Appa could not stop laughing. 'Look, you fool, look,' he said, pointing at all the money. He too laughed along with Appa. It seemed as if the entire liquor store was covered with money. They collected the money, stuffed it in his pocket and sent him away. Those who were at the liquor shop took some of it too. Who knew how much was taken from him that day? The next morning, this was the talk of the town. 'He's suddenly become rich but is still so cheap. He is even capable of making a garland with his money and wearing it everywhere. The way he dances around with his money, the whole liquor shop dances with him.'

The little boy served them the rose milk. Another group drank lemonade. The little boy was very energetic. He went around checking for orders and serving everyone. He kept track of the money properly.

There were a lot of youngsters inside. Annan was with them. Because the shop was adjacent to the bus stand, the boy was familiar with the rowdy gang. Bringing bottles of liquor and drinking inside the shop had become the norm. Annan gave them company. He had gone with them on a tour where they took ten chickens and lots of bottles of alcohol in a Matador van and drank themselves silly before returning home. Even now, he used the excuse of having to mix cool drinks to go inside and drink some more.

The boy had no desire to go inside to see his brother. Lately, even the few words they used to exchange had been reduced to almost nothing. He just wanted to leave. Vasu too was waiting for him. He slowly took leave only from his father and they both headed out.

They went towards the rides. There was one like a train carriage. And one like a helicopter in a round carousel. His head felt giddy and his eyes were spinning. He forgot about himself. He wanted to melt into the air along with the spinning ride.

He couldn't step out without feeling embarrassed. Stabbing words spoken behind his back were making his ears bleed. In spite of how hard Amma tried, she couldn't manage to keep Annan's drinking habit a secret. 'A fart released under water has to but come out in the open.' Amma was still bearable. She reduced her frivolous ways of the past and focused a little more on her work. Perhaps it was her guilt at losing the two of them like this. Where could they find a girl for Annan? Who would give him one in marriage? Who would willingly want the ill fate of being married to a habitual drunk?

He had to somehow snap out of this trap and get away. He couldn't take it any longer, the fights and the stinging words. He wanted the peace that Gopal's house or Kadhir's house had, even though their families had less income than his. He longed for togetherness in peace and happiness. But here in his house, as money kept coming in, disorderliness grew.

They left the rides, walked through all four streets and left. It felt good to keep walking. All the problems were left behind. He could walk anywhere without thinking a single thought. All he wanted was to get away from them. Free his mind from the stings of the scorpion. Free from the worms that crawled into his ears. Free from the stench of all the shit that was piled up around him. Freedom.

The crowds began to gather around the chariot to pull the rope at evening time.

Chapter 10

The day was about to break. The crows at the goat pen cawed incessantly. If anyone went near the trees, 'plop!', and they would have to take care of a head full of a crow's mess first thing in the morning. Was it only when people passed under them that the crows ever felt the urge to defecate? The boy bypassed the trees and went into the village. It had not yet fully woken up. Only the ladies who delivered milk were seen, like insects buzzing about. They carried bags within which were different varieties of milk packets. Three-rupee ones, four-rupee ones, four-and-a-half-rupee ones. Their knuckles got calloused just from knocking on the doors of the houses whose inmates slept even through daybreak. Nubile young women were dampening front yards with water that had a little cow dung mixed in it for sanitation. Their faces still had plenty of sleepiness smeared on them.

From there, he could see only the lamps on the hill that looked like a carelessly tossed rope. The mountain still lay fully hidden in the darkness.

He walked over to Veeran's house. The kiluva trees surrounding their house looked like the lamps in a Perumal temple—narrow at the bottom and broad at the top. It was a small thatched-roof house, thatched with dried coconut

fronds and covered with millet straw that had been in use
for a long while now. It had lost its colour to multiple rains
over the years and lay in oblivion. In front of the house
were four or five black nightshade berry shrubs that stood
like headless chickens. When he went there, only Veeran's
mother was at home. She asked him to sit on the plinth
outside. She had lost all her teeth and was toothless. She
wore a white sari that was dirty in colour with patches of
cow dung on it. She grabbed her frizzy and unkempt hair
into a bundle as she said to him, 'Veeran . . . He just left
to go to the colony. He said he had to take some boy to
college today.'

'Will it take a long time for him to return?'

'I don't think so . . . he told me he will come back soon.
You wait.'

This was the time of year when Veeran made a killing.
He was educated and had a few good connections. All the
boys went seeking him for this reason. He must be over
thirty-five years old. His younger brothers were all married
but he had chosen to be single. Maybe no one he found
agreeable was willing to give his daughter to him.

He moved about a lot in the name of the party. He
balanced himself with a stick but walked majestically. When
he went on a cycle pedalling with one foot, his slightly bent
posture and twisted moustache made him look like an older
vulture passing by with its wings spread wide. He didn't fear
anything. If someone opposed him, he'd land a thunderous
slap on their cheek. He was the first one to show up for any
work related to the village that involved fighting.

He had been maintaining an unblemished story of how he got wounded when he fought against the spread of Hindi. When he got drunk, he spewed threats and spat out words recklessly. He would be found lying by the roadside or even at the liquor shop sometimes. Still, everyone was proud when they talked about him. 'Even our village had a hand in the protests!' 'One of our villagers is a soldier who fought against Hindi!' Comments like these certainly painted a picture of his heroism.

He was out of town most of the time. He travelled to some place or the other claiming party-related work or some such thing. If the two of them ever saw each other, the boy would wish him, 'Hello, Maama.' Veeran would respond with a 'Maaple . . .' and that would be the extent of their exchange. The boy didn't know anything about his work. Only Sevathaan would bring him up in conversation and say unpleasant things about his arrogance at being in the ruling party. If only he had participated in any protest like Veeran he would understand what it took. It was money that made him a leader. A lot of people talked about that protest against Hindi imposition. Even Sevathaan spoke about it animatedly when he had had enough to drink.

At that time, Veeran was studying for the Secondary School Leaving Certificate or SSLC in a Karattur high school. In those days, there were no student leaders. In an awakening that exploded everywhere in Tamil Nadu, students protested and got their rights to vote and selected leaders for themselves. Veeran could be found at the forefront of such activities. All the school buildings looked perpetually saddened, having buried these activities within themselves. The boy was very eager to find out which building Veeran had studied in and to see it for himself. He even wondered if the two of them had sat in the same classroom. Somehow, he never asked him about that.

In 1965, an uprising spread across schools and colleges, true to the slogan 'Spread the fire of protests'. All the students assembled at the high-school grounds with a courageous few, including Veeran, in the lead. The protest started at the high-school grounds, launched by students in their teens wearing white and khaki with the itch of a blossoming moustache above their upper lips. Their faces were all red; their plan was to sweat it out. The juggernaut of a crowd that spread from the high-school grounds all the way to Keezhur Road remained energized with slogans, and would have scared a person standing at the bus stop, watching a sea of white rush down.

'Hindi! Down, down!'

'Stop it, stop it!'

'Stop the 17th government division.'

'Make the people's language the official language.'

'Make all the languages official languages!'

'Monkey making this decision, give up your position!'

The din made by those in the front spread quickly through the crowd. Sounds soared from the otherwise orderly crowd. Acrimony and bitterness dripped from each word. There was anger against this entity that they couldn't see but that sat on their heads and directed them like puppets, hatred as if they were being dragged by their hands to be fed shit. All the voices sounded determined. Every face had the glow of hope. The procession moved forward. Banners floated over the heads like some sort of protection. The words of the leaders echoed everywhere as if gospel. The procession went on.

The school had more than a thousand students. Added to that was the endless train of people who came from elsewhere. The procession couldn't be seen even at the end of Therur Road. A piece of news arrived that the police, carrying weapons, were going to stop the procession. The leaders came forward with the intent of protecting the protesters without having to disperse them, their eyes glimmering with the confidence of being able to handle any situation. Floating in that dream, even their lives didn't matter. Just after the bus station came the snarl of the police force. Right where the north and west streets intersected was a statue of Aringyar Anna, pointing towards the direction of the north street. A warning was put forth that anyone taking a step beyond that would trigger police action.

The young, tender hearts hardened themselves like stone. They worked hard to make themselves so tight that bullets would bounce off them. They took a step and crossed the statue. Then, a second and a third . . .

In the blind shooting that followed, two people died on the spot. With hands shot or legs shot, the crowd of students floated in a flood of wounds and gore. Some jumped, some ran away. What exactly happened, what happened to the others—everyone was in a flurry with no answers. The screams and the noises made the whole town shiver. They took the wounded to the hospital. A bullet sat lodged in Veeran's right thigh and struggled to come out. He lay unconscious. An order reached the government-run hospital. 'There is no need to treat the wounded immediately. Take a day or two to attend to them.'

He kept drifting in and out of consciousness. He writhed in the pain he was suffering. The wound remained exposed and blood-bathed. There were protests across the nation, and lives sacrificed. After everything settled down, they cut off the festering leg and threw it away. If they had treated him as soon as he was brought to the hospital, they could have saved it. But as the days passed, the leg became weak and dry and eventually died.

The dawn broke into morning. Veeran's mother was lighting the stove to make coffee. The women were rushing towards the well at the entrance to the village to get their fill of good water. There was still no sign of Veeran. Every time the boy went to Karattur, his eyes would wander at the foot of Anna's statue looking for dried drops of blood. He imagined blood spread across the base of the statue. Veeran too must have lain fallen somewhere close by. Sunk in blood. The father of one of the students who lost his life was now a secretary in the ruling party. When their only son died in the protests, they tried for another child and had one. That boy studied with him. They all referenced him only as 'the single'.

'Why is there no sign of Maama still?'

Veeran's mother brought coffee powder from inside the house, left it next to the stove and then responded.

'He said he was going only somewhere nearby. But he still hasn't returned. I can't even ask him what he is up to. If I do, he will only say "I will chop you up" and carry on. You should see how angry he gets at that time. I just shut up.'

She then softened her voice and said, 'What is the point in running around so much for the *katchi*, the political party. He doesn't have it in him to earn a handful of money. Did you see how far the others who went to work for the party have risen? Every day, he keeps jumping about for it. As if that is paying enough to feed this house. But don't go telling him all this. He will want to chop me up in his anger.'

'That must be to simply threaten you.'

'What do you know? He has held me by a clump of my hair, pounded my back and kicked me down. And do I have any strength? If you shove me like this, I will lie fallen like a pile of grains. He hits me, of all people, dear.'

She cried softly. Her voice faded to a murmur. He didn't know what to say to console her. But she continued. The coffee grew cold.

'I think of going to the younger son's house but I feel bad for this one. There is no one to feed him a meal. That's why

I grind my teeth and bear all this for the sin of giving birth to him.'

She handed him the coffee. It was black and went in leaving a trail of mild bitterness. It warmed his body, which had got cold. Veeran's mother relished the coffee, drinking it with her toothless mouth as she blinked her deeply sunken eyes. A cycle sped towards the house as if it was going to crash into the entrance steps and stopped in the nick of time. Veeeran pulled out the rounded staff from the cycle carrier and straightened himself with its support as he engaged the cycle's stand. He jumped on to the plinth in one leap.

'When did you get here, Maaple? Has it been long?'

'I came some time ago. Where had you gone, Maama?'

He flicked his moustache as he took the coffee his mother handed him.

'A boy from the colony wanted to be admitted in the polytechnic college. He says he wants to go there after finishing high school. I went to meet our taluk secretary regarding this. That guy is a bottom-feeder. They got him the post because he was known to the Therur folks. Doesn't know a thing. I went because I know someone he knows. Didn't even bother to talk to me.'

'He dared to play his tricks with you, Maama?'

'Yes, my Maaple. But that fellow hardly knows anything about me. These fellows got their posts just now. Is it enough if you have only money? Let them be, those stingy buggers. Why do I need them to get my work done? I will go directly to Thalaivar and talk to him about this.'

'. . .'

'Don't think I can't do this. I have direct connections to the professor himself. He will do anything for me. Here, I will bring you the letter that he wrote for me.'

Veeran appeared to regret telling him about his initial setback and wanted to change that impression by proving himself. He went inside and came back with an old diary. He pulled out a folded piece of paper and showed it to him. The folds had collected dust and become dirty. He gently opened the sticky folds. It certainly was on the professor's letterhead and was signed by him too. He grabbed the letter and tucked it back in immediately.

'You think I'm some small-timer working with crumbs? I have connections everywhere. Did you get an interview card yet?'

'Not yet, Maama.'

'There are two people I know in CM College. I will tell them and get this done. I'm anyway going there today. Give me a hundred rupees. Only if I stuff some here and there will any work get done.'

'I didn't bring any with me right now, Maama. I will go home and get the money. If I get the interview card then I can get in somehow, can't I?'

'Don't you worry, I'm here for you.'

He left on his cycle. It had been more than twenty days since the results came out. Even if he got only into CM College, that's all he wanted. That too hadn't happened yet. The sun had begun to sting already. He got the money from his father and rushed to give it to Veeran. He noted that the application was for BSc chemistry and gave him the application number. Meanwhile, Veeran had showered and was ready to leave, dressed in his veshti and *thundu* with coloured borders. He took the money from the boy and assured him, 'I'll take care of it, don't worry.'

If he somehow got accepted there, that was enough for him. He could escape from his house and all the troubles. Even though the college was in Odaiyur and he could commute by bus every day, he decided he would join the hostel there. That was the only way he could focus at least a little bit on his studies. He wouldn't have the trouble of taking with him all the burdens from his house every morning and rushing back in the evening, wondering what state his house was in. He was sure that Veeran would somehow get him admission. After all, he did have a few connections he could tap into. And it did count for something that he had a special letter from his professor. Surely he knew a few people around there, especially with all the years of experience he had doing this? His thoughts about Veeran were favourable.

With these thoughts through the day, he waited for the postman expectantly. Until the colony was built, everyone had been receiving their mail properly even though there was only one postman delivering to ten villages. After the colony was built, the postman had time only to deliver mail to all the houses there. The mail delivery reached at eleven every day. After it was opened and distributed, he had to collect all the letters from the letter boxes and take them back by two in the afternoon when the collection truck arrived. The post office was in Seppur, which was three miles away. Within that short frame of time, how much could the postman do? How could he deliver to all ten villages? He didn't. If he saw someone from any of those villages, he would hand the whole bundle of post for that village to that person. Sometimes, the mail reached after a whole month.

So he waited along the postman's route and asked him if it was a yes or a no every day. Veeran had told him that he would receive the interview card within a week's time.

The card arrived after two days. It was a notification for him to come in person the following week. He took the card and went to see Veeran. Veeran was eating when he got there. So the boy sat on the exterior plinth and flipped through a book that was lying there. It was an anthology of poems with a foreword by Thalaivar. The front cover and the title pages were all torn. When Veeran finished eating and came out, he saw him reading the book. He seated himself next to him immediately and straightened his moustache, making the droplets of water trapped in it drip down.

'This is how you should read, Maaple! People skip the introduction and preface and go somewhere to the middle of the book directly. I can see you are interested in reading. And you know how to read.'

His praise had the boy wrapped in shyness. He tittered as an acknowledgement. Seeing the card spread happiness on Veeran's face. He shook his head as he spoke.

'It arrived, didn't it! That's what I thought. They all do as discussed and agreed upon. They name the price

shamelessly for doing it, don't they? Now you can go and
join the college, Maaple.'

'I will join the hostel, Maama.'

'Getting into the hostel is a bit tough, Maaple. They
may say that you are from Karattur and need to be a day
scholar. Mm . . .'

'Get me into the hostel somehow, Maama! Only then
can I study properly. If I have to commute from here, it is
not going to be possible.'

'Okay, you get ready to pay the fees. Only if we push
two hundred or three hundred to those fellows can we get
into the hostel. Let's see.'

He brought three hundred to get into the hostel. Veeran
made another trip just for that purpose. The next week,
they paid the fees and got him admitted. Appa went with
them too. They bought his bed and baggage at Odaiyur,
dropped him off at the hostel and went back.

~

Even if he tried lifting it with both his hands, the trunk box
still felt heavy. The boy had put everything in it and locked
it. He would have to get off slowly in Aattur. Knowing that
the bus driver was always in a hurry, not really halting even
at a stop, he had told him beforehand about his trunk box.
The breeze blew wild inside the bus, messing up his hair. It
fell on his face. *The first order of business after reaching home
is to snip this burden off my head*, he thought to himself. He
didn't like even getting his hair cut in Odaiyur. Only if he

got it done in his usual place would it be to his satisfaction. In the month that passed, was there anything that was to his satisfaction?

After he was dropped off at the hostel, he felt as if everything around him dried up. Being in a college and the happiness and excitement it brought on all got deflated within half an hour of being there. The dreams that had sprouted and grown burned down to their roots. He was hurting more there than the place he had escaped.

The campaigning for the college elections was in progress: support that party, support this party. They were competing for power. His room was upstairs. Number 27. The din that started at eight in the evening went on till as late at twelve or one at night. The contestant for the post of student council chairman, Venkatachalam, bought everyone a pen. Ravichandran gave them shaving sets. The ones standing for various executive posts made sure that booze flowed through the hostel; every room got a bottle. The boy had the habit of sleeping at ten and was in constant fear that even if he covered himself from head to toe to sleep, they would wake him up and offer him a drink that he had to drink.

The newcomers were made to strip down to their underwear and run up from the ground floor all the way to the terrace and back tooting like a train. If they refused, they were made to remove even their underwear and do it. If he came across a senior student, his heart pounded in fear as he wondered what he was going to make him do.

The ordinary kind of ragging did not faze him much. But when each of their sadistic and torturous minds began to be displayed in the name of ragging, he couldn't take it any more and ran away as fast as he could with his bag and baggage. Venkatesan was in the BCom line in his final year. His eyes were always bloodshot. His nickname was 'Mabban', and he was always drunk. The way he laughed at the juniors made them shit in their pants.

The ragging that happened in the open usually involved running like a train or pretending to play cricket. But what he did behind closed doors in his room went way beyond all this. The boy too got caught in that trap once.

That room was painted in blue. It felt 'edgy', and with the night lamp turned on it became a very private set-up. He felt like he was levitating. On the cot and the chair were three people. On the table was a bottle and a packet of snacks. He was told to 'sit on the floor'. Sipping on his tumbler, Venkatesan asked, 'Do you want to drink?'

'Mm.'

'What is "mm"? Open your mouth and answer the question.'

'Yes, I will.'

'You will? Can a student drink? Why have they sent you here? To study or to drink?'

'To study.'

'Then why did you say you will drink?'

The only way to deal with them was to remain silent. But simply keeping silent didn't help in all situations. He had to talk a little and that too in a very measured way. If he had a look of fright on his face, that thrilled them to no end and made them want to continue. He figured out all these things in a very short amount of time.

They told him to hold his palms like a cup and poured brandy into that. If any drop spilt out they made him lick it up like a dog. Every time they made him do anything, they laughed brazenly. It was as if a tiny little mouse was being teased by a few cats. With just their gaze, the cats would skin the mouse. The mouse struggled, its body bloodied.

'Have you clapped before?'

'. . .'

'Mm?'

'. . .'

'Clap. Clap now!'

They let the mouse run and then trapped it again. They dragged it back, digging their long, sharp nails into it and flipped it over. The stench of the open wounds! The mouse fell, broken into pieces. They grabbed it by their mouths, tore it apart and devoured it.

He caught a fever, with the temperature so high it set off sparks of fire. For two days he didn't get out of bed, except to visit a doctor nearby and buy medicines. He couldn't stay there any longer. He was glad that his fascination for staying in the hostel had worn off.

The bus stopped. He moved the trunk box slowly and got down from it. His mind was sparkling bright, like the sun after a torrential rain. As he walked carrying his trunk box, Vasu walked over from the tea shop.

'What is this, you show up suddenly with your bag and baggage?'

'I'll tell you all that later. It's a long story.'

'Okay, come, let's have some tea.'

He turned and looked behind the tea shop and was shocked. The back wall of the temple was ruined and gaping, with its mouth wide open.

'What happened at the temple, Vasu?'

'You don't know about it? A lorry driver rammed into it. Nothing happened to him. They are going to demolish the whole wall and rebuild a new one.'

'Leave this trunk box in the buffalo centre. I will pick it up when I go there. I am going to go to the temple now.'

Vasu took the trunk box and asked him, 'How are you going to go to college from now?'

'I'm thinking of becoming a day scholar.'

'Why, what happened?'

'Will tell you later.'

The back wall of the temple had crumbled to dust. It happened once every couple of years. The motorists seem to be driving with their eyes closed. The villagers would have collected money from the person who ran into the wall. But what could they do with that money? How many times could they rebuild that wall? The whole village was tired of this. They could build a bigger and better temple a little farther away.

He heard voices from the front plinth. He walked around to the front. Sevathaan and the village leader, Nallan, were talking about something. When Sevathaan saw him, he said, 'Welcome, welcome, Maaple! Wait, we can go home together. Let me finish this discussion.'

The boy too sat next to him. They were discussing a village problem.

'The water he drew has already been drawn. Getting the village together now and chiding him is not going to work.'

'But look at how defiant Kodukkan has gotten!'

'What does the village have of his to deduct anything? Does he pay anything? He doesn't. We don't pay him any annual labour gratuity either. That's why he dared do it.'

'Okay, okay, let's talk about this later. I have some work to take care of.'

Kodukkan Rangan, who was from a lower caste, had drawn water from the village's common well. Up until then, if someone was drawing water, he would put his pot down and have them fill it for him. Now, he was evidently drawing the water from the well by himself. That was the problem. He sold bags, winnows, brooms and so on from market to market. No one in the village bought anything from him. Nor did they pay him an annual labour token. But still, how could he draw water from the common well?

They would find a way to bring a sense of lawfulness.

Sevathaan walked along with the boy, with his arm around his shoulder. His shirt smelt nice, of mothballs. The veshti he was wearing went all the way to the ground and parted slightly with each step before falling back into place. He brought him into the shade of the tamarind tree and asked him a question slowly. With the sound of the passing lorries, his voice sounded even more secretive.

'Did you see Veeran?'

'No, Maama.'

The mocking tone of his voice became a smile on his face.

'How much did he grab from you?'

'Grab what, Maama?'

'Money, of course.'

Sevathaan's voice was full of mischief. But the boy understood too. He needn't have given Veeran any money to join the hostel. Nor was CM College so well-known that people from the nooks and corners of Tamil Nadu knew about it and wanted to study there. Very few students stayed in the hostel. There were many empty rooms that came in handy when anyone wanted to take a piss in the middle of the night. Those who stayed on the upper floors didn't spoil their sleep by coming all the way down just to use the toilet. They simply let it drip on the walls of the unused rooms. With so many vacancies, there was no need to bribe anyone to get in. Even for day scholars, there were some rooms available to play truant or get a drink. Those rooms had locks but even the warden of the hostel had no clue about who kept the keys to them.

The three hundred rupees that Veeran took from him had stayed right in his pocket itself. Within a few days of joining the college the boy had realized that he had been cheated. But what was he going to do knowing that? For a person who had never seen a college or had any inkling of how the admissions worked, getting swindled in the process was not uncommon. It was as if the person who said 'I will take you there and show you around' was walking behind him with his eyes closed. But Veeran being the one doing this was quite a shock to the boy. Only with experience was he beginning to understand people.

His face was full of silliness as he responded to Sevathaan.

'He took me there and got me admitted. He may have taken a little for himself. But why are you bringing it up, Maama?'

His response made Sevathaan's face serious. He held on to the tamarind tree with one hand. He didn't pay any attention to the ants that were climbing up his legs as he spat out the words.

'He is wretched! He steals from the village. Nobody knows where he is right now. And gullible boys like you, the educated fools, you all go seeking him.'

Sevathaan was offended because the boy hadn't come to him instead.

'Where is he now?'

'He lives somewhere . . . He cheated two or three lads from the colony. One was promised a seat in a polytechnic. And the other in a college in Kottur. He took a thousand or two thousand. Those boys are literally crying. He has disappeared. There is no trace of him.'

'Is that so?'

His surprise served to encourage Sevathaan. Someone on the street put his hands together as a sign of respect to

Sevathaan. He nodded ever so slightly in acknowledgement to the other man as he patted him.

'I know Nallaiyan from Odaiyur really well. His is my man. He will do anything for me, whatever it is. We could have admitted you in that college without any expense. But you rushed to him and got trapped. At least from now on use your brains.'

'How did he become so cheap?'

His question made Sevathaan excited.

'That is fate. His party itself is like that. What did he really achieve from protesting against Hindi? A two-hundred-rupee token and a bus pass? And what can he do with that? Each person makes himself a lot of money even when his party is not in power. And fools like him only grin and bear all that.'

The boy's throat became parched. He couldn't swallow even his saliva. He felt like killing himself by jumping from atop some place really high. For Veeran's livelihood, the party became useful. He had the letter from the professor. He had the identity of the person who fought in the Hindi protests. With all that, he was able to beg for money with dignity from a few people. And he could still walk right back after disappearing like this. He could still stroke his moustache after getting drunk. He could still yell and challenge anyone. His body could handle all that. But Veeran's sacrifices were oozing out. The blood that Veeran shed in the soil of Karattur was now in a large sewage pond. Thinking of him was making the boy want to cry. Which faceless force was behind this?

He hung his head to hide his tears. Sevathaan consoled him half-heartedly.

'It's okay, Maaple, now you go. Your grandfather isn't doing well. They were going to bring you home today or tomorrow anyway. Go see him. If there is anything you need in the future, discuss with me before you do anything. Learn to survive. Go now.'

As soon as he mentioned his grandfather, the boy forgot everything else and hastened his pace.

Chapter 11

Thatha looked like a food-poisoned goat on the brink of death. His face was shrivelled and sagging. He was lying down with his mouth wide open, like someone snoring with fatigue. Before he died, he was breathing only through his mouth. The 'nggkr, nggkr' sound that he was making since the previous night was the only sign of life in him. He sounded like he wanted to say something badly but instead was yelling in frustration because words didn't join him in his effort. He kept his legs folded. Even if they kept straightening his legs, they didn't stay straight. His hands moved up and down with his breath. His body was covered with sores. The soul was fighting to shake itself away and somehow escape the body that was holding on to it. They thought of ways to put to an end to that fight that carried on through dawn.

'All his life, he never carried a money purse on his hip. That may be what Appa is still yearning for. It must be his desire for money. Let's strike a rupee coin with water and give him that water.'

Everyone thought what Periappa said was reasonable. The water that they fed him stagnated in his throat. There was a 'kara kara' sound. The water then went through swiftly. The 'nggkr nggkr' sound resumed. Paati sat next to

his head and cried. She often placed her hand on Thatha's
forehead and stroked him gently.

'Thatha had a lot of liking for arrack. Should we try that?'

'Let's try toddy. If he wasn't fasting, he always preferred
toddy.'

They called for Chinnaan and had him give Thatha
some toddy. The toddy went through him like buttermilk.

'Just what does he desire so much?'

'Wonder what his fragile soul has its mind set on?'

Periamma, who was sitting on the plinth with her head
against a pillar, spoke up. 'It is the land that he craved. How
much he lamented that the land was being taken away for
the colony. It was only after that that he began to give up.
Look at him, does he seem like one who should be dying
now? His love for his land isn't letting him move on. This
is a body that sprouted from that soil. Bring some of that,
mix it in water and give him.'

For two days and nights, they all had taken turns to
stay by Thatha's side all the time. The weariness had begun
to show on everyone's faces. They sent the boy to bring
some soil. If they gave that with water to Thatha, his throat
would be blocked. The 'nggkr' sound would stop.

The love that Thatha had for the land where the
colony had been constructed was indescribable. The boy
still remembered the wounds his Thatha suffered, crying
inconsolably when they filled their well with soil. Where
the well was, they had built a large water tank and a park
around it. A single coconut tree still stood there. It used to
belong to his Chithappa. It was a short tree, and its fruits

alone 'would have prevented all this misery'. He took some soil from between the roots of that tree.

The soil was going to go into Thatha. The soil that was already soaked in him. That soil was mixed with water, and his beloved grandchildren poured a little of that mixture into his mouth, one by one. When Chithappa's son Muthu was done, the sound subsided. Paati's lament was the first to be heard. Everyone else sniffled softly. Appa's eyes kept oozing tears uncontrollably. He stood with his hand over his mouth.

Periappa began to provide instructions for each step that had to take place next. Thatha's mouth was tied up with a white cloth, the body was covered and laid in the middle of the covered porch. The message had to be communicated to relatives from other villages. Chithappa went to the Aalkudi valavu looking for help. They sent the boy to town to arrange for the audio system and petromax lights. As he started moving ahead on his cycle, he ran into his Chithappa.

'Payya, no one is willing to deliver the message to other villages. "Who will go in this heat to deliver the news of death, Saami," they say. They certainly weren't going to do it for one or two rupees. I even tried to give them five, but they still wouldn't. If you saw them in their vetti and thundu, you couldn't tell they are labourers. A man with some land is all but ruined!'

'Okay, what needs to be done now?'

'You go inform your grandmother's family. I will send our boys to other places.'

'Raakur Maama will be in the paddy godown. He has
a phone there. If someone knows the number, couldn't we
just call him?'

'That's right, Payya. Your Annan knows the number.
Get it from the shop.'

The boy's cycle moved faster the deeper he sank into his
thoughts. He was enveloped with the sadness that the one
lap that lay open for him was now folded and tucked away.
That lap was sown with love. On the days that Thatha
went to the market, a savoury mixture and murukku would
unfailingly show up from the folds of that lap. Thatha
would offer it to him with his shaky hands and with his
drunk drawl. That shakiness made the snacks taste even
better. Thatha even brought him little packets of the spicy
bean snack from the arrack shop.

How did it matter how big a boy he was? To his
grandfather, he would always remain a little boy who crawled
on to his lap to play with him. 'Ponnaiyyan.' The old man
couldn't pronounce the name that everyone else called him
by. He had a special name for him to call with love.

'Ponnaiyya . . .' he would call even when he was a
distance away, as he staggered in his tipsy darkness. The
boy had to run over and guide him, holding his hand.
The man who knew how to get to that point didn't know
the direction beyond it. It was the boy's grasp that had to
show him the way.

He would buy white baby goats from somewhere. He
would look for his Ponnaiyyan to bring them. When the
boy walked in front with the goat, he would tease him.

'With Ponnaiyya's touch, I'm sure we got a *polar*!'

'Surely it must be Ponnaiyya's fortune that we got ourselves a *thattai*?'

Thatha's praises were in the jargon of goat-sellers. If he got more profit than he expected, Thatha would hand him two rupees. 'Go buy something and eat.' Those two rupees had so much value. At the end, when Thatha lay sick on his cot, they made him sit and bathed him in hot water. Both his legs had swollen like pillows. His face was bright. The limbs had stretched out like nerves. Appa and Chithappa poured water on him and scrubbed him. 'Why are you bothering me like this . . .?' he had whined. As the exhaustion from that spread throughout his body, he had begun to lose consciousness. One by one they had gone to him to get his blessing and a wish. Paati had asked, with her tear-filled eyes, 'What blessing are you going to give me?'

He had stayed quiet. Paati had shaken him and asked again. He had gathered all his strength and had spat out, '*Masuru.*' My foot.

For many, his silence had been his word. The boy had gone and stood next to him. Thatha had looked at him until his eyelids could not stay open any more. He had stretched out his arm and held him. A hold that felt akin to being caught under an iron wheel.

'Ponnaiyya . . . live smartly . . .'

Those were his last words. After that, it was only the 'nggkr' sound till the end. That voice wouldn't be heard any more. The sound of him clearing his throat as if to spit out the never-ending sediments of impurity was no more.

At night, he would pat the boy's back gently and wake him up. 'Do you want to pass urine?' he would ask. That support was no longer available. The hand that enveloped him while sleeping would now do so only in spirit. It was as if the boy was collecting all his memories of his grandfather in a little box to protect them.

By the time he finished all the work assigned to him and returned home, a pandal had been installed outside. Under it were two benches. A group of men had come from Chinnur to play the drums. They had lit up a heap of dead leaves to temper the *thappattai*, a small percussion instrument. The group hadn't started playing the drums yet.

'Saami . . .' they bent their bodies and wished the few people who arrived. As people gathered, they would wish them by their names and ask for money. The people who came to see the dead before the body was taken away usually brought some money specifically to give the percussionists.

The women began the customary lamenting. Incense sticks burned by Thatha's head. His face was devoid of any care. His eyes seemed full of determination. That determination did not leave him till the end. He was careful to not let his problems affect anyone else. Twice or thrice he had defecated on the cot without his knowledge. The daughters-in-law refused to clean it. It was clear that until Atthai arrived and cleaned it, he was going to lie there in the smell. He had no sensation of the urge to defecate. Appa and Periappa had each held one end of him and transferred him to another cot. They had removed his loincloth and poured water on him. They had poured water on the other cot and Paati had scrubbed hard with a broomstick. Thatha had watched everything that happened without batting an eyelid. He hadn't said anything then but after that he had refused to eat anything.

The drummers began to play the drums. The loudspeaker was being set up. The women's laments were inconsistent. People from both villages joined them. Periappa, Appa and Chithappa stood in a row outside and demonstrated their sorrow by crying loudly with their faces in their towels. Sevathaan and the village head arrived and sat down. The drummers wished them by their names and asked for money. When Sevathaan heard the voice say 'Saami . . .' he looked at them carefully. He then took Periappa alone to the side.

'Maama, where are you planning to bury your father?'

'In the graveyard in our village, of course, Maaple. Where else will we bury him?'

'I was wondering if you were maybe going to take him to the Chinnur one.'

Sevathaan slipped away from him and spoke to the village head. The people of Aattur gathered together and spoke in hushed tones amongst themselves. In an instant, they got on their vehicles and left. Nobody knew what was going on. How could the funeral continue without a gathering? The labourers also left with them. Nowadays, no one came to collect old clothes. No one came to give haircuts. They didn't come to collect the annual gift money too. They gathered only when there was an occasion, happy or sad. Even then, they didn't want anything in kind.

They took a fee instead. Appa asked them, 'Where are you going? How can we not have anyone around for the moaning?'

'What can we do, Ayya? A few people from the village told us not to be here. If the villagers tell us to stay, we will. Come to the village and talk to them.'

The family did not understand what the problem was. The front yard of the house with a dead body was devoid of any people. Even the lamenting stopped and the women followed the men out. Someone stepped on the tail of the dog that was lying crumpled in a small ball and it got up and ran, yelping loudly. Unable to run or walk properly, it stood with one foot lifted. Poor Mani. Usually it lay in a pit it dug for itself. Vengan had ridden his bike out of control and run over Mani, severely wounding its hip. It didn't go anywhere else but stayed close to home after that. Mani licked the wound over and over again, and walked slowly and quietly without disturbing the dispersing crowd. It sat in the garbage pit, curling its body back into a ball.

~

They parked the vehicle outside the village head's house and Periappa and the boy walked in. The old place had been demolished and in its place was a larger and more spacious house divided into four or five rooms. The design of the window grilles oozed sophistication. The vernacular roof tiles had been replaced with cement and mortar. The old, large ancestral doors made with timber had been removed and in their place were pairs of smaller doors that stopped people from entering. The village head walked over from a corner of the house. He was a tall man with his face full of a greying beard.

'What is this, Maama . . . you all just left in an instant without saying a word? What are we expected to do with a corpse lying in front of our house?'

Periappa's face seemed as if he was on the verge of bursting into tears. His eyes were filled and about to give any minute. His hands were nervous and struggling to stay calm. They couldn't comprehend the reason why the villagers had walked away. The village head, an older man, spoke with a straight face.

'How did you think this was going to happen without a problem, Maaple?'

'If you tell us what the problem is and the village tells us what we should comply with, will we not obey you?'

'Okay, Maaple, why don't you go meet with Sevathaan?'

'If you can tell me what the problem is . . .'

'That's why you have to go see him, Maaple.'

Periappa didn't know what to do. He was worried more about gaining the wrath of the village than losing his father. They needed the village. After all, the village people were their people. The village stood by them through good and bad. The village harboured them. They could not live in isolation without its support. If they could lean on anything, it was the village.

Sevathaan's house was recently constructed. The doors were finished in laminate and shined smooth. The window grilles curved here and there and formed a circular pattern.

Lamps hung around beautifully. There was a dining table and small porcelain dolls on display. It felt like a little palace. The house was built with the money from selling the land. Periappa was so upset he didn't seem to notice anything. The boy, on the other hand, felt uncomfortable being there. He stood close to his Periappa. Sevathaan was seated on an easy chair.

'What is the matter, Maaple? I asked the village head and he sent me here to ask you about it.'

'Maama . . . if you do anything without thinking it through, this is what will happen. The grand old man had built a shack for himself adjacent to your younger brother's house. Okay. Now, which village does that land come under?'

'Chinnur, of course.'

'Are you paying taxes to that village, though?'

'Even though we bought land and moved there, this village is where our heart is. The temple taxes are all paid to this village, our village.'

'Why the change in the village, Maama? To this side of the panchayat road is our village. The other side is the other village. So then, will Maama's house not belong with that village?'

'No, Maaple . . . we are going to bury Appa in our village graveyard only.'

The boy could not bear to listen to Sevathaan's stances. *Why all this pretence? How many convoluted questions is this man going to ask before he speaks of the problem? Is he using Thatha's death to play games and seem like an important man?*

He needs to be kicked so hard that his testicles go flying. He sits there lounging, showing no signs of moving, what sort of a show is this? Bloody rascal.

'The temple wall got damaged. We collected thousands of rupees around the village and are rebuilding it now. Will we even ask the colony people? They could put any donation in the temple donation box if they feel so inclined. Our people are our people no matter where they are. Yes. But it takes something to be part of a village, isn't it?'

'Maaple, everything you said is right. Tell us what the problem is.'

Periappa was losing his patience. The boy's face flushed red as he stared at Sevathaan. Sevathaan spoke as if he understood their emotions.

'You pay taxes to this village. You are going to bury the body in the graveyard of this village. But you bring the drummers from that village?'

Finally, the issue was clear. No one had thought that such a problem would come up. They were struggling, being caught between two villages. How did it matter where the drummers were from? They beat the drums. They got some money. The Aattur drummers came from a place close to Sornavur. Someone had to go there to inform them but they didn't have anyone to send. There was no need to make such a big deal about this. Sevathaan continued, 'If you tell these drummers to leave and send for the other drummers, the villagers will come back.'

Periappa did not know how to respond to him. The two of them returned home. There was a lot more sorrow around the house that no one was there mourning the dead than for the loss itself. There were a couple of people from Chinnur, and a few relatives. Periappa asked them for their advice.

'As soon as he died, I was the one who sent for the drummers. Who expected that that would lead to something like this? Do we not pay the Aattur drummers their annual labour gift? Will they keep quiet if we didn't? So why did this have to become such a big issue?'

Appa clarified his actions to avoid blame. To see a house with the dead so empty made the women weep over and over. The boy didn't want to interrupt the elders who were in discussions, but he had ideas. *Why are they thinking like this? What can the villagers do? Their absence is not going to stop the body from being buried. Were they going to expel them from the village? No, that was all in those days. These days, nothing like that would happen. What did they do to Kodukkan for drawing water from the village well against the village rules? They are still only watching him do it. They cannot move and shake like they used to be able to. Sevathaan is jumping around as if everything is in his hands. He prods and creates problems that were never there.*

'Doing the rites without the village is not such a big deal.'

'How can that be? Don't we still have to go to the graveyard?'

'So what if we don't take him to that graveyard? Isn't there a spot right here in this land for him?'

The drumming became louder in the background. The drummers were nervous they would be sent home and started beating the drums faster. They were very focused on not giving up their rights. 'We'll see how someone else enters the boundaries of Chinnur and plays here. How will they allow that?'

Chithappa went to them and told them to stop playing. Wait till the problem was discussed and resolved and play after that, he said. They stopped and sat down. 'We'll deal with it then when they ask us to leave. We have the people of Chinnur on our side,' they decided.

'We can't simply go against the village just like that, Maaple.'

'Why, what can they do to us?'

Annan's face was glowering.

'It's not like that, da. The temple, the tank, people, caste, everything belongs to the village. Can we claim a relationship with Aalkudi instead? Those are our people. We cannot simply brush them aside today, we have to think about tomorrow as well.'

'We cannot ask the drummers who are already here to leave. That is not fair either. Moreover, they won't leave even if we ask them to. What else can we do? Tell me.'

Periappa's face displayed a lack of clarity. Chithappa seemed like he was ready to carry the body like a gunny sack and bury it right then. The women whimpered quietly. They were all frustrated that even after Thatha was dead, he had to go through all this. The stereo was switched off too.

'We did this by mistake. Let us go and ask the villagers for forgiveness and try to cajole them to join us.'

'Why the hell should we ask them for forgiveness? Did we go into the village and pull anyone by their hand? Or did we steal something from them? Whatever we do, I will not agree to the business of asking them for forgiveness.'

Chithappa's point did seem to make sense. Appa tried to advise him nicely but both the boy and his Annan were on Chithappa's side.

'Whatever it is, we don't want to get into a fight with the village. Go. Go and tell them . . . all this happened by mistake. And ask them what we should do. We cannot ask the drummers to leave now. We cannot ask the other drummers to come now either. Ask Sevathaan himself what other option we have.'

Chithappa said, 'I will go this time', and left. The boy seated himself on the pillion seat. Sevathaan was expecting them.

'What have you decided, Maama?'

'What can we do? Whatever the village decides, we will accept that. Let me gather a few people and I will ask them . . .'

Sevathaan interrupted him hurriedly, 'You don't have to call any of them. If I say something, they will all agree to it.'

'Then just tell us,' said Chithappa, a little sternly.

'I already said what needs to be done. Send them back and get these drummers.'

'That is not possible, Maaple. If we send the ones that are already there back, will their villagers keep quiet? They are already ready with their armours. Give us another option.'

'There is no other option.'

Chithappa's face shrunk. He flapped his towel vigorously and got up. He then looked at the boy and said, 'Get up now, let's go. How much has my father done for this village. These are dogs with no gratitude. If you can come, come. Otherwise, his sins will come after you.'

'Don't rush out, Maama,' said Sevathaan, immediately grabbing his hand and making him sit.

'Will this get resolved with your anger? This ritual involves the village. We must think before acting. If you say something today, you would not want some others to blame you for anything tomorrow, do you?'

'There is no need for insinuations. Just tell me what needs to be done. How many people has my father helped settle disputes? And today, you have made that man himself ask for a mediation, haven't you?'

'Maama . . . I understand your state completely. I have a thought. See if this will work out for you.'

'Only if you say it can I do that.'

His voice was laced with urgency. He would not wait any longer. He went to the vehicle and stood holding it.

'Pay the amount that was agreed upon to the ones who are already there. Give the ones from our village an amount that they deserve as well. I will tell the villagers to show up.'

'How can we pay the fellows who aren't there?'

'Maama, they should have been the ones called for this rightfully. But you didn't call them. Even though they don't collect annual wages like they used to, we still need them for all the good and the bad, don't we? Therefore, give them what they should have been given. Why don't you give about two hundred? That should do.'

'Fine.'

Chithappa agreed. As long as the rites could go on. He gave the money to Sevathaan.

'This man is something else, da. Even if it's a cat's hair, he seems to want a cut from it. As long as everything goes on smoothly now,' said Chithappa after they left Sevathaan's house.

The boy did not condone giving any money to Sevathaan. Still, he didn't say anything. What was going to change even if he did say something? Even before they reached home, the villagers had started trickling in one by one.

Chapter 12

The moon was bright. He was lying down watching only the moon. There was noise all around—discussions about the drama. The temple kumbabhishekam was next week. The plan was for the youngsters to perform a play at the festival. For the past two or three nights, they had been getting together and talking only about this.

The more he stared at the moon, the more he yearned—if he had been living on his ancestral lands, it would have been as bright as day there. He could have put a cot outside the house and stared at the sky, comfortably lying on his back. The light would have gradually dimmed as the moon moved behind the blossoming clouds before slowly making its way out. There would have been darkness everywhere for a brief moment. In a jiffy, it would have become bright again. This game of hide-and-seek would have continued on and on. Here, in the colony lit with electric lights, the full brightness of the moon wasn't appreciable at all. He became sad when the thought of the farms filled him.

'The people from the colony conducted games during the festival of Thai Pongal. They showed a movie too. On top of that, they built a temple there and performed a play. We are not less than them, are we?'

That's how Balu started the conversation with him. He wanted to put up a play one way or the other. And he had to play the role of the protagonist. He wanted to be able to flaunt that around the colony. He had a general store in the colony. He looked like a dark ghost when he sat at the cash counter. He believed that the colony boys were depriving him of his ability to be a hero in real life. He was fully determined to at least act as a hero in a play and establish his heroics.

'Sure, we can put up a play. Our guys have to agree to it and participate. Who will come forward?'

'If we get started, they will all join. Who has the play book?'

They heard the sound of a vehicle. Its lights were blinding. The ones who were lying around, the ones who were discussing the play, all stood up in an instant. It was Sevathaan's bike. The main focus of this gathering was to meet with him, tell him about the play and get the posters started off. He had seen them and stopped his vehicle.

'What is going on at this hour?'

'We have to talk to you about something, Maama.'

He put down the bike's stand and seated himself on the temple plinth. He had fatigue written all over his face.

'We are planning to perform a drama for the temple kumbabhishekam.'

His face showed no expression.

'Who all?'

'Us boys together.'

'Who is "us"?'

Balu pointed around him: 'Me, he, Ravi, Muthu . . . and the rest of the boys.'

That was not the answer he was expecting. He grimaced and dug his nose with a finger.

'Is there someone to write the play?'

'Raman's son Shaktivelu is writing it.'

He became quiet after hearing that. He lifted his head up and looked as though he was thinking about something. Shaktivel had written a handful of plays. They had decided to pick one from among those to perform. He was going to direct the play too. He had gone to Chennai for two months claiming he was going to act in the movies. He had sent them a letter from there: 'Please send two hundred rupees immediately for me to return to the village.' Raman scrambled the money together and sent it to him. His two-month experience acting in the movies had made him write plays. He had photos of himself in a banian showing his armpit. He showed them around and claimed he would get called to act in the movies. He had stopped going to work at Periappa's loom completely. He had resigned from there.

Sevathaan's voice broke the silence.

'You have decided to join those guys. Tomorrow, will you also be okay marrying one of their women?'

They all got annoyed with him for mixing one thing with another.

'Are we talking about marrying women right now?' There was anger in the boy's voice. It had irritated him too.

'Today you say drama. Tomorrow you will say wedding. Why should our boys go down this road? You come up with one together. Can you not write a play? M—'

'Sure . . . but isn't it way better to marry a girl than to call her to the shed at night?'

Ravi snuck that in when no one expected it. Instantly, a very palpable silence enveloped them all. Sevathaan's face was glowering. He couldn't respond to this in that awkward moment. Trying hard to alleviate the awkwardness, Balu said in a lifeless voice, 'He's a fool, ignore him. We can also write a play. But Shaktivel has experience in the cinema industry.'

'What cinema experience does he have? Some experience indeed! If you let me, I will write four plays for you tonight. You guys are hanging on to him like he is something. As it is, they barely respect what we say. They walk over our heads. If we go to them asking for a drama and this and that, they will climb on top of us.'

'Why are you bringing up all that, Maama? You say all these irrelevant things. We are including them because they too are part of our village. They too have a share in this. What do you have to say?'

'They have a share, do they . . .? If you fellows cannot write a play, then conduct a kabaddi contest. Show two movies on your behalf. Who is stopping you from doing any of that?'

As if there was nothing else to talk about—if he did, it would get more awkward. Sevathaan shook his towel, put it on his shoulder and got up. He had an air about himself as if he had to make all decisions. He wanted everyone to come to him for everything. The thought that he had been the one to cause all the problems when Thatha died fired up anger in the boy.

'The fact is that we are going to put up a play. If the village accepts, we will be there. If not, don't call us to be part of anything else.'

Sevathaan started his vehicle, listening to what was said. He softly swallowed his words, 'Well then, do as you wish.'

Even those words were taken as a big approval. Things began to move in earnest after that. They got the script from Shaktivel and every one of them read it. Because it would take longer if they read it out individually, they listened to Shaktivel read it aloud. He read with emotion and dramatization. Everyone liked the story.

~

When the character casting was ongoing, they were on the verge of a bloodbath, or so it seemed. Balu and Mani competed for the role of the protagonist. For a couple of days, they were roaming about fighting like cat and dog. Across Balu's general store was Mani's 'contemporary tailoring' shop with a billboard and an illustration of a woman with a welcoming smile on it. Balu and Mani looked at each other as if they were going to set the other in flames and burn him down. They attacked each other, making indirect references.

When Mani crossed by Balu's store, Balu would say, 'Useless fellows roam around believing they are hero material', sitting at his cash counter.

To the people who came to his store, Mani would say, 'Look at that blob of a face. Like a soot-covered pot. He doesn't make the cut even for the role of a comedian!' and laugh mockingly.

This became such a big problem that it was beginning to jeopardize the play. They had support on both sides. Shaktivel became nervous. He was worried that the one opportunity he was getting to showcase his talent was going to vanish. He was eager to put all his dreams of being in cinema into the play and make it a grand success, but this fight was threatening all that.

The boy was the one who came up with the idea. It was announced immediately.

'The play is going to have two heroes and two heroines. Whoever provides the higher sponsorship amount will be the lead hero.'

Everyone agreed to this. Balu donated two hundred rupees and became the lead hero. Mani was the second hero. There was a similar problem for the role of comedian. The comedy part also involved an actress. That's why it was in demand too. Shaktivel had a solution for that as well.

'You have all watched *Vasantha Maligai*, right? That movie had both Nagesh and V.K. Ramasamy for comedy. We will do that here too.'

Shaktivel got the villain's role. He refused to give that to anyone else. The villain had two henchmen. Because they had two heroines now, the villain got two dream scenes, one with each of the heroines. Pacchaami, who was assigned the role of a father, created a ruckus about wanting a dream scene too. How could a father have a dream scene? There was no way for that. Nothing could be modified to include that. But Shaktivel was a smart cookie and managed to resolve that too.

'Okay, don't worry. The father character wishes for a second marriage. When he sees the heroine, he dreams about how it would be to marry her. We can add a dream scene there.'

The boy got four or five scenes as a manager. He had a respectable role. All because of the respect he got as a college student. Apart from that, he was the treasurer. Another four or five lads from Shaktivel's Aalkudi valavu were given character roles. Finally, the rehearsals started. Everyone assembled at eight. The director alone walked in at nine, draped in a long shawl.

Each of them had finished their work by evening and rushed over to be at the rehearsal. Shaktivel didn't have a job. He had stopped going to the loom under the pretext of wanting to become a cinema actor and did not ever go by that side again. Other than floating around in his dreams, he did not do any work. He had sent mails to a few advertisements seeking people to work in cinema and had gone to places for that. In each place, they had made him pay two–three hundred rupees in the name of a 'make-up test', handed him a few photographs and sent him home. So, he stopped responding to those too. He sent his stories to magazines like *Rani* and *Kumudham* but nothing was published yet.

He hoped that if this play went well, he would get opportunities in the neighbouring villages. In spite of that, he made everyone wait just to show his importance. The rest of them lost patience with him walking in late day after day and began rehearsals without him. There was a dance for a duet song. The rehearsal started with the comedian Ravi doing the part of the heroine. Shaktivel had written the lyrics too.

> In my heart a storm blows
> Cheer me up, come close
> I can't bear this rain, my lover
> Shall we tuck in together under a cover?

In their hoary voices they sang the lines over and over as they practised the steps. Then, Shaktivel arrived.

'Who started the rehearsal without me?'

He yelled as though a great blunder had been committed. Not because he felt that they disrespected him or his talent, but because he was afraid there may be no need for his position.

'You take your own sweet time to appear every day. And we have to sit around and wait for you to show up?'

From the next day onwards, he was there before anyone else. He was adamant on only one thing: that they listened to what he said. He had the role of the villain. When he delivered his bit shaking his hands and legs, he looked like a clown.

'Dei . . . Motte. She has insulted me. I have to have her, otherwise my name is not Karkotakan!'

'Master, our Sotte has something to say.'

'Dei Sotta, let me get her and you get the leftovers.'

Gajendran and Keerthi had the roles of Motta and Sotta. They could not bear being bossed around.

'Whatever it is, we cannot accept that he addresses us disrespectfully with a "da".'

'This is a drama, da!'

'But still, how can he?'

The boy tried to pacify them and then burst out in exasperation. 'Fools. Does your pride hurt just because he addresses you with a 'da'? He has been directing us all the while, telling us to 'do this' and 'do that' and we all listen. Where is this self-esteem then? Stop talking rubbish. Either do your roles properly or pack your bags right now.'

Even though he belonged to another valavu, because Shaktivel knew a thing or two about acting, they tolerated him. They decided to stay quiet at least till the drama was over. As it is, there was enough jealousy when someone from among one's own people rose up in life. On top of that, they had to tolerate him, someone from another valavu, making them dance to his tunes. Sevathaan and the other villagers didn't miss a beat to build on that animosity.

'Till yesterday they addressed us as "Saami" and stood bowing in front of us with their hands crossed as a sign of respect. With all the latitude you are giving them today, they are going to come to our homes tomorrow seeking brides for their grooms. At that time, feel free to offer your sisters. You all don't understand the need to keep someone at the status that he belongs to.'

Those words were largely ignored for their want to perform a drama.

A few from the group went to Therrur to find actresses, negotiate and sign the deal. Four times. Each time they went, they spent a hundred. They all had a glow on their faces that wasn't there before, like that of a new groom. They gathered together often, whispered something to each other and laughed. 'Actresses are a rare commodity . . . We have to roam around looking for them . . . If you go out and look, you will know. Even just finding out where they live itself is a big problem. By the time we find a few of them, we get exhausted. If they are good-looking, they are not available, if they are available, they look terrible.' And many such excuses were made to justify more trips.

As the treasurer, the boy updated everyone on the accounts at the rehearsal one day.

'The four trips you made cost us four hundred. You still haven't booked anyone. Therefore, those who went need not go again. I will go with two others and find someone to book.'

When they heard him, they became nervous. Balu became very angry with him. 'He behaved like a friend but dug a grave for us instead,' he told himself. When the few got together and shared chuckles, they should have included the boy in at least one of the trips. If they had done that, perhaps this situation wouldn't have risen.

The boy, meanwhile, had the satisfaction of taking revenge on them. Balu tried to keep the clique from falling apart and said, 'We will go this one time. If we don't accomplish what we set out to, you can go the next time. Why waste more money on this?'

'Who wasted money on this? It's you fellows! Did you have to use the common funds to go touch and tickle those women?' barked Ravi.

Bringing Ravi in on the expenses beforehand and singing to him the song of their misbehaviour was paying off.

'Dei . . . don't speak indecently.'

'What did I say that didn't happen? Isn't it because you went to some woman that you all gather and cackle? There, you flaunt the money from common funds as your own, don't you? Find someone else to cheat.'

Balu got up and slapped Ravi. Ravi smacked him back and the two of them got into a fight, rolling on the floor. The boy stood with a sly smile on his face. The rest tried to separate them. Shaktivel mitigated the situation.

'Both of you have hit each other. No need to take this further. After all this work, you are going to get the play stopped.'

'Why did he slap me first?'

'If he accuses me of going to a prostitute, will that not peeve me?'

'Of course! As if you are the epitome of good behaviour. We can go to that street and find out about that.'

They each washed the other's dirty laundry. Shaktivel was in a pickle. He shut his mouth and stayed quiet. The stench gave the boy the biggest satisfaction. He felt relief, as if he had accomplished something great, and got a sense of calm like the feeling of having taken revenge. Somehow, the two of them were pacified and the rehearsal continued. As they got closer to the day of the show, they wrote down all the dialogues on a forty-page notebook, fearing that they may forget their lines, and memorized them.

Then there was the job of getting the temple kumbabhishekam notices printed. They drew up the notice for the play and gave it to Sevathaan. He took one look at it and said, 'Come to the finance office, I will review it and let you know.' He treated the finance office as his own.

Finance companies had sprouted all across Karattur like mushrooms. Putting money in financing yielded a lot of interest money. Investing in one paid bountiful dividends. The allure of the big returns made everyone scrape together all the money they had and dump it in one of these companies. Even if one sold a buffalo the money went directly to a finance company, without spending a paisa on anything else. Not having the heart to spend the money earned from interest, they collected a few months' worth of dividends and when that added up to about five thousand, they invested that back in. The women didn't have an ounce of gold on them.

There were people who sold their lands and put the money in finance after paying their debts. Of what use was keeping land? In a year, they barely got two or three showers of rain. When they sowed groundnuts, the land was wet. By the time they sprouted, dust blew around. Clearing the land of weeds was an endless chore. To cultivate flowers, they needed rain. Eventually, something or the other managed to grow. At the end, though, what did the land tally up to? A man with land could barely feed himself. And that was after working the skin off his back day and night. Selling land made better sense. It was going at a good price. Gone were the days when they were getting a mere thousand or two thousand for an acre. The lands were transformed to plots for homes. The unit of sales changed from acres to square feet. If they sold the land and put the money in finance, the money from interests reached them promptly. They could build a house. Buy a vehicle. Wear a bright white shirt and a veshti. Do as they pleased. What else did they want?

People like Sevathaan took full responsibility for the transactions. The finance companies were like their second homes. Whatever the dealing was, he said, 'Come to the finance office.' When the lads went to the office, he pulled out the notice and read it. They said that the play should be mentioned on the last page of the kumbabhishekam pamphlet.

'Should the play be included in the pamphlet? Looks like this will use up a whole page,' he grumbled but finally agreed to it. The way he poked his nose into every business was becoming highly intolerable.

Thalaivar had been unwell and had moved to the USA. Only if that man died would this man's dance stop, the lads groused behind Sevathaan's back. When they talked to him, though, they talked politely and quietly, as if whispering a secret.

Unable to hide his frustration, the boy said a bit loudly, 'We collected money for the drama. We have been rehearsing for it all these days. If you can't even include us in the pamphlet, then what is the point in having us boys in this village?'

'Okay, okay, Maaple. Why are you getting angry? Am I saying no? We will put it in there, we will put in it there.' He was only keen on getting them out of there.

Even though he had agreed to including the notice in the way they had drawn it out, there was only a small mention of the drama when the pamphlets arrived. The boys were all so infuriated they wanted to tear him apart. All of them were eagerly waiting to see their names on the pamphlet for the first time in their lives and were supremely disappointed.

Chapter 13

'Why did you not print what we gave you?' a few of them surrounded Sevathaan and demanded. He seemed a little taken aback. His face started to sweat. He pulled himself together and got off his vehicle.

'Nothing against printing all that. We ran out of space.'

'How can you say there was not enough space, Maama? We told you right in the beginning, didn't we? What did you tell us then?'

'I said we will print all that. There was a lot of the temple matter that needed to be included, you saw that, didn't you?'

Balu had the pamphlet in his hand. Ravi snatched it out of his hand and thrust it in front of Sevathaan.

'You know how much space could have been saved? Look.'

Without taking the pamphlet in his hand, Sevathaan said, 'Yes, I saw. This was all written by the temple priest. How can we edit that, tell me? Come, let's get some tea and continue talking.'

He walked quickly towards the tea shop. That was one way to escape from the boys. And it would help him control his anxiety too. The boys followed him to the shop. They were clearly enraged. He did everything just the way he wanted. Everyone in the village, including the village head, took his word as gospel and agreed to everything he did. There was never any opposition to him. It was as though he held everyone under his spell and controlled them.

Whatever the concern, the answer was always, 'Go, ask Sevathaan.'

'Does he have two horns? Selfish man. Once the kumbabhishekam is over, he is going to pay for a *lakshaarchanai*, a special elaborate pooja, for the well-being of Thalaivar apparently. Everything is just a sham,' the boys thought to themselves before they squabbled aloud.

'They have printed such a big photo of Dhanappaswamy. Why couldn't you put us in there?'

'That fellow is a fraud and a rogue who cheats the village in the name of god. And he gets three-quarters of a page.'

'It seems when he sees women he acts like a monkey and whistles at them. Does he deserve so much respect?'

Their bickering began to annoy Sevathaan. He pulled out a pamphlet from his pocket and showed it to all of them. 'Here, read this.' It was a biography of the holy man Dhanappaswamy.

'Even though he lives in Vagunarur, he comes to Aattur once every week. When we approached him to help with our temple, he got a statue made. Read that. Then you won't talk so badly about him.'

Ravi stood reading it in the light of the lamp. A couple of boys from the colony seated across the road from them on a little elevation kept looking at them. Sevathaan wanted to say anything that would get him away from the boys and away from there.

'The holy Dhanappaswamygal is about five feet tall and has good bodily features. He has dense hair, a small forehead, eyebrows like a bow, mercy-filled eyes, a prominent nose, a natural smile, a mouth that wishes well, two hands that bless, two golden feet on legs that stand on wooden slippers as if to claim that they were created for their duty, which is to reach any devotee in need of help. His gaze is full of benevolence. Firm words that are sweeter than honey came together to create the holy Dhanappaswamygal's body, making it of extraordinary beauty. The elegance of his thoughts, the calmness within him and the sweetness of his words would make one wonder if the great god Mansamy himself was standing in front of them. He is a rare sight. His love, holy vision, striking smile and the calm glow of beauty that his face exudes will bring happiness to our minds and open our eyes.'

'Stop it!' Balu grabbed that pamphlet from his hands, tore it up and threw it away. Sevathaan got on his vehicle and started it. They went and stood around him again.

'Come home, all of you. We can discuss this further.'

'Let's talk right here. Get off your vehicle.'

He got off his vehicle quietly and sat on the temple bolster. The boys continued standing.

'Dhanappaswamy is a woman in man's clothes. A transvestite. We have all seen him in person. You give that wastrel so much space. Here we are, putting so much effort into our play. Give us a viable option and then leave.'

He held Balu by his shoulder and made him sit next to him.

'You are all young fellows. What do you know? Today, the biggest seer around this area is Dhanappaswamy. You can check this out for yourself. There is always a crowd around him. Whether what he predicts actually happens or not, he rakes in a lot of money. He has built a big house in Aattur itself. You all have seen it, right? He has a voice. Who knows if he is a cheat or not. But he has given fifty thousand for our temple and made a statue for us. Not one or two rupees. A full fifty thousand. Just like that. All the pages and spaces belong to him. You will put up a drama with the help of some motherfucker. And we need to give you a whole page for that?'

'Again, don't keep mixing issues here.'

'If we youngsters remain united, you all can't bear that, can you?'

But the force in their words began to diminish. It was the fifty thousand doing its job. The money the godman had donated stifled their voices. And this worked to Sevathaan's benefit.

'You foolish boys, just where doesn't this difference come up? Today, that is what gets anything done. Dhanappaswamy is from our caste, da. That is why when we asked for a donation for our temple, he gave us money immediately. Otherwise, will he give any?'

'All that is okay, but we want space in the pamphlet.'

'Why do you want that? So their names appear in large fonts and the names of our boys get printed in tiny letters? Do you all have any brains? Even the government gives all the unlimited subsidies only to them. Guru's son is studying in Madurai. The government is bearing all his expenses. If any of our boys go to study like that, do you think they will do the same? Here, this Maaple is going to college. How much is the government giving him? It is the hard-earned money from toiling in the lands yesterday that pays for him instead. Keep all that in your minds.'

Gajendran suddenly began to talk as if he agreed with what Sevathaan was saying.

'I told them all this a while ago. That Shaktivel is addressing me with the disrespectful "da". And he acts up just because he is the director of the play. Even the other guy who comes with him from his valavu hardly respects us. He after all works in my family's looms. Yet, he thinks it's okay to put his arm around me and talk to me as if he is my equal.'

Sensing that Sevathaan was gaining traction to pull them all towards his side, the boy wanted to shift the focus back to getting their goal accomplished.

'Let all that be. Now, how are we to perform the play without any publicity? We will get our own handouts printed then.'

'When the boys from the colony put up a play, they had handouts. Do you think we are worth less than them?'

Sevathaan stayed quiet, seemingly thinking. The flies swarmed around the temple lamps and fell down charred. All around, little night lamps glowed in various colours. The old structure with the clay-tiled roof had disappeared. The temple stood shining in its newly painted hues. Its tower had new sculptures added. The lamp that glowed on top of it hugged everything around with its light.

'Come to Kasog Finance tomorrow morning. Just two of you will suffice. I will make the arrangements for your handouts. But I have a condition . . .'

'Tell us.'

'It should be our councillor who inaugurates the play. He is standing in the upcoming elections. What do you say?'

'Sure, why not. Let him come. We are good if we get the handouts.'

'The handouts will be ready in a day.'

The next day, the handouts arrived as promised. Just the way they had written it out. Not a thing had been changed.

With the blessings of Sri Saamiyayi
Long live the world of Tamil, long live the world of art

At the Karattur, Aattur villages'
Sri Saamiyayi Temple's
Consecration ceremony

On the 21st day of the month of Thai (3-2-85), Sunday, at 9 p.m., at the beautiful stage located adjacent to the great Saamiyayi's temple

Presenting the first work of art by the Red Rose Youth Club

In Wedding Attire Again?

A social drama

Production and Management by the Red Rose Youth Club, Aattur	Stage set-up, sound and light set-up: Manimegala Scene Company, Paruvur	Music direction: Rainbow Orchestra, Odaiyur
Actors: K.M. Balu K.S. Mani K.R. Shaktivel K.V. Ravichandran K.K. Gajendran K.N. Keerthi K.A. Murugesan K.G. Pacchaami K.E. Sellappan and more	Actresses: J.G. Shyamala, Therur M.D. Nadhiya, Therur R.C. Sumathi, Therur	Story: Screenplay, lyrics, Direction: K.R. Shaktivel, Aattur

Opposite Karattur's Annasalai, in the Rangusamy supermarket building, is Sri Suryabhavan, a vegetarian restaurant. Tea, coffee, tiffin, meals, curd rice, lemon rice, tomato rice, veg biryani, etc. are available here.

By Suryabhavan, K. Aarumugam, Karattur

Note: We are delighted to share that we process any orders in your name for sweet, savoury or tiffin varieties on the spot.

Sri Velmurugan Printers, Main Street, Karattur

The temporary shed with the stage was bursting at its seams. Women and children fell over each other trying to watch them. It was like a cinema shooting. The men tittered looking at the actresses again and again. A rehearsal was under way. The final rehearsal. The whole village's eyes were only on them. Even those in a rush slowed down to take a quick peek at them before moving on. Nubile women watched the young men on stage with both shyness and enthusiasm, whispering with their eyes. Looking at them, the men on stage thought they were big superstars and began to put on airs. And when they forgot their lines, they blinked cluelessly. There was so much commotion. No one could distinguish between the sounds of the actors and the chatter of the viewers. In the middle of all this, the music crew was sitting in a corner practising the songs. They were all new songs. They had to be set to new tunes. The three actresses looked like *karagaatam* dancers in their excessively glittery clothes. They delivered their lines, adapting them to the scene themselves. The love scene took place in the park. Balu kept pinching the actress' cheeks as he said his lines.

'Yow, talk without touching me. If you keep touching me, I will walk out. You better watch out.'

'Like you are some devoted wife. Do I not know about you?'

'If you speak like this, I will not act.'

She walked away and sat in a corner. The comedian Ravi had the music crew stay by him and had them play his song. As they played it, he danced with the comedy actress.

Don't go, my pristine rose,
Don't leave, I'll be morose.

As he chased after her, trying to hug her, she kept running away coyly.

O flower goddess who dances in my heart
If you don't love me, my soul will depart
This heart is full of love, talk sweet, my dove . . .

The more she struggled to release herself from his grasp, the tighter he held her. She finally bit him to free herself and ran away. Pacchaami, who had the father role, also wanted to practise his song. Shaktivel was pulling his hair out. It was so chaotic. Unable to take the disorder, the boy yelled at everyone.

'Stop all this. Everyone, stop talking and stand to the side. If the final rehearsal doesn't go properly, we will end up forgetting our lines and our scenes on stage. Start the rehearsal from the first scene. All the viewers, please leave now. Come back tonight and watch the show.'

They managed to send everyone away and start the rehearsal from the first scene. For those who forgot their lines, he held the book with all the lines and gave them cues. Even then, Shaktivel was directing them to act this way and that. For his scene, he shouted loudly and made a scene. A villain he had to be.

The actresses decided to drink water and went into a changing room built with a few braided coconut fronds.

Keerthi tried to peep through the gaps in the fronds. One of the women was changing her clothes there. The boy gave Keerthi a hard kick on his bottom. 'Hee hee,' Keerthi giggled as he straightened himself and asked him, 'Do you want to see too?' 'Go, da, your scene is coming up.' Keerthi reluctantly walked to where the rehearsal was going on.

The boy had a headache and wanted to have a cup of hot tea. Thinking about the others made him angry. They looked like they were going to pick the actresses apart and devour them piece by piece. But did they observe the 'exquisite' bodies of their beloved actresses? Did they notice the gestures of these beloved actresses with skins devoid of firmness or sensitivity? Their faces sparkled with beauty created with layers of make-up. And here the boys were trying to make real the imaginary lives that they were acting out. *Che . . . why do I alone have no interest in all this? Is it really a lack of interest or is it my sense of superiority over the rest that I am continuing my studies? If not, would I have been behaving worse than them? What was the reason I went seeking Ramayi? Do I think that these boys also are not my equals, just as I thought about Murali and Gopal? If not, would I have been like this too? Inside, every atom is lust in all its arrogance. It draws everything to it. And guffaws boisterously like there is nothing beyond. If bettered, it flips itself and stays down adamantly. Ppa! . . .* His mind full of thoughts, he didn't feel like going back to the shed and decided to walk home instead. The drama could be managed somehow. Getting there in the evening should be enough.

Starting in the morning, programmes related to the kumbabhishekam took place one after the other. A Thalaivar movie was going to be screened on a 35 mm screen in the evening. After that was the drama. It was going to be inaugurated by K.K. Murugayyan, known better as *vettukaaran*, 'the Slicer'. There was talk that he was going to stand in the next election for the position of panchayat head. He was related to the minister Kandhasamy by way of his wife. He had opened an industrial training unit near Mullur and business was going well. Efforts to upgrade it to a polytechnic were in the works. The man was extremely thin, barely noticeable on the chair. He wore glasses that looked like mirrors. The white veshti, shirt, gold chain, watch, ring, minor chain, car—all this helped give the man a presence. Sevathaan wanted to run for the post of president. That was why he was acting subservient to K.K.M.

As soon as the car arrived, they all rushed to greet him. The Slicer climbed the stage, swaying like a pendulum. He sat on a chair arranged for him. On one side was Sevathaan and on the other was a village senior and Veeran. Balu delivered the welcoming address. He then opened a shawl and handed that with a garland to the village head, who then placed them on the Slicer. After Sevathaan spoke highly of him, the Slicer gave his speech to inaugurate the show. He could barely deliver a speech—of the words that came stuttering out, he swallowed half of them. As soon as the Slicer finished, it was the boy's turn to present the vote of thanks. 'I am going to talk for a couple of minutes,' Shaktivel whispered in his ears.

'The director of this show, Shaktivel, will say a few words in front of you. Following that will be the vote of thanks,' the boy announced and moved over to the side. Shaktivel put his hands together and bowed to the crowd. He spoke elaborately about how he had worked day and night without sleep to put the play together and that it was all because of his passion for the art. Even if he had stopped there, it wouldn't have been a problem. But he went on to speak about Sankaradas Swamigal and Sambhandha Mudhaliar and their contributions to the field of drama. He cited the examples of Balachandar and Sridhar, about their origins in this field before becoming big in the cinema industry, and talked about his own experience in cinema. Everyone began to get restless. Sevathaan's face stayed frozen in shock. In a different context, he may have even slapped him for it. Still, all that jabber was within some bounds. Until Shaktivel grabbed the garland that was lying on the table.

'The wonderful leader that we have obtained for our region, the respectful K.K. Murugayyan sir. We all know that in this region where there isn't even a high school, he promised to bring an industrial training institute and delivered his promise by building one here. As a consequence, we enjoy the importance our village has gained and are prospering from that. Not only am I very honoured that such a man should preside over this function, since he follows the footsteps of Thalaivar—everyone knows that Thalaivar started performing in drama first and then grew step by step. For us too to achieve such heights, I request

Sir to produce a movie and make this region even more famous. To add to that, it is indeed my great pleasure to bestow this flower garland, that I imagine to be a garden of gold, again on this great man's golden shoulders.'

As the Slicer stood up reluctantly, Shaktivel garlanded him and took both his hands to his eyes in reverence. If at all a movie was made in the future, that he should be made director was written all over it. But the episode didn't end with his speech. Rather, it stayed smouldering through the play. When the play ended, it opened again. Sevathaan walked in like a storm, fuming. They had put the actresses on a bus early in the morning, seen them off and were all seated on the plinth of the temple.

'Where is that rascal? Garlanding the guest. The glares I got from the chief guest! I wanted to kill myself right there. My dignity is all but destroyed!'

The boys from that valavu had gone back already. Sevathaan looked at Balu, and holding himself back from hitting him, said, 'How could he reuse the garland that was already given to the guest? The Slicer was furious at me for allowing that fellow to garland him in the midst of so many people. Why, Balu, when I warned you all, you got angry at me, didn't you? See how he showed his cheap thinking now? Will that man ever come this side now? You all stood in the corner, he walked over and garlanded that man. "The director of the show will speak now!" Isn't that what our Maaple announced over the mic? If I see you get together with those guys again, I will become the Devil to you all, you better watch yourselves.'

Everyone including the village head got together and scolded them to no end. All the fatigue they felt disappeared completely. Gajendran and Keerthi kept saying, 'We told them so many times' at every pause. The next day, all the boys called Shaktivel and interrogated him with fury.

'Apparently, you worked on the play giving up your sleep? So only you gave up your sleep? What about us?'

'Why did you garland him with the garland that was already given to the guest?'

'Quite the temerity you have to do what you did, don't you?'

There was no one to placate them. Balu stepped out quietly. They asked the boy to leave too. Gajendran and Keerthi led the rest. Shaktivel got angry.

'Don't speak disrespectfully. If it wasn't for me, would you have written a play yourselves?'

'Dei . . . you used to stand in the corner of our streets in respect, we'll break all your bones, watch your tongue now . . .'

Shaktivel grabbed Keerthi's shirt, Keerthi retaliated and the two of them fought rolling on the ground. That was it. The dam broke. Everyone joined in to kick Shaktivel. He was caught like a mouse amidst hungry crows, struggling in pain. Finally, when he managed to escape from them, he ran as fast as he could and then stopped at a safe distance. His shirt was torn to bits. His lungi was torn at the back and hung loose. His hair was completely dishevelled. He waved his hands as he spoke. His face was covered with dust. Tears were fighting their way out. He looked like a madman.

'Dei . . . you all brought me here and beat me up, didn't you! If I don't make it big in cinema and make you all stand in subservience to me . . . I wasn't born to my father . . .'

The other boys jeered. 'As if you are your father's son now. Maybe it was my father, or my grandfather,' they shouted and pretended to throw up, mocking him all the way.

Gajendran and Keerthi started writing the play for next year's drama.

said, 'To sell.' It was as if he was callously spitting at the whole village.

Veeran was provoked to get to the bottom of the situation. 'Who asked you to cut these trees down?'

They responded with an attitude of 'no one here will listen to your orders'.

'The ones who can give such a direction.'

How audacious these men who came from Asalur were! They treated the villagers like dust.

Whenever they auctioned manure, the village heads consulted the entire village. The auctioning of trees fallen from rain or wind also included all the villagers. Why did they not ask anyone about cutting down the trees? Veeran dug his stick deep and limped over to the buffalo centre.

He stood outside the centre and shouted loudly. The way he stroked his moustache and twisted it and shook his head as he spoke scared the people across him to the core.

'Why the hell did you have to bring the men from Asalur? If you are the government, do you think you can do anything? If I come at night and untether a couple of the buffaloes, what will you do?'

He spoke as if he was flinging stones at them. Two people came hurrying from inside, gesturing to Veeran that the reason was 'something else' and took him inside. After that, the real reason spread across the village via Veeran. Everyone was shocked.

After the colony was built, the land prices for the forests in this region had risen to unimaginable heights. Whoever had money simply stacked up cash and bought it at any price that they could get it for—nothing short of multiples of lakhs. The lands could be sold, the money invested in the finances and one could relax, relieved of land labour. Much of the land was sold off. Unable to see government land with so much value lying around unused, the minister Kandhasamy decided to appropriate it. They said that the land had been leased to the Office of Animal Husbandry several years ago and that he had bought it from the grandson of the original owner. The land was in Kandhasamy's benami's name. He was the one who brought the men to cut down the trees and put a fence around the land. Once he heard about it, the doctor in charge of the buffalo centre decided he didn't want to be in the middle of this and went away on a leave of absence. Only if another officer was instated could any action be taken against the land usurper.

'Who is that doctor? That transvestite!'

Veeran dug deep with his stick and limped across again. He whispered something to all the youngsters in the village. He had them bring the rest from their homes. They went to the arrack shop en route.

'Did you see how Sevathaan disappeared without a trace? All those fellows are but women, just like their Thalaivar.'

Veeran held an intimidating machete in his hand. Each person held an axe, a short-handled hoe, a staff or some sort of a weapon. A few trees fell quickly. They surrounded the men chopping the trees and the youngsters called out for them. 'Come out!' Veeran stood right in the front, like the leader of the group.

'One more cut and the next will be one of your heads.'

'You people from Asalur think you can show us such attitude. Come out!'

The tree-cutters, who were about twenty or thirty in number, stood stunned. They didn't know how to react to the strong, drunk, angry and naked youngsters standing there with weapons. They were surrounded by fire. They couldn't bear the heat but they couldn't run out of the forest either and struggled, being trapped in between.

Annan stood swooshing his machete. From his eyes flew red sparks. 'Dei . . .!' A blood-curdling warning emerged from him. His face reflected the rage of hunter dogs when chasing rabbits. The women stood separate in a tight group, anticipating a possible fight.

'Thalaivar, indeed! This must be Sevathaan's mastermind. He choreographed everything and snuck into his house to hide? Go, see if he is there. If he is, drag him over here.'

The boys hesitated. Annan stood there quietly. A few big men waved their staves as they walked away. 'Until yesterday he was a drunkard, roaming around like a rowdy, and today he has elevated himself to the post of a leader? Has he become a big mover and shaker? We'll see.'

Deeply jealous of his growth, they walked over and knocked on his door. He wasn't there. He didn't want to be found at the forefront of the problem and had gone into hiding. The few men, wearing nothing but strips of cloth to cover their privates, swung their staves at the glass panes. The panes came down crumbling. The coloured bulbs all around were smashed to smithereens. Whatever things were left outside all became dust. They broke anything they could lay their hands on. The whole place looked as if large pigs from a sewer had rampaged through it.

Veeran, who had sent those burly men there, also assigned work to the seething youngsters.

'So many people are here cutting these trees. But look, not one person came out of that office building. Go, go and serve them some.'

An army marched towards the buffalo centre. In fact, this was on top of the configuration of youngsters surrounding the woodcutters that hadn't changed at all. The women watched, wondering with fear what was going to happen. A mother who tried to pull her son out of the group got a forceful push in return. The noise was like Armageddon.

The buffaloes that were tethered amongst the neem trees with fat braided ropes that pulled them through their nostrils finally found freedom. Using the energy that was suppressed until then to make themselves nimble, they ran everywhere on the roads, and made their way into the colony. Fearing the buffaloes, many houses shut their doors. The men from the buffalo centre ran in all directions. Inside the centre, everything, including the semen tubes, eggs and refrigerators were destroyed.

'Instead of letting the buffalo spend the night when asked for, you insist that you will only provide injections.'

'Dei . . . putting up a show for us, weren't you?'

No one could be identified in all that frenzy. There was running, screaming. Wherever there was an enemy, there

Chapter 14

The vadhanaram trees mimicked human voices as they fell with an 'o' sound. These were trees that were so tall that one couldn't see their tops even if one looked all the way up. These were saplings that had withstood the trampling over years to become mature at great heights. They were the best part of the goat farm. Even after the goat farm became the buffalo centre, the trees stood tall. Only on the western corner of that land stood four or five pitiable Delhi buffaloes, tethered. They always had an expression of being hungry no matter what time of day. They frothed at their mouths and breathed loudly. It they spotted a cow or another buffalo at a distance, they tried to tug on the trees with a grunt. They ate the food they were given by weight and sat quietly. Other than the space that the buffaloes occupied, it was all trees with the crows reigning over them.

The boys who grazed the goats would drive them here and climb up the trees to play woodpecker. Watching these strong boys climb higher and higher up the trees in no time was frightening. They grabbed a branch and hopped from one to the other with the verve of wanting to snatch the moon. Sometimes, they broke a few branches from the top and dropped them down for the goats. In the month of Chithirai, when the trees adorn a fresh young green, the sight would rejuvenate the whole village. Aside from the land where the trees stood, a strip of land shaped like the map of south India lay open by the north side of the road that went past the temple. The villagers had assigned that land to the temple. In the beginning, they would cook pongal there together. Later one year, they built a little podium and placed two stones on it. The temple priest hung two bells for them. The officers of animal husbandry didn't seem to mind it.

They were chopping those trees down too. The crows fluttered over in limbo and cawed away. The goats saw the fallen branches and ran towards them. With twenty big men whose torsos were built like tree trunks chopping and dragging, work went ahead in haste. Everyone thought it was the officers who had arranged for the trees to be cut. But why did they suddenly wake up to this after staying quiet for all these days? Were they going to fill that land with more buffaloes?

The men cutting the trees kept mum. They were not from around here. They were surely from elsewhere. The men who had worked with axes and short-handled hoes were no longer to be seen in the village. They had brought these men from outside. The little ones climbed on the fallen trees and danced in glee. Men and women stood around and gaped at the newly exposed sky with wonder and curiosity.

'Why are you cutting them?' Rangamma asked loudly.

One of the men looked up and, with a gesture that looked like he was going to spit his betel leaves on her face, were attacks. Any unsettled disputes, even if they were burning within just as small, ordinary flames, were being avenged. A tray of eggs from the buffalo centre went to the arrack shop's pantry. The people at the arrack shop also feared the spread of the attacks but not even a little bit of the chaos reached them, despite the fact that the shop belonged to Sevathaan.

At the bus stop that was always crowded, not a soul could be found; it was completely deserted. Usually, a bus left every minute, but the buses had been halted a distance away. There were no bicycles, motorcycles or vehicles on the road. The shops were all shut. Noises arose from all around. No one knew what anyone else was doing or what was going on. The men trapped within the circle tried to escape amidst the commotion—they were chased with staves and axes. Holding their lives in their hands and with their eyes filled with the fear of death, they ran in all directions.

The snout of a police van appeared in the distance. Veeran tried to pull the crowd back to the spot where they had dispersed from. He didn't realize that he had long lost control of the mob. His yells resonated far beyond their ears. Annan was shirtless, and missing his lungi. Like a ruffian, he held a staff in his hand and wandered around in his shorts. His hair was completely dishevelled, like a beggar's. Not caring about any of that, he ran towards the mud road, and tripped on a stone and fell down. He got up and ran again.

A week had passed since the shop had been open for business. There were no ingredients to make soda in the shop either. He was two months behind on the rent. For a week, Annan had been loafing around like this. Like fishing out every morsel of soaked rice from water, he used up all the money. Appa pretended not to notice anything and kept himself busy visiting finance offices frequently. Even at that moment, he was at a finance office to arrange five thousand for someone to borrow. He had gone to co-sign the document for that person. The boy had gone to college. Annan ran aimlessly but managed to run towards home.

Before the police arrived, the whole place was empty. No one heard Veeran say, 'Let's get arrested.' They all disappeared without a trace. In the end, Veeran too vanished from there. As for the one or two people who got caught, the police laid it on them. The woodcutters who escaped from the mob were brought back and the cutting of trees continued with police protection. They installed a fence all around that land.

The buffaloes that were freed, though, were still roaming about in rage.

~

Annan came home running, so intoxicated that he didn't know what had happened. He was full of fear from his hallucination of being chased by a faceless person. He tripped on stones. He pulled himself off the ground and continued to run. 'Who's that?' he mouthed uncertainly. No one was at home. Only Paati was sitting on the plinth, winnowing rice. Unable to bear the state in which he returned home, she put the winnow aside and went running to hold him. 'Chi, get lost, you old lady,' he said and shoved her down. Paati got herself off the ground using her hands to support herself and sat on the plinth again. When she realized she didn't have strength in her arms to control him, she tried to accomplish that with words.

'Payya . . . would even you approve of what you have done? We are such a decent family. How many people have we advised to better their lives? How can you do such a thing and make us seem like we preach to the world but let our house crumble?'

'Go, ask your son all this. If you continue to talk to me, I will only kick you.' He spat out words at Paati with a drunken drawl. Paati couldn't see properly. She had been getting some interest money that she used to feed herself. After Thatha passed away, she couldn't do any manual labour. With none of her past strength still in her, she lived on the edge of life and death, like the male calf of a milkless buffalo.

'Think about this, da. If you continue like this, who will give you a girl in marriage? Your father too has looked in several places. The whole village calls you a drunkard. How will any father give his daughter to you? Are you going to stay single like this your entire life? No matter how much we tell you, you don't listen. If you give advice to a good person, he will use his brain and remember it. If you give advice to the devil, it is but useless.'

'Ey, old lady. Even today, I can find a girl and marry her. You shut it and keep it that way.'

Paati's eyes filled up. Her body had become desensitized from all the insults she had borne through her life.

'I will shut it, my dear. If you buy a couple of towels for your grandmother, I will shut it happily. Mm . . . the women who deliver milk talk amongst themselves about how you visit someone in the colony every day. Why this habit? There are bitches in the colony who simply want to spoil all our youngsters. Ever since the colony was created, a plant is snapped out even before it sprouts a couple of leaves.'

'I will go anywhere I want and live however I want to. What do you care? Do you cook, eat? Stop with that. If you breathe any more than that, I will kill you. I will step on your throat and crush you.'

He sat on the stone mortar and flung a piece of firewood at her. It fell on the plinth and split into pieces. Paati, who lifted her legs away from them, said as she dug out the muck from her eyes, 'Of course, you can kill me and you all can live well . . . I too am waiting for my life to end. But my fate is such that I have to live to see all these horrible things. He sold the land and gave you a lump of money. You insisted on keeping a shop. Here we are, expecting you to double the money. Instead, you stand here with nothing. How much more can he do to help you? If one has good children, he can walk with his head held high. Otherwise he only has to continue to bear the burden. But do you even feel a little gratitude that someone is saying and doing all this for you? Mmm. If one walks on his two feet, he will get to some place. If he insists on walking on his head, he will only collapse.'

He stood up and lit a beedi. It kept getting snuffed out by the wind. He went to the plinth. Mani lay curled at one end of it. Since being wounded by the bike, it had lost all its vigour. The wound in its testicles was not healing at all. Mani kept licking it all the time. But the wound kept growing in size. The dog was growing bald and looked pitiable. 'And you need the plinth, do you?' he said and kicked the dog. The hapless animal had no energy even to yelp. It rolled its tail, got down slowly from the plinth and went towards the garbage pit.

'Hey, old lady . . . feed yourself and stay quiet the rest of the time. If you keep saying this and that, I will light your funeral pyre today.'

Annan struck a match to light his beedi. His hand shook and his head couldn't stay still. The matchstick kept slipping from his fingers.

'Look at how you have drunk yourself beyond comprehension, you fool . . .' she said, getting off the plinth to pour the water that was in a mud pot over his head. But she couldn't reach the top of his body; it had grown taller than her. He pushed the pot away in an instant. It slipped from her hand and shattered to pieces. Paati struck her stomach in grief as she saw the broken pot. He sat in the cow shed and flicked the lit matchstick. It fell on Paati's thatched roof.

The wind was blowing hard. Seeing the tiny little flame stoked its enthusiasm. The very dry thatch began to crackle and burn. Paati was still grumbling about the broken mud pot. Annan was lying in the cowshed. The fire burnt with nothing to stop it. It spread at a relaxed pace, as though crunching on a snack. Even though someone yelled, 'Aiyyoo, fire!' from afar, Paati didn't realize what was going on. Her eyes were so bad that even if the fire had been right behind her, she couldn't have seen it. Only after she noticed a few people rushing over shouting did she get up and come out, and see the fire with her blurry vision. She didn't feel like crying. Instead, a deep guttural 'aang' sound rose from within her. A few village oldies surrounded her and wailed, striking their foreheads and their stomachs. Then the tears began. And her mouth split open like a palmyra sprout. For a while, sounds rose on and off from her.

Some ladies surrounded her and tried to console her. 'Whatever is gone, is gone, Aaya. Don't cry now.' The fire came together on the roof as if someone had their hands clasped together above their heads, and the smoke bellowed through the village. Seeing the smoke, more people came running.

'I was standing by the temple and chatting. And then I look up and see the smoke of all smokes! At first, I too thought it may have been in a village street and came running.'

'I was by your land then. I saw the smoke and thought it was the mango forest and rushed over.'

The winds spread the fire everywhere. The men tried to stop it from spreading to the other sheds in the vicinity, and doused it with pots and pots of water from the well. The fire was at its peak. No one was home. In order to save the other two sheds, they organized themselves in a line from the well to the house. Men, women, all stood in a line and passed pots of water back and forth. They couldn't put out the fire but they could stop it from spreading.

Someone broke into Paati's shack. The top of the door was in flames. They brought two pots from inside. Spirals of smoke pressed through the door. The stench made it hard to breathe. The smoke pushed away anyone who tried to enter the house. They tried to push through the smoke but returned defeated, rubbing their eyes. In a wide-mouthed container that they managed to bring out were her saris and clothes, still burning, and nine one rupee coins in a little knot. They handed that to Paati.

'Toss these also in there to burn . . .' she shouted. The sugar had burnt into caramel. The groundnuts were completely charred. The rice crackled in the fire as it burned. Everything was gone. Nothing that could be called Paati's possessions was saved. Only the cot escaped because it was outside.

When the boy got down from the bus at the stop, the news about the fire reached him. He rushed home. His stomach fluttered when he saw Paati. If all these people had not helped that day, everything would have been lost. *Just because he was drunk, would he eat shit? Wouldn't he at least be cognizant enough to know that he was setting the house on fire? That scum of a brother! The one born to destroy everything.* The boy wanted to pick him up and throw him in the fire too. He grabbed him by his hair and pulled him up. He slapped him on his face. Annan hissed, skewing his face as if an ant was bothering him. The boy kicked him.

Let him die of broken testicles. He punched him on his back. *Let him suffer from breathlessness. The rogue of a rascal.*

He was held back by people he didn't even know. Paati too hugged him. He hugged Paati back and cried. The fire was not completely put out yet. It softened but flared up occasionally, as if to check what was going on. They heard the palm beams falling, destroyed by the fire. Everything around was getting charred. What else was left?

Oblivious to any of this was Annan on the floor of the cowshed, with his face in the mud and saliva oozing from his mouth, lying like a mendicant.

Chapter 15

Appa's voice hid deep inside him. Words came out dead, without any sound. The man was seated on the plinth against the wall and could not be moved from there. He sat there in shock. The only sounds he emitted were like the sobs of a weeping child. He refused to even set eyes on food, as though he had decided to loathe the very idea of it. All that he had managed to save from before was now completely gone. Grief, that had come to hide in the house as though afraid of being sent to the netherworld, wasn't letting go of him easily. Even the people who came to visit him threw words at him, intending to torment him more. His heart suffered to the point of being scalded.

All his frivolous arrogance came to a grinding halt. The way he took the Swega and sped on it with no control; his chutzpah when he flung wads of cash in the arrack store; when he bought fifty coconut saplings and planted them, claiming conceitedly that 'they will grow with just my touch' when there was no water in the wells; the way he acted as if he was strong like a tiger, striking anyone as soon as they raised their voices when speaking to him, regardless of who they were—everything was now interred. Now he was reduced to going out only in the dark or inconspicuously, with a towel on his head, if he needed to venture out during the day.

He felt too disgraced to even respond properly to people who came to see him. He shrunk into himself and spoke diffidently. People who had lent him money asked him stinging questions. Sitthan from Soliakaadu had given him five thousand. He came over and said the nastiest things to Appa.

'I thought to myself, I am lending it to Maama, he's not going to run away with my money. You received the whole amount in crisp notes, didn't you? Shouldn't you be giving it back the same way? If you don't give back the money, I will destroy everything . . . I am warning you. I will come back this Thursday.'

The way he spoke, waving his hands, seemed like he was going to kick him. Why did Appa borrow from these dogs, who had no empathy or compassion, to invest in the finance company? Anger rose within the boy.

'I will pay back the money even if I have to sell my head, Payya. Bear with me for a wee bit. I am not going to eat others' money the way some dogs ate mine.'

'There is not a thing to sell. You can wave your hands and say all you want. You think I sat there making money while chewing on betel leaves? Only if I toil and sweat will I see a little money.'

'I am not denying all that, da. I have borrowed from a few people, including you. I didn't think something like this would happen even in my dreams. But what happened has happened. Bear with me. I will return your money.'

'When you say wait for a bit, how long is that?'

'You go on and on about your five thousand. I have lost fifty thousand. Who can I go and demand it from?'

Appa's voice faded. He started crying. Sitthan waited for a bit and left after warning him.

Appa had borrowed from five or six people to invest in the finance company. Two thousand from Kandhan. Four thousand from the Paati with a moustache . . . the list went on. Close to thirty thousand in all. Everything had been swept away like a flood. From now on, Appa was nothing more than a devil with his hands on his head.

The finance companies that had sprung up like mushrooms all across Karattur now withered away just as swiftly. Everyone had kept praising them but no one really cared to find out where the money went after they put it in those companies. Every street had ten, twenty finance offices. Still, there was not enough money. Even if there was a deposit of five thousand one minute, it disappeared the next minute. They charged them a twenty-four per cent fee, stamp fee, this fee, that fee and deducted a lot of that money. No matter how much money they deducted, no one bothered to understand how it all worked. No one gave a thought to it. They were all happy to receive the interest payments.

But then the whole village was filled with lorries. Rickshaw services encroached the northern districts. Power looms sprung up everywhere. All the lands in the region transformed into blocks of houses and the area lost its original identity. New faces from unknown places began to settle there. The finance companies were ready to give any amount of money for anything. Everything was seemingly prosperous. The ones who borrowed money were paying it back properly. The ones who invested in the finance companies went to a monthly meeting and came back with bagfuls of money. There was no evidence of any problems.

Until someone somewhere filed an insolvency petition: the yellow notice. The next minute, hundreds of yellow notices piled up on the desks of the finance companies. The ones who took loans kept their assets in the names of their wives and their mistresses. Even if they had assets on their own names, nothing could be done with that. Even if the loan amount was small, they claimed to be insolvent. The bonds and deeds that the finance companies held became worthless sheets of paper. Nothing worked. No legal action was favourable. Fearing their own conscience, a handful of people paid back their loans. The rest didn't feel an iota of guilt that they were swindling the savings of the public. They had become numb to all that. Few of the guarantors with some self-respect paid the loans. Others, like Mohan Master, consumed poison and killed themselves. Suicides became commonplace. And there were more who saw that and tucked a smile in the corners of their lips as they walked on.

For the last month or so, the only stories floating around were that of dying finance companies. Running from pillar to post to get any of the money back resulted only in leg aches. The smell of money had disappeared from across Karattur, replaced now with the stench of corpses.

Appa had joined two groups. In the beginning, he had put in fifty thousand from selling land. Then there was the money, the smaller amounts that were given to him by a few who were single or poor but had a tiny bit of money tucked away that they could invest. They gave him the money only because they trusted him. He had also signed as a guarantor for a loan of ten thousand rupees. Every bit of it had vanished into thin air.

His own money was gone but no one else cared about that. And the money that he had collected from around the village, did he really need to pay that back? Well, there was no bond. No papers. But there was pride—and his conscience. That was why he was vehement about returning all of it. But where was he going to find that money? Amma had about ten sovereigns of gold around her neck. But she had said she was not going to part with it even if it meant death.

'That bottom-feeder! He took the money from anyone and everyone in town and put it all in finance. That day, when my brother asked for money, he refused him flatly. Today, everything is gone with no trace. Had he joined with them then, today he would be running twenty looms. That dog in heat. Now, he wants my jewellery, yes, mine! We will see about that the day this Pacchiappan Pillai dies.'

She had no sense of what to say when. At any time, her words tended to sting.

Annan added a salvo of his own. 'That day, didn't you all yell at me for setting the old lady's house on fire? Now look at what has happened. That must have caused damages of maybe a couple of thousands. Now we have lost in the order of lakhs, haven't we? No one sees an elephant go by. But everyone picks on the mouse. That's how it is. Let me see if anyone dares say anything about me now. I will tear them—tear them apart!'

There was no new shed set up for Paati. They had arranged for her to stay with each of her sons for a month each time. The spot where the shed stood was covered with ashes. The mud walls were broken and smeared with soot like a cooking utensil.

Annan stayed on his cot for ten days straight without getting up once. As soon as Appa's financial troubles came up, he got up to mock him for it.

Within a week of the onset of this trouble, Appa lost all of himself. No one knew what to do. The ones who lent him money came home every day to ask him about it. He just stayed quiet. To offer the money that was in an account on the boy's name only amounted to a speck of salt in an ocean of loans. Appa had no interest in touching that money either. He never brought it up. The boy was going to finish his BSc soon. He hadn't decided what to do next. He too was very confused.

The house now seemed like it was haunted most of the time. There was no cheer on anyone's face. No one talked to another with any mirth. Everyone carried on with their work as if they had no option.

The boy's mind was always in turmoil. He kept on worrying about something or the other. He imagined he would run away from all these troubles. But where? What would he do? Even before he set one foot out, trouble stuck to his face. He couldn't get rid of it no matter what he did. They had to watch Appa closely at night. What if he resorted to something untoward? If money is lost, one can earn it back. If a life is lost, what can crying, wailing, shouting, fighting do to get it back? It is lost forever. When the boy went out, he felt as if people snickered at him. *Well, if their stories are looked at closely for their virtuosity, then we will see who snickers at whom*, he thought to himself as his anger crept up. Scared of unpleasant consequences, Paati kept an eye on Appa day and night, just like she did with Akka.

In all this, Appa was very determined about one thing. No matter what happened, he was going to return the money to those he had borrowed from. Once, it was a new-moon day, so dark that one couldn't see the face of the person sitting next to them. Appa called them all together and said, 'Shall we sell the land?'

'Right. Sell whatever is left and you can take a bowl to beg around to eat.' Amma talked loudly to squelch the already defeated voice of Appa.

Appa got irritated. Even though he was crushed, his old passion wasn't diminished. 'Don't stir my anger now. You speak like you bring bags and bags of money from your house. Like I took the lakhs you brought from your house and bought the lands, yes?'

'As if my father died without giving me anything. Even when he died, he gave me whatever he saved from working so hard, he didn't send me here naked.'

'Yes, yes he gave, didn't he? Like giving to a beggar. Only because I touched that money have I been cursed to roam around here and there. Have I been able to complete a job fully and properly? Has anything gone right since the time that money set foot here? Who knows how many sins that house committed? My father and my mother asked for your hand only to keep the relationship going, even though they were approached here locally for Virumaayi who lives in the valavu on the west.'

'So, go to her if you want . . . Keep seven mistresses in every place you go.'

Amma got beaten. Every time they opened their mouths, it always ended in hitting and kicking. It looked as though it had become a habit for Appa to hit and for Amma to get hit. No fight got resolved with words. Annan pulled Amma away.

'Why are you hitting Amma? Just watch what happens if you do it again. I will deal with having to respect you as my father later. You take all the money and lose it and you think you can get angry at the ones here? Who is going to help you out?'

'Ask him that first . . . I have to bear the brunt of everything.'

Appa went outside and sat on a rock. The boy followed him and sat on another rock. He asked him, 'What do you say?'

'What can I say? It is your decision.'

'Follow your dad holding his tail,' said Amma, cracking her knuckles as if to curse Appa. 'He will find a deep well to push you in.'

'You keep quiet, Amma . . . If each one keeps interrupting the other, what good is that?'

'Okay. If you decide to sell the land, I will not come to sign the documents,' said Annan staring at the lamp.

'The property is in my name. You can come if you want, or get lost.'

'You think you can sell the land without us?'

'If I can't sell it, I will take a loan against it. I have to answer to the people coming here asking for money. It's my land, my money. I will sell it, hold on to it. If you want to come with me, do that. Or else, I will proceed on my own.'

Seeing Appa talk like he had given up on everything and everyone brought tears to the boy's eyes. But Annan was in no state to understand him.

'Give me one acre of land. I will sell it myself.'

'How will you alone get one acre of land? There are only two acres. I can sell both together and pay all my debts. There is a house in the colony that we can buy and live in. Whatever we need to buy for the shop, we will and at least take care of that properly. You too obliterated all the money that we got by drinking with those rogues. Maybe he is going to study further? Otherwise, we three can take care of the shop together. If we take good care, we are but going to see some money. Don't dance to your mother's tunes.'

Annan became quiet listening to what Appa said. After seeming deep in thought for a while, Appa spoke again.

'There is house available for fifty thousand next to the triangle near the mango forest itself. We will give him five thousand more and buy it. What else to do? It is what it

is. That whole land was ours. Now we cannot afford to buy
even one house over there . . . Of what is left over, we will
give the girl ten thousand. We haven't given her anything
since she had the boy. We can also arrange for you to be
married if you mend your ways. Are you going to continue
to loaf around like this?'

There was no opposition to what Appa said. It was
decided that they would buy a house in the colony and move
there. Appa embarked on finding a good price for the land.

~

The milkmaids informed them that Mani lay dead in the
colony ditch. After looking for the dog everywhere for two
days, they had assumed that it chose the colony as its refuge
to live in from then on and stopped looking for it. The
boy had thought he should check at the few houses that it
frequented in the colony but Appa and Amma didn't think
that was needed. With all the human-related problems
they had to deal with, who wanted to add this to the pile?

At first, he thought he would bury it somewhere in the
colony and set out with a basket in hand. Everyone laughed
at him for bothering to bury a dog. They looked at him
in bewilderment. The dog is lying dead somewhere. Why
bother burying it? 'Who knows where that corpse lies?' It
had been two days since it had died. Apparently, it was full
of worms. Should he risk getting infected himself?

He didn't pay attention to anything that they said. The
dog had spent most of its days in the forests. When it knelt

down and affectionately licked his face, he didn't notice its stench then. When it curled its tail and laid on the lap, that love was needed. When it followed him around everywhere in the forest, he wanted to pick it up and cuddle it. Today, just because it was infested with worms, should he get squeamish about burying it? He was getting irritated with the people mocking him.

Mani had not been well for a few days. After it got injured by the bike, the wound on its testicles never healed and became a lump instead. Even then, it used to go to the colony, limping all the way and back. It lost a lot of weight and came close to weighing nothing. It was shrinking slowly. If it had lived a little longer, they themselves would have moved into the colony. But, it ostensibly was in a hurry. Unless it was the sorrow of not having a speck of land ever again that pushed it over. That it couldn't roam around the fields freely. Nor drag over bandicoots again. It couldn't round up the goats that wandered away while grazing and bring them back. There wouldn't be any connection left with the land. It would have had to stay confined within the four walls of the house. Maybe roam about in a couple of streets, perhaps. That would have been it. Maybe it feared all that and decided to die instead?

He didn't know which ditch it was in. He asked Thanaya Paati who was bringing sewage water. She pointed to a ditch down below.

'Look in there. The wretched stench is unbearable.'

The dog's life had begun on four square measures of land. It ran to all sorts of places, fell, got wounded and finally went back to the same place to meet its end. Its world was very small. Home, the goat pen and the cool shadow of the coconut trees. It roamed only within these spots. Sometimes, it did not get any food for a couple of days. Occasionally, someone would add water to old rice and pour that for the dog. Drooling, it would lick that clean. Ticks had taken over its body. Unable to bear the pain, it howled with irritation and bit itself in several places to assuage the pain.

Once, during mating season, it went looking for bitches. When it was in the throes of mating, it got stuck in some thorn and struggled to free itself. Like tugging lizards from a fence, it pulled in one direction to free itself from the thorn and the female dog pulled the other way. The whole thing was one embarrassing situation. Young boys who came with their grazing goats flung stones at it and snickered with their palms over their mouths. Towards the end of the mating season, it was covered in rashes. The dog was terrible to look at. They used to try smothering it with kerosene and other different ways to cure its afflictions. It lost all its hair, became bald and looked like it was going to die. By the time they brought it back to normalcy, offering prayers on its behalf, it seemed as though it had been rescued from the jaws of death.

It knew every nook and corner of the fields. It would keep going back to the same spot over and over again, sniffing at it. The dog would spot all the rat burrows. If it spotted bandicoot tracks, it would bark and oust them. Those four measures of land were its life. It didn't know anything beyond it. It had intertwined itself with that soil.

It would kick up dust and enjoy the scent of the soil. If the wind kicked up the dust, though, it would close its eyes and howl sadly. But it would still breathe in that air and enjoy it. Even the buses that go up and down the tar road were unknown to him. It had one place for itself. One attachment. All the world's emotions and experiences were within that space for Mani. It had never liked coming out of that world. It wanted to become one with that soil. But who let it be?

He looked at the spot where the dog lay dead. He couldn't recognize it. Only its teeth helped identify it. The dog's skin looked like a wet black cloth, and the stench choked his insides. There was nothing there that could possibly have been identified as Mani. Worms squirmed around. The bloated body looked damp and overripe. The swollen stomach had burst open and the whole place was reeking of putrid flesh. For a second, even the boy felt defiled. Later, when he thought about it, he had tears in his eyes. He wanted to burst into tears and let it all out. Even if he did, there was not a hand to console him in that concrete jungle. He couldn't tolerate the smell in spite of all the love and affection he had for the dog. He looked up to get some fresh air, then bent down a little uncertainly to pick up the dog's corpse and put it in the basket. He felt as if he had accomplished something of great significance. Finding his spirit again, he made a cloth pad, placed that on his head and mounted the filled basket over it. He started walking.

The problems the dog faced ever since it was thrown out of those lands danced like ghosts in front of his eyes.

He recalled how, when they moved from their lands into the valavu and he had to go in search of the dog, it would keep slipping from him through the thorn bushes. Now it felt as if that had happened hardly a while ago. How many events had occurred and disappeared into oblivion. And throughout its life, the dog had suffered, always seeking stability but never achieving it. First the lands, then the valavu, one after the other, the changes were constant. Even after the colony was inhabited, it didn't stop seeking its world. It tried to belong to the houses in the colony. But how many times it was hit! The last one was by the motorcycle—that was the final straw. Perhaps it would have lived a few more days if not for that incident.

Uprooting the little dog that was content in its little world and putting it in the middle of an expanse and asking it to breathe had overwhelmed it. It struggled to breathe. It tried various ways to stabilize itself but it just couldn't. The gasping continued until the end. The protection the four measures of land gave it, the wide open outside didn't. Yes, there were troubles in its little world too but the ones outside were far worse. The most severe had been the suffering that came from the dog's inability to adapt from an accustomed life to one completely alien and unknown. That was what had finally defeated the dog. Licked it clean and tossed it out. And now, only in death could the dog's life find redemption.

He placed the basket down and dug a hole. He folded his lungi up. His torso was bare. The soil was loose around a young coconut sapling. He dug deep. Otherwise, some dogs may drag it out. Let it lie in peace in one spot at least in death. Let it remain drunk with the smell of the earth. He checked once if the length was sufficient and then positioned the dog in the grave. The worms scattered everywhere. His hands ached to cover his nose. Once he reminded himself how he used to hold that body with his own arms as he placed it in the grave, he was able to bear the smell. He pushed the soil back in the hole. Little by little, the body was covered. He felt dizzy. His eyes glazed over. His hands trembled. He pushed in all the soil, placed a few stones on top of it and pulled himself up straight. In the middle of the day, he straightened his weary body and stood up.

On his back, covered with a sheen of sweat, he felt the stinging heat of the sun.

Glossary

Aaya	grandmother; grandmother-like elderly woman
Akka	elder sister; any older, sister-like female
Aiyo	exclamation of concern or distress
Amma	mother
Annan	elder brother
Appa	father
Atthai	father's sister; mother's brother's wife
arivalmanai	cutting instrument with a wooden or metal base and a vertical, curved metal blade with a coconut scraper at the free end
Ayya	sir
Chithappa	father's younger brother
Chitthi	father's younger brother's wife; mother's younger sister
Da, dei	term used in casual conversations amongst male contemporaries but disrespectful or degrading when used at a male who is older or from a higher caste or strata of society

Di   term used in casual conversations amongst female contemporaries but disrespectful or degrading when used at a woman who is older or from a higher caste or strata of society

dosai   crepe-like dish made with rice and lentils

Ey   disrespectful way of calling someone, especially someone older or of a higher caste

kali   thick porridge made with millet flour

kallu   alcoholic drink made of fermented toddy

Karagaatam   folk dance involving balancing pots on one's head

komanam   strip of cloth held in place by a string around the waist to cover the private parts of a man

Kumbabhishekam   temple consecration festival that occurs once in twelve years, usually preceded by renovation of the temple

kuzhambu   spicy stew often made with vegetables and/or meat

lungi   long piece of cloth wrapped around the waist that covers the whole lower half from waist to ankles, similar to a sarong. Usually casually worn by men. It has patterns or prints; the cut ends are sown together

Maama	mother's brother; a polite term for addressing or referring to an older, distant relative or person from the same caste
Maamoy	casual, endearing way of saying 'maama'
Maaple	nephew; son-in-law; brother-in-law
mani	bell
Paati	grandmother
pandakaran	potter; one who works with clay
Payya	son; boy
Periappa	father's elder brother
Periamma	father's elder brother's wife; mother's elder sister
Pille	daughter; girl
Saami	respectful way of addressing landlords and their family members, and people holding important positions in society
Thalaivar	leader; a term that the late Dr M.G. Ramachandran came to be known as fondly by the people of Tamil Nadu
Thambi	younger brother
Thatha	grandfather
Theluvu	non-alcoholic sweet-palm toddy
thundu	towel
valavu	cluster of houses very close to each other, sharing a common street; sometimes all the houses are located within a fenced area

veshti   long piece of cloth wrapped around the waist that covers the body's whole lower half from waist to ankles. It is formal attire and usually white with thin stripes along the top and bottom edges. The cut ends are loose

Yow   annoyed and impolite way of addressing a man by a woman

Acknowledgements

My foremost thanks to writer Ambai and Kannan Sundaram from Kalachuvadu for aligning the start for the successful completion of this work. I am immensely grateful to them for this opportunity.

I am very grateful for the tremendous resource in Indumathi Mariappan who helped with the nuances of the Konganadu Tamil dialect, to Ashima Unni for being not only the much-needed second pair of eyes but also for her voice of reason when doubts filled my mind. I am thankful to my dear mother for spending several hours of her very sparse time checking my work, in the midst of planning and arranging a wedding.

I thank the editorial team at Penguin Random House—Ambar Sahil Chatterjee, Manasi Subramaniam and Shreya Chakravertty were not only kind and patient in their guidance, but also professional and highly attentive to detail. The cover art is fabulous.

I save my deepest gratitude for my family but most of all, for my husband, Shankar Radhakrishnan, who continues to fill the voids I create with immense patience. And last but in no measure the least, to my wonderful little boy, Vishak, for being a boundless source of joy and for inspiring to always rediscover.

Los Angeles   Janani Kannan
22 February 2020

ALSO BY PERUMAL MURUGAN

One Part Woman

 Kali and Ponna's efforts to conceive a child have been in vain. Hounded by the taunts and insinuations of others, all their hopes come to converge on the chariot festival in the temple of Ardhanareeswara, the half-female god. Everything hinges on the one night when rules are relaxed and consensual union between any man and woman is sanctioned. This night could end the couple's suffering and humiliation. But it will also put their marriage to the ultimate test.

ALSO BY PERUMAL MURUGAN

Trial by Silence

At the end of Perumal Murugan's trailblazing novel *One Part Woman*, readers are left on a cliffhanger as Kali and Ponna's intense love for each other is torn to shreds. What is going to happen next to this beloved couple? In *Trial by Silence*—one of two inventive sequels that picks up the story right where *One Part Woman* ends—Kali is determined to punish Ponna for what he believes is an absolute betrayal. But Ponna is equally upset at being forced to atone for something that was not her fault. In the wake of the temple festival, both must now confront harsh new uncertainties in their once idyllic life together.